Glass Houses

The Morganville Vampires

Book One

RACHEL CAINE

Allison & Busby Limited
12 Fitzroy Mews
London W1T 6DW
www.allisonandbusby.com

First published in Great Britain by Allison & Busby in 2008.
This paperback edition published by Allison & Busby in 2012.

Copyright © 2006 by ROXANNE LONGSTREET CONRAD

A CIP catalogue record for this book is available from
the British Library.

24

ISBN 978-0-7490-7951-2

Typeset in 11/17 pt Sabon by
Allison & Busby Ltd.

The paper used for this Allison & Busby publication
has been produced from trees that have been legally sourced
from well-managed and credibly certified forests.

Printed and bound by
CPI Group (UK) Ltd, Croydon, CR0 4YY

RACHEL CAINE is the bestselling author of over thirty novels, including the *New York Times* bestselling Morganville Vampires series. She was born at White Sands Missile Range, which people who know her say explains a lot. She has been an accountant, an insurance investigator and a professional musician, and has played with such musical legends as Henry Mancini, Peter Nero and John Williams. She and her husband, fantasy artist R. Cat Conrad, live in Texas with their iguana Pop-eye, a *mali uromastyx* named (appropriately) O'Malley, and a leopard tortoise named Shelley (for the poet, of course).

www.rachelcaine.com

To Liz, who asked.

To my dad, Robert V Longstreet,
who dared to dream – and to be a dreamer –
when it wasn't cool.

To my mom, Hazel Longstreet, who took
on the tough job of being practical in a family of
impractical people, and did it brilliantly and with
love. I love you both. Miss you, Dad.

Acknowledgements

Every teacher and student at Socorro High School
in El Paso, Texas, and every student and professor
at Texas Tech University.

None of you are in this book, but heck, if you
can't acknowledge your alma maters...!
You gave me the tools and the passion.
Thank you.

CHAPTER ONE

On the day Claire became a member of the Glass House, somebody stole her laundry.

When she reached into the crappy, beat-up washing machine, she found nothing but the wet slick sides of the drum, and – like a bad joke – the worst pair of underwear she owned, plus one sock. She was in a hurry, of course – there were only a couple of machines on this top floor of Howard Hall, the least valued and most run-down rooms in the least valued, most run-down dorm. Two washing machines, two dryers, and you were lucky if one of them was working on any given day and didn't eat your quarters. Forget about the dollar-bill slot. She'd never seen it work, not in the last six weeks since she'd arrived at school.

'No,' she said out loud, and balanced herself on the edge of the washer to look down into the dark, partly rusted interior. It smelt like mould and cheap detergent. Getting a closer look didn't help.

One crappy pair of underwear, fraying at the seams. One sock.

She was missing every piece of clothing that she'd worn in the last two weeks. Every piece that she actually *wanted* to wear.

'No!' She yelled it into the washer, where it echoed back at her, and slumped back down, then kicked the washer violently in the dent made by all the other disappointed students before her. She couldn't breathe. She had some other clothes – a few – but they were *last-choice* clothes, oh-my-God-wouldn't-be-caught-dead clothes. Pants that were too short and made her look like a hick, shirts that were too big and too stupid, and made her look like her mom had picked them out. And she had.

Claire had about three hundred dollars left to last her for, well, months, after the latest round of calling out for pizza and buying yet *another* book for Professor Clueless Euliss, who didn't seem to have figured out yet what subject he was teaching.

She supposed she could find some clothes, if she looked around, that wouldn't totally blow her entire budget. After all, downtown Morganville, Texas, was the thrift shop capital of the world. Assuming she could find *anything* she could stand to wear.

Mom said this would happen, she thought. *I just have to think. Keep my cool.*

Claire threw herself into an orange plastic chair, dumped her backpack on the scratched linoleum, and put her head in her hands. Her face felt hot, and she was shaking, and she knew, just *knew*, that she was going to cry. Cry like the baby they all said she was, too young to be here, too young to be away from Mommy.

It sucked to be smart, because this was where it got you.

She gulped deep, damp breaths and sat back, willing herself not to bawl (because they'd hear), and wondered if she could call Mom and Dad for an extension on her allowance, or use the credit card that was 'just for emergencies'.

Then she saw the note. Not so much 'note' as graffiti, but it was addressed to her, on the painted cinderblock wall above the machines.

Dear Dork, it read, *We found trash in the machines and threw it down the chute. If you want it, dive for it.*

'Shit,' she breathed, and had to blink back tears again, for an entirely different reason. Blind, stupid rage. *Monica.* Well, Monica and the Monickettes, anyway. Why was it the hot mean girls always ran in packs, like hyenas? And why, with all the shimmery hair and long tanned legs and more of Daddy's money than Daddy's accountants, did they have to focus on *her*?

No, she knew the answer to that.

She'd made Monica look stupid in front of her friends, and some hot upperclassmen. Not that it had been all that hard; she'd just been walking by, heard Monica saying that World War II had been 'that dumbass Chinese war thing'.

And by simple reflex, she'd said, 'It wasn't.' The whole lot of them, slouched all over the couches in the dorm lobby, looked at her with as much blank surprise as if the Coke machine had just spoken up. Monica, her friends, three of the cool older frat boys.

'World War II,' Claire had plunged on, panicked and not quite sure how to get out of what she'd gotten herself into. 'I just meant – well, it wasn't the Korean War. That was later. World War II was with the Germans and the Japanese. You know, Pearl Harbor?'

And the guys had looked at Monica and laughed, and Monica had flushed – not much, but enough to ruin the cool perfection of her make-up. 'Remind me not to buy any history papers off of you,' the cutest of the guys had said. 'What kind of dumbass doesn't know that?' Though Claire had been sure none of them had, really. 'Chinese. Riiiiight.'

Claire had seen the fury in Monica's eyes, quickly covered over with smiles and laughter and flirting. Claire had ceased to exist again, for the guys.

For the girls, she was brand-new, and unwelcome as hell. She'd been dealing with it all her life. Smart and small and average-looking wasn't exactly winning the life lottery; you had to fight for it, whatever *it* was. Somebody was always laughing at, or hitting, or ignoring you, or a combination of the first two. She'd thought when she was a kid that getting laughed at was the worst thing, and then – after the first couple of school-yard showdowns – getting hit jumped up to number one. But for most of her (brief, two-year) high school experience, being ignored was worse by far. She'd gotten there a year earlier than everybody else, and left a year ahead of them. Nobody liked that.

Nobody but teachers, anyway.

The problem was that Claire really *loved* school. Loved books, and reading, and learning things – OK, not calculus, but pretty much everything else. Physics.

What normal girl loved *physics*? Abnormal ones. Ones who were not ever going to be hot.

And face it, being hot? That was what life was all about. As Monica had proved, when the world had wobbled off its axis for a few seconds to notice Claire, and then wobbled right back to revolve around the pretty ones.

It wasn't fair. She'd dived in and worked her ass off through high school. Graduated with a perfect 4.0, scored high enough on the tests to qualify for admission to the great schools, the legendary schools, the ones where being a brainiac mutant girl-freak wasn't necessarily a downside. (Except that, of course, at those schools, there were probably *hot tall leggy* brainiac mutant girl-freaks.)

Didn't matter. Mom and Dad had taken one look at the stack of enthusiastic thumbs-up replies from universities like MIT and Caltech and Yale, and clamped down hard. No way was their sixteen-year-old daughter (nearly seventeen, she kept insisting, although it wasn't really true) going to run off three thousand miles to go to school. At least not at first. (Claire had tried, unsuccessfully, to get across the concept that if anything would kill her budding academic career worse than being a transfer student at one of those places, it was being a transfer student from *Texas Prairie University*. Otherwise known as TPEwwwwwwww.)

So here she was, stuck on the crappy top floor of a crappy dorm in a crappy school where eighty per cent of the students transferred after the first two years – or dropped out – and the Monickettes were stealing her wet laundry and dumping it down the trash chute, all because Monica couldn't be bothered to know anything about one of the world wars big enough to rate a Roman numeral.

But it isn't fair! something in her howled. *I had a plan! An actual plan!* Monica slept late, and Claire had gotten up early just to do laundry while all the party crowd was comatose and the studious crowd was off to classes. She'd thought she could leave it for a couple of minutes to grab her shower – another scary experience – and she'd never even thought about anybody doing something so incredibly *low*.

As she bit back her sobs, she noticed – again – how quiet it was up here. Creepy and deserted, with half the girls deep asleep and the other half gone. Even when it was crowded and buzzing, the dorm was creepy, though. Old, decrepit, full of shadows and corners and places mean girls could lurk. In fact, that summed up the whole town. Morganville was small and old and dusty, full of creepy little oddities. Like the fact that the streetlights worked only half the time, and they were too far apart when they did. Like the way the people in the local campus stores seemed *too* happy. Desperately happy. Like the fact that the whole town, despite the dust, was *clean* – no trash, no graffiti; nobody begging for spare change in alleyways.

Weird.

She could almost hear her mother saying, *Honey, it's just that you're in a strange place. It'll get better. You'll just have to try harder.*

Mom always said things like that, and Claire had always done her best to hide how hard it was to follow that advice.

Well. Nothing to do but try to get her stuff back.

Claire gulped a couple more times, wiped her eyes, and hauled the arm-twisting weight of her backpack up and over her shoulder. She stared for a few seconds at the wet pair of panties and one sock clutched in her right hand, then hastily unzipped the front pocket of the backpack and stuffed them in. Man, that would kill whatever cool she had left, if she walked around carrying those.

'Well,' said a low, satisfied voice from the open

door opposite the stairs, 'look who it is. The dumpster diver.'

Claire stopped, one hand on the rusted iron railing. Something was telling her to run, but something always told her that: fight-or-flight – she'd read the textbooks. And she was tired of flighting. She turned around slowly, as Monica Morrell stepped out of the dorm room – not hers, so she'd busted Erica's lock again. Monica's running buddies Jennifer and Gina filed out and took up flanking positions. Soldiers in flip-flops and low-rise jeans and French manicures.

Monica struck a pose. It was something she was good at, Claire had to admit. Nearly six feet tall, Monica had flowing, shiny black hair, and big blue eyes accented with just the right amount of liner and mascara. Perfect skin. One of those model-shaped faces, all cheekbones and pouty lips. And if she had a model's body, it was a Victoria's Secret model, all curves, not angles.

She was rich, she was pretty, and as far as Claire could tell, it didn't make her a bit happy. What did, though – what made those big blue eyes glow right now – was the idea of tormenting Claire just a little more.

'Shouldn't you be in first period at the junior high by now?' Monica asked. 'Or at least *getting* your first period?'

'Maybe she's looking for the clothes she left lying around,' Gina piled on, and laughed. Jennifer laughed with her. Claire swore their eyes, their pretty jewel-coloured eyes, just glowed with the joy of making her feel like shit. 'Litterbug!'

'Clothes?' Monica folded her arms and pretended to think. 'You mean, like those rags we threw away? The ones she left cluttering up the washer?'

'Yeah, those.'

'I wouldn't wear those to sweat in.'

'I wouldn't wear them to scrub out the boys' toilet,' Jennifer blurted.

Monica, annoyed, turned and shoved her. 'Yeah, you know all about the boys' toilet, don't you? Didn't you do Steve Gillespie in ninth grade in there?' She made sucking sounds, and they all laughed again, though Jennifer looked uncomfortable. Claire felt her cheeks flare red, even though it wasn't – for a change – a dis against her. 'Jeez, Jen, Steve Gillespie? Keep your mouth shut if you can't think of something that won't embarrass yourself.'

Jennifer – of course – turned her anger on a safer target. Claire. She lunged forward and shoved Claire back a step, toward the stairs. 'Go get your stupid clothes already! I'm sick of looking at you, with your pasty skin—'

'Yeah, Junior High, ever heard of sunshine?' Gina rolled her eyes.

'Watch it,' Monica snapped, which was odd, because all three of them had the best tans money could buy.

Claire scrambled to steady herself. The heavy backpack pulled her off-balance, and she grabbed on to the banister. Jen lunged at her again and slammed the heel of her hand painfully hard into Claire's collar-bone. 'Don't!' Claire yelped, and batted Jen's hand away. Hard.

There was a second of breathless silence, and then Monica said, very quietly, 'Did you just hit my friend, you stupid little bitch? Where do you think you get off, doing things like that around here?'

And she stepped forward and slapped Claire across the face, hard enough to draw blood, hard enough to make flares and comets streak across Claire's vision, hard enough to make everything turn red and boiling hot.

Claire let go of the banister and slapped Monica right back, full across her pouty mouth, and for just a tight, white-hot second she actually felt *good* about it, but then Monica hissed like a scorched cat, and Claire had time to think, *Oh crap, I really shouldn't have done that.*

She never saw the punch coming. Didn't even really feel the impact, except as a blank sensation and confusion, but then the weight of her backpack on her shoulder was pulling her to one side and she staggered.

She almost caught herself, and then Gina, grinning spitefully, reached over and shoved her backward, down the stairs, and there was nothing but air behind her.

She hit the edge of every stair, all the way to the bottom. Her backpack broke open and spilt books as she tumbled, and at the top of the stairs Monica and the Monickettes laughed and hooted and high-fived, but she saw it only in disconnected little jerks of motion, freeze-frames.

It seemed to take forever before she skidded to a stop at the bottom, and then her head hit the wall with a nasty, meaty sound, and everything went black.

She later remembered only one more thing, in the darkness: Monica's voice, a low and vicious whisper. 'Tonight. You'll get what's coming to you, you freak. I'm going to make sure.'

It seemed like seconds, but when she woke up again there was somebody kneeling next to her, and it wasn't Monica or her nail-polish mafia; it was Erica, who had the room at the top of the stairs, four doors down from Claire's. Erica looked pale and strained and scared, and Claire tried to smile, because that was what you did when somebody was scared. She didn't hurt until she moved, and then her head started to throb. There was a red-hot ache near the top, and when she reached up to touch it she felt a hard raised knot. No blood, though. It hurt worse when she probed the spot, but not in an oh-my-God-skull-fracture kind of way, or at least that was what she hoped.

'Are you OK?' Erica asked, waving her hands kind of helplessly in midair as Claire wiggled her way up to a sitting position against the wall. Claire risked a quick look past her up the stairs, then down. The coast looked Monica-clear. Nobody else had come out to see what was up, either – most of them were afraid of getting in trouble, and the rest just flat didn't care.

'Yeah,' she said, and managed a shaky laugh. 'Guess I tripped.'

'You need to go to the quack shack?' Which was college code for the university clinic. 'Or, God, an ambulance or whatever?'

'No. No, I'm OK.' Wishful thinking, but although basically everything in her body hurt like hell, nothing felt like it had broken into pieces. Claire got to her feet, winced at a sore ankle, and picked up her backpack. Notebooks tumbled out. Erica grabbed a couple and jammed them back in, then ran lightly up a few steps to gather the scattered textbooks. 'Damn, Claire, do you really need all this crap? How many classes do you have in a day?'

'Six.'

'You're nuts.' Erica, good deed done, reverted to the neutrality that all the non-cool girls in the dorm had shown her so far. 'Better get to the quack shack, seriously. You look like crap.'

Claire pasted on a smile and kept it there until Erica got to the top of the stairs and started complaining about the broken lock on her dorm room.

Tonight, Monica had leant over and whispered. *You'll get what's coming to you, you freak*. She hadn't called anybody, or tried to find out if Claire had a broken neck. She didn't care if Claire died.

No, that was wrong. The problem was, she *did* care.

Claire tasted blood. Her lip was split, and it was bleeding. She wiped at the mess with the back of her hand, then the hem of her T-shirt before realising that it was literally the only thing she had to wear. *I need to go down to the basement and get my clothes out of the trash*. The idea of going down there – going anywhere alone in this dorm – suddenly terrified her. Monica was waiting. And the other girls wouldn't do anything. Even Erica, who was probably the nicest one in the whole place, was scared to come right out on her side. Hell, Erica got hassled, too, but she was probably just as glad that Claire was there to get the worst of it. This wasn't just as bad as high school, where she'd been treated with contempt and casual cruelty – this was worse, a lot worse. And she didn't even have any friends here. Erica was about the best she'd been able to come up with, and Erica was more concerned about her broken door than Claire's broken head.

She was alone. And if she hadn't been before, she was scared now. Really, really scared. What she'd seen in the Monica Mafia's eyes today wasn't just the usual lazy menace of cool girls versus the geeks; this was worse. She'd gotten casual shoves or pinches before, trips, mean laughter, but this was more like lions coming in for the kill.

They're going to kill me.

She started shakily down the flights of stairs, every step a wincing pain through her body, and remembered that she'd slapped Monica hard enough to leave a mark.

Yeah. They're going to kill me.

If Monica ended up with a bruise on that perfect face, there wasn't any question about it.

CHAPTER TWO

Erica was right about the quack shack being the logical first stop; Claire got her ankle wrapped, an ice pack, and some frowns over the forming bruises. Nothing broken, but she was going to be black-and-blue for days. The doctor asked some pro forma questions about boyfriends and stuff, but since she could truthfully say that no, her boyfriend hadn't beaten her up, he just shrugged and told her to watch her step.

He wrote her an excuse note, too, and gave her some painkillers and told her to go home.

No way was she going back to the dorm. Truth was, she didn't have much in the room – some books, a few photos of home, some posters... She hadn't even had a chance to call it home, and for whatever reason, she'd never really felt safe there. It had always felt like...a warehouse. A warehouse for kids who were, one way or another, going to leave.

She limped over to the Quad, which was a big empty concrete space with some rickety old benches and picnic tables, cornered on all sides by squat, unappealing buildings that mostly just looked like boxes with windows. Architecture-student projects, probably. She heard a rumour that one of them had fallen down a few years back, but then, she'd also heard rumours about a janitor getting beheaded in the chem lab and haunting the building, and zombies roaming the grounds after dark, so she wasn't putting too much stock in it.

It was mid-afternoon already, and not a lot of students were hanging around the Quad, with its lack of shade – great design, considering that the weather was still hovering up in the high nineties in September. Claire picked up a campus paper from the stand, carefully took a seat on the blazing-hot bench, and opened it to the 'Housing' section. Dorm rooms were out of the question; Howard Hall and Lansdale Hall were the only two that took in girls under twenty. She wasn't old enough to qualify for the coed dorms. *Stupid rules were probably written when girls wore hoop-skirts*, she thought, and skipped the dorm listings until she got to OFF CAMPUS. Not that she was really allowed to be living off campus; Mom and Dad would have a total freak-out over it, no question. But...if it was between Monica and parental freakage, she'd take the latter. After all, the important thing was to get herself someplace where she felt safe, where she could study.

Right?

She dug in her backpack, found her cell phone, and checked for coverage. It was kind of lame in Morganville, truthfully, out in the middle of the prairie, in the middle of Texas, which was about as middle of nowhere as it was possible to get unless you wanted to go to Mongolia or something. Two bars. Not great, but it'd do.

Claire started dialling numbers. The first person told her that they'd already found somebody, and hung up before she could even say, 'Thanks.' The second one sounded like a weird old guy. The third one was a weird old lady. The fourth one...well, the fourth one was just plain weird.

The fifth listing down read,

THREE ROOMMATES SEEKING FOURTH, *huge old house, privacy assured, reasonable rent and utilities.*

Which... OK, she wasn't sure that she could afford 'reasonable' she was more looking for 'dirt cheap' – but at least it sounded less weird than the others. Three roommates. That meant three more people who'd maybe take up for her if Monica and company came sniffing around...or at least take up for the house. Hmmmmm.

She called, and got an answering machine with a mellow-sounding, *young*-sounding male voice. 'Hello, you've reached the Glass House. If you're looking for Michael, he sleeps days. If you're looking for Shane, good luck with that, 'cause we never know where the hell he is' – distant laughter from at least two people – 'and if you're looking for Eve, you'll probably get her on her cell phone or at the shop. But hey. Leave a message. And if you're looking to audition for the room, come on by. It's 716 West Lot Street.' A totally different voice, a female one lightened up by giggles like bubbles in soda, said, 'Yeah, just look for the mansion.' And then a third voice, male again. '*Gone with the Wind* meets *The Munsters*.' More laughter, and a beep.

Claire blinked, coughed, and finally said, 'Um…hi. My name is Claire? Claire Danvers? And I was, um, calling about the, um, room thing. Sorry.' And hung up in a panic. Those three people sounded…normal. But they sounded pretty close, too. And in her experience, groups of friends like that just didn't open up to include underage, undersized geeks like her. They hadn't sounded mean; they just sounded – self-confident. Something she wasn't.

She checked the rest of the listings, and felt her heart actually sink a little. Maybe an inch and a half, with a slight sideways twist. God, I'm dead. She couldn't sleep out here on a bench like some homeless loser, and she couldn't go back to the dorm; she had to do something.

Fine, she thought, and snapped her phone shut, then open again to dial a cab.

Seven sixteen Lot Street. *Gone with the Wind* meets *The Munsters*. Right.

Maybe they'd at least feel sorry enough for her to put her up for one lousy night.

The cabbie – she figured he was just about the only cabdriver in Morganville, which apart from the campus at TPU on the edge of town had only about ten thousand people in it – took an hour to show up. Claire hadn't been in a car in six weeks, since her parents had driven her into town. She hadn't been much beyond a block of the campus, either, and then just to buy used books for class.

'You meeting someone?' the cabbie asked. She was staring out the window at the storefronts: used-clothing shops, used-book shops, computer stores, stores that sold nothing but wooden Greek letters. All catering to the college.

'No,' she said. 'Why?'

The cabbie shrugged. 'Usually you kids are meeting up with friends. If you're looking for a good time—'

She shivered. 'I'm not. I'm – yes, I'm meeting some people. If you could hurry, please…?'

He grunted and took a right turn, and the cab went from Collegetown to Creepytown in one block flat. She couldn't define how it happened exactly – the buildings were pretty much the same, but they looked dim and old, and the few people moving on the streets had their heads down and were walking fast. Even when people were walking in twos or threes, they weren't chatting. When the cab passed, people looked up, then down again, as if they'd been looking for another kind of car.

A little girl was walking with her hand in her mother's, and as the cab stopped for a light, the girl waved, just a little. Claire waved back.

The girl's mother looked up, alarmed, and hustled her kid away into the black mouth of a store that sold used electronics. *Wow*, Claire thought. *Do I look that scary?* Maybe she did. Or maybe Morganville was just ultra-careful of its kids.

Funny, now that she thought about it, there was something missing in this town. Signs. She'd seen them all her life stapled to telephone poles... advertisements for lost dogs, missing kids or adults.

Nothing here. Nothing.

'Lot Street,' the cabbie announced, and squealed to a stop. 'Ten fifty.'

For a five-minute ride? Claire thought, amazed, but she paid up. She thought about shooting him the finger as he drove away, but he looked kind of dangerous, and besides, she really wasn't the kind of girl who did that sort of thing. Usually. It was a bad day, though.

She hoisted her backpack again, hit a bruise on her shoulder, and nearly dropped the weight on her foot. Tears stung at her eyes. All of a sudden she felt tired and shaky again, scared... At least on campus she'd kind of been on relatively familiar ground, but out here in town it was like being a stranger, all over again.

Morganville was brown. Burnt brown by the sun, beaten down by wind and weather. Hot summer was starting to give way to hot autumn, and the leaves on the trees – what trees there were – looked grey-edged and dry, and they rattled like paper in the wind. West Lot Street was near what passed for the downtown district in town, probably an old residential neighbourhood. Nothing special about the homes that she could see...ranch houses, most of them with peeling, faded paint.

She counted house numbers, and realised she was standing in front of 716. She turned and looked behind her, and gasped, because whoever the guy had been on the phone, he'd been dead-on right in his description. Seven sixteen looked like a movie set, something straight out of the Civil War. Big greying columns. A wide front porch. Two stories of windows.

The place was huge. Well, not *huge* – but bigger than Claire had imagined. Like, big enough to be a frat house, and probably perfectly suited to it. She could just imagine Greek letters over the door.

It looked deserted, but to be fair every house on the block looked deserted. Late afternoon, nobody home from work yet. A few cars glittered in the white-hot sunshine, finish softened by a layer of dirt. No cars in front of 716, though.

This was such a bad idea, she thought, and there were those tears again, bubbling up along with panic. What was she going to do? Walk up to the door and beg to be a roommate? How lame-ass was that? They'd think she was pathetic at best, a head case at worst. No, it had been a dumb idea to even blow the money on cab fare.

It was hot, and she was tired and she hurt and she had homework due, and no place to sleep, and all of a sudden, it was just too much.

Claire dropped her backpack, buried her bruised face in both hands, and just started sobbing like a baby. *Crybaby freak*, she imagined Monica saying, but that just made her sob harder, and all of a sudden the idea of going home, going home to Mom and Dad and the room she knew they'd kept open for her, seemed better, better than anything out here in the scary, crazy world...

'Hey,' a girl's voice said, and someone touched her on the elbow. 'Hey, are you OK?'

Claire yelped and jumped, landed hard on her strained ankle, and nearly toppled over. The girl who'd scared her reached out and grabbed her arm to steady her, looking genuinely scared herself. 'I'm sorry! God, I'm such a klutz. Look, are you OK?'

The girl wasn't Monica, or Jen, or Gina, or anybody else she'd seen around the campus at TPU; this girl was way Goth. Not in a bad way – she didn't have the sulky I'm-so-not-cool-I'm-cool attitude of most of the Goths Claire had known in school – but the dyed-black, shag-cut hair, the pale make-up, the heavy eye-liner and mascara, the red-and-black-striped tights and clunky black shoes and black pleated miniskirt...very definitely a fan of the dark side.

'My name's Eve,' the girl said, and smiled. It was a sweet, funny kind of smile, something that invited Claire to share in a private joke. 'Yeah, my parents really named me that, go figure. It's like they knew how I'd turn out.' Her smile faded, and she took a good look at Claire's face. 'Wow. Jeez, nice black eye. Who hit you?'

'Nobody.' Claire said it instantly, without even thinking why, although she knew in her bones that Goth Eve was in no way bestest friends with preppy Monica. 'I had an accident.'

'Yeah,' Eve agreed softly. 'I used to have those kinds of accidents, falling into fists and stuff. Like I said, I'm a klutz. You OK? You need a doctor or something? I can drive you if you want.'

She gestured to the street next to them, and Claire realised that while she'd been sobbing her eyes out, an ancient beater of a black Cadillac – complete with tail fins – had been docked at the curb. There was a cheery-looking skull dangling from the rearview mirror, and Claire had no doubt that the back bumper would be plastered with stickers for emo bands nobody had ever heard of.

She liked Eve already. 'No,' she said, and swiped

at her eyes angrily with the back of her hand. 'I, uh – look, I'm sorry. It's been a really awful day. I was coming to ask about the room, but—'

'Right, the room!' Eve snapped her fingers, as if she'd forgotten all about it, and jumped up and down two or three times in excitement. 'Great! I'm just home for break – I work over at Common Grounds, you know, the coffee shop? – and Michael won't be up for a while yet, but you can come in and see the house if you want. I don't know if Shane's around, but—'

'I don't know if I should—'

'You should. You totally should.' Eve rolled her eyes. 'You wouldn't believe the losers we see trying to get in the door. I mean, seriously. Freaks. You're the first normal one I've seen so far. Michael would kick my ass if I let you get away without at least trying a sales pitch.'

Claire blinked. Somehow, she'd been thinking that she'd be the one begging for them to consider *her*...and normal? Eve thought she was normal?

'Sure,' she heard herself say. 'Yeah. I'd like that.'

Eve grabbed her backpack and slung it over her own shoulder, on top of her black silver-studded purse in the shape of a coffin. 'Follow me.' And she bounced away, up the walk to the gracious Southern Gothic front porch to unlock the door.

Up close, the house looked old, but not really run-down as such; weathered, Claire decided. Could have used some paint here and there, and the cast-iron chairs needed a coat, too. The front door was actually double-sized, with a big stained-glass panel at the top.

'Yo!' Eve yelled, and dumped Claire's backpack on a table in the hallway, her purse next to it, her keys in an antique-looking ashtray with a cast-iron monkey on the handle. 'Roomies! We've got a live one!'

It occurred to Claire, as the door boomed shut behind her, that there were a couple of ways to interpret that, and one of them – the *Texas Chainsaw Massacre* way – wasn't good. She stopped moving, frozen, and just looked around.

Nothing overtly creepy about the inside of the house, at least. Lots of wood, clean and simple. Chips of paint knocked off of corners, like it had seen a lot of life. It smelt like lemon polish and – chilli?

'Yo!' Eve yelled again, and clumped on down the hall. It opened up to a bigger room; from what Claire could see, there were big leather couches and book-shelves, like a real home. Maybe this was what off-campus housing looked like. If so, it was a big step up from dorm life. 'Shane, I smell the chilli. I know you're here! Get your headphones out of your ears!'

She couldn't quite imagine *Texas Chainsaw Massacre* taking place in a room like that, either. That was a plus. Or, for that matter, serial-killing roommates doing something as homey as making chilli. Good chilli, from the way it smelt. With...garlic?

She took a couple of hesitant steps down the hallway. Eve's footsteps were clunking off into another room, maybe the kitchen. The house seemed very quiet. Nothing jumped out to scare her, so Claire proceeded, one careful foot after another, all the way into the big central room.

And a guy lying sprawled on the couch – the way only guys could sprawl – yawned and sat up rubbing his head. When Claire opened her mouth – whether to say hello or to yell for help, she didn't know – he surprised her into silence by grinning at her and putting his finger over his mouth to shush her. 'Hey,' he whispered. 'I'm Shane. What's up?' He blinked a couple of times, and without any change in his expression, said, 'Dude, that is a badass shiner. Hurts, huh?'

She nodded slightly. Shane swung his legs off the couch and sat there, watching her, elbows on his knees and hands dangling loosely. He had brown hair, cut in uneven layers that didn't quite manage to look punk. He was an older boy, older than her, anyway. Eighteen? A big guy, and tall to match it. Big enough to make her feel more miniature than usual. She thought his eyes looked brown, but she didn't dare meet them for more than a flicker at a time.

'So I guess you're gonna say that the other chick looks worse,' Shane said.

She shook her head, then winced when motion made it hurt even more. 'No, I – um – how did you know it was—?'

'A chick? Easy. Size you are, a guy would have put you in the hospital with a punch hard enough to leave a mark like that. So what's up with that? You don't look like you go looking for trouble.'

She felt like she ought to take offence about that, but honestly, this whole thing was starting to feel like some strange dream anyway. Maybe she'd never woken up at all. Maybe she was lying in a coma in a hospital bed, and Shane was just her lame-ass equivalent of the Cheshire cat. 'I'm Claire,' she said, and waved awkwardly. 'Hi.'

He nodded toward a leather wing chair. She slid into it, feet dangling, and felt a weird sense of relief wash over her. It felt like home, although of course it wasn't, and she was starting to think that it really couldn't be. She didn't fit here. She couldn't actually imagine who would.

'You want something?' Shane asked suddenly. 'Coke, maybe? Chilli? Bus ticket back home?'

'Coke,' she said, and, surprisingly, 'and chilli.'

'Good choice. I made it myself.' He slid off the couch, weirdly boneless for his size, and padded barefoot into the kitchen where Eve had gone. Claire listened to a blur of voices as the two of them talked, and relaxed, one muscle at a time, into the soft embrace of the chair. She hadn't noticed until now, but the house was kept cool, and the lazy circle of the ceiling fan overhead swept chilly air over her hot, aching face. It felt nice.

She opened her eyes at the sound of Eve's shoes clomping back into the room. Eve was carrying a tray with a red and white can, a bowl, a spoon, and an ice pack. She set the tray on a coffee table and nudged the table toward Claire with her knee. 'Ice pack first,' she said. 'You can never tell what Shane puts in the chilli. Be afraid.'

Shane padded back to the couch and flopped, sucking on his own can of soda. Eve shot him an exasperated look. 'Yeah, man, thanks for bringing me one, too.' The raccoon eye make-up exaggerated her eye roll. 'Dork.'

'Didn't know if you wanted zombie dirt sprinkled on it or anything. If you're eating this week.'

'*Dork!* Go on and eat, Claire – I'll go get my own.'

Claire picked up the spoon and tried a tentative bite of the chilli, which was thick and meaty and spicy, heavy on the garlic. Delicious, in fact. She'd gotten used to cafeteria food, and this was just...wow. *Not.* Shane watched her, eyebrows up, as she started to shovel it in. ''Sgood,' she mumbled. He gave her a lazy salute. By the time she was halfway through the bowl, Eve was back with her own tray, which she plunked down on the other half of the coffee table. Eve sat on the floor, crossed her legs, and dug in.

'Not bad,' she finally said. 'At least you left out the oh-my-God sauce this time.'

'Made myself a batch with it,' Shane said. 'It's got the biohazard sticker on it in the fridge, so don't bitch if you get flamed. Where'd you pick up the stray?'

'Outside. She came to see the room.'

'You beat her up first, just to make sure she's tough enough?'

'Bite me, chilli boy.'

'Don't mind Eve,' he told Claire. 'She hates working days. She's afraid she'll tan.'

'Yeah, and Shane just hates working. So what's your name?'

Claire opened her mouth, but Shane beat her to it, clearly happy to one-up his roomie. 'Claire. What, you didn't even ask? A chick beat her up, too. Probably some skank in the dorms. You know how that place is.'

They exchanged a look. A long one. Eve turned back to Claire. 'Is that true? You got beat up in the dorm?' She nodded, hastily shovelling more food in her mouth to keep from having to say much. 'Well, that totally blows. No wonder you're looking for the room.' Another nod. 'You didn't bring much with you.'

'I don't have much,' she said. 'Just the books, and maybe a couple of things back at my room. But – I don't want to go back there to get stuff. Not tonight.'

'Why not?' Shane had grabbed a ratty-looking old baseball from the floor and tossed it up toward the tall ceiling, narrowly missing the spinning blades of the fan. He caught it without effort. 'Somebody still looking to pound you?'

'Yeah,' Claire said, and looked down into her fast-diminishing chilli. 'Guess so. It's not just her, it's – she's got friends. And... I don't. That place just – well, it's creepy.'

'Been there,' Eve said. 'Oh, wait, still there.'

Shane mimed throwing the baseball at her. She mimed ducking.

'What time is Michael getting up?'

Shane gave her another mock throw. 'Hell, Eve, I don't know. I love the guy, but I don't *love* the guy. Go bang on his door and ask. Me, I'm gonna go get ready.'

'Ready for what?' Eve asked. 'You're not seriously going out again, are you?'

'Seriously, yeah. Bowling. Her name's Laura. If you want more details, you're gonna have to download the video like everybody else.' Shane rolled off the couch, stood up, and padded off toward the wide stairs leading up to the second floor. 'See you later, Claire.'

Eve made a frustrated sound. 'Wait a minute! So what do you say? You think she'd do OK here, or what?'

Shane waved a hand. 'Whatever, man. Far as I'm concerned, she's OK.' He gave Claire one quick look and a crooked and oddly sweet smile, and bounded up the stairs. He moved like an athlete, but without the swagger she was used to. Kind of hot, actually.

'Guys,' Eve sighed. 'Damn, it'd be good to have another girl in here. They're all like, *Yeah, whatever,* and then when it comes to picking up the place or washing dishes, they turn into ghosts. Not that you have to, like, be a maid or anything, I mean…you just got to yell at 'em until they do their part or they walk all over you.'

Claire smiled, or tried to, but her split lip throbbed, and she felt the scab break open again. Blood dribbled down her chin, and she grabbed the napkin Eve had put on the tray and applied pressure to her lip. Eve watched in silence, frowning, and then got up from the floor, picked up the ice pack, and settled it gently against the bump on Claire's head. 'How's that?' she asked.

'Better.' It was. The ice began to numb the ache almost immediately, and the food was setting up a nice warm fire in her stomach. 'Um, I guess I should ask…about the room…'

'Well, you have to meet Michael, and he has to say yes, but Michael's a sweetie, really. Oh, and he owns this place. His family does, anyway. I think they moved away and left him the house a couple of years ago. He's about six months older than I am. We're all about eighteen. Michael's sort of the oldest.'

'He sleeps days?'

'Yeah. I mean, *I* like to sleep days, but he's got a thing about it. I called him a vampire once, 'cause he really doesn't like being up in the daytime. Like, ever. He didn't think it was real funny.'

'You're sure he's not a vampire?' Claire said. 'I've seen movies. They're sneaky.' She was kidding. Eve didn't smile.

'Oh, pretty sure. For one thing, he eats Shane's chilli, which, God knows, has enough garlic to explode a dozen high-quality Dracs. And I made him touch a cross once.' Eve took a big swallow of her Coke.

'You – what? *Made him?*'

'Well, sure, yeah. I mean, a girl can't be too careful, especially around here.' Claire must have looked blank, because Eve did the eye-roll thing again. It was her favourite expression, Claire was sure. 'In Morganville? You know?'

'What about it?'

'You mean you don't *know*? How can you not know?' Eve set her can down and got up to her knees, leaning elbows on the coffee table. She looked earnest under the thick make-up. Her eyes were dark brown, edged with gold. 'Morganville's full of vampires.'

Claire laughed.

Eve didn't. She just kept staring.

'Um...you're kidding?'

'How many kids graduate TPU every year?'

'I don't know... It's a crappy college, most everybody transfers out...'

'Everybody *leaves*. Or at least, they stop showing up, right? I can't believe you don't know this. Didn't anybody tell you the score before you moved in? Look, the vamps run the town. They're in charge. And either you're in, or you're out. If you work for them, if you pretend like they're not here and they don't exist, and you look the other way when things happen, then you and your family get a free pass. You get *Protection*. Otherwise...' Eve pulled a finger across her throat and bugged out her eyes.

Right, Claire thought, and put down her spoon. *No wonder nobody rented a room with these people. They're nuts.* It was too bad. Except for the crazy part, she really liked them.

'You think I'm wacko,' Eve said, and sighed. 'Yeah, I get that. I'd think I was, too, except I grew up in a Protected house. My dad works for the water company. My mom is a teacher. But we all wear these.' She extended her wrist. On it was a black leather bracelet, with a symbol on it in red, nothing Claire recognised. It looked kind of like a Chinese character. 'See how mine's red? Expired. It's like health insurance. Kids are only covered until they're eighteen. Mine was up six months ago.' She looked at it mournfully, then shrugged and unsnapped it to drop it on her tray. 'Might as well stop wearing it, I guess. It sure wouldn't fool anybody.'

Claire just looked at her, helpless, wondering if she was the victim of a practical joke, and if any second Eve was going to laugh and call her an idiot for buying it, and Shane would go from kind of lazy-sweet to cruel and shove her out the door, mocking all the way. Because this wasn't the way the world worked. You didn't like people, and then have them turn up all crazy, right? Couldn't you *tell*?

The alternative – that Eve wasn't crazy at all – just wasn't anything Claire wanted to think about. She remembered the people on the street, walking fast, heads down. The way the mother had yanked her little girl off the street at a friendly wave.

'Fine. Go ahead, think I'm nuts,' Eve said, and sat back on her heels. 'I mean, why wouldn't I be? And I won't try to convince you or anything. Just – don't go out after dark unless you're with somebody. Somebody Protected, if you can find them. Look for the bracelet.' She nudged hers with one finger. 'The symbol's white when it's active.'

'But I—' Claire coughed, trying to find something to say. *If you can't say anything nice…* 'OK. Thanks. Um, is Shane—?'

'Shane? Protected?' Eve snorted. 'As if! Even if he was, which I doubt, he'd never admit it, and he doesn't wear the bracelet or anything. Michael – Michael isn't, either, but there's sort of a standard Protection on houses. We're sort of outcasts here. There's safety in numbers, too.'

It was a very weird conversation to be having over chilli and Coke, with an ice pack perched on the top of her head. Claire, without even knowing she was going to do it, yawned. Eve laughed.

'Call it a bedtime story,' she said. 'Listen, let me show you the room. Worst case, you lie down for a while, let the ice pack work, then bug out. Or hey, you wake up and decide you want to talk to Michael before you leave. Your choice.'

Another cold chill swept over her, and she shivered. Probably had to do with the bang on the head, she figured, and how tired she was. She dug in her pocket, found the package of pills the doc had prescribed for her, and swallowed one with the last gulp of Coke. Then she helped Eve carry the trays into the kitchen, which was huge, with stone sinks and ancient polished counters and two modern conveniences – the stove and the refrigerator – stuck awkwardly in the corners.

The chilli had come from a Crock-Pot, which was still simmering away.

When the dishes had been washed, trays stacked, trash discarded, Eve retrieved Claire's backpack from the floor and led her through the living room, up the stairs. On the third riser, Eve turned, alarmed, and said, 'Hey, can you make it up the stairs? Because, you know—'

'I'm OK,' Claire lied. Her ankle hurt like hell, but she wanted to see the room. And if they were likely to throw her out later, she at least wanted to sleep one more time in a bed, however lumpy and old. There were thirteen steps to the top. She made every one of them, even though she left sweaty fingerprints on a banister Shane hadn't even bothered to touch on his way up earlier.

Eve's steps were muffled here by a rich old-looking rug, all swirls and colours, that ran down the centre of the polished wood floor. There were six doors up here on the landing. As they passed them, Eve pointed and named. 'Shane's.' The first door. 'Michael's.' The second door. 'He's got that one, too – it's a double-sized room.' Third door. 'Main bathroom.' Fourth. 'The second bathroom's downstairs – that's kind of the emergency back-up bathroom when Shane's in there moussing his hair for like an hour or something...'

'*Bite me!*' Shane yelled from behind the closed door. Eve pounded a fist on the door and led Claire to the last two on the row. 'This one's mine. Yours is on the end.'

When she swung it open, Claire – prepared for disappointment – actually gasped. For one thing, it was huge. Three times the size of her dorm room. For another, it was on a corner, with three – *three!* – windows, all currently shaded by blinds and curtains. The bed wasn't some dorm-sized miniature; it was a full-sized mattress and box spring with massive wooden columns at the corners, dark and solid. There was a dresser along one wall big enough to hold, well, four or five times the clothes that Claire had ever owned. Plus a closet. Plus...

'Is that a TV?' she asked in a faint voice.

'Yeah. Satellite cable. You'd pitch in, though, unless you want to take it out of the room. Oh, and there's Internet, too. Broadband, over there. I should probably warn you, they monitor Internet traffic around here, though. You have to be careful what you say in messages and stuff.' Eve put the backpack on top of the dresser. 'You don't have to decide right now. You probably ought to rest first. Here, here's your ice pack.' She followed Claire to the bed and helped her pull back the covers, and once Claire had pulled off her shoes and settled, she tucked her in, like a mother, and put the ice pack on her head. 'When you get up, Michael'll probably be awake. I have to get back to work, but it'll be OK. Really.'

Claire smiled at her, a little fuzzily; the painkillers were starting to take effect. She got another chill. 'Thank you, Eve,' she said. 'This is – wow.'

'Yeah, well, you look like you could use a little wow today.' Eve shrugged, and gave her a stunning smile back. 'Sleep well. And don't worry, the vampires won't come in here. This house has Protection, even if we don't.'

Claire turned that over in her mind for a few seconds as Eve left the room and shut the door, and then her mind wandered off in happy clouds of noticing the softness of the pillow and how good the bed felt, and how crisp the sheets were...

She dreamt about the strangest thing: a silent room, with someone pale and quiet sitting on a velvet sofa, turning pages in a book and weeping. It didn't scare her, exactly, but she felt cold, on and off, and the house...the house seemed like it was full of whispers.

Eventually, she fell into a deeper, darker place, and didn't dream at all.

Not even about Monica.

Not even about vampires.

CHAPTER THREE

She woke up in the dark with a panicked flinch that sent the ice pack – water sloshing in a bag now – thumping off her pillow and onto the floor. The house was quiet, except for the creaky, creepy noises houses made at night. Outside, wind rattled the dry leaves on the trees, and she heard music coming from the other side of the bedroom door.

Claire slid out of bed, fumbled for a lamp, and found one next to the bed – Tiffany-style glass, really nice – and the colourful glow chased away any nightmare fears she'd been trying to have. The music was slow and warm and contemplative, kind of guitar alternative. She got her shoes on, took a look in the dresser mirror, and got a nasty shock. Her face still hurt, and it was obvious why – her right eye was swollen, the skin around it purple. Her split lip looked shiny and unpleasantly thick, too. Her face – always pale – looked even paler than normal. Her short pixie-cut black hair had a serious case of bed-head, but she fluffed it out into something like order. She'd never really been much for make-up, even when she'd been stealing Mom's to try on, but today maybe a little foundation and concealer couldn't hurt... She looked ragged, and beaten, and homeless.

Well. It was nothing but the truth, after all.

Claire took a deep breath and opened her bedroom door. Lights were on in the hall, warm and glowing gold; the music was coming from downstairs, in the living room. She checked a clock hanging on the wall at the far end; it was after midnight – she'd slept for more than twelve hours.

And missed all her classes. Not that she'd have wanted to show up looking like this, even if she hadn't been so paranoid about Monica following her around...but she'd need to hit the books later. At least the books didn't hit back.

Her bruises felt better, and in fact her head hurt only a little. Her ankle was still the worst of it, sending sharp glassy jabs of pain up her leg with every step down the stairs.

She was halfway down when she saw the boy sitting on the couch, where Shane had been sprawled before. He had a guitar in his hands.

Oh. The music. She'd thought it was a recording, but no, this was real, this was live, and he was playing it. She'd never heard live music before – not really *playing*, not like this. He was...wow. He was wonderful.

She watched him, frozen, because he clearly didn't even know she existed yet; it was just him and the guitar and the music, and if she had to put a name to what she could see on his face, it would be something poetic, like *longing*. He was blond, his hair cut kind of like Shane's, in a careless mop. Not as big as Shane, and not as muscled, though he was maybe as tall. He was wearing a T-shirt, too, black, with a beer logo. Blue jeans. No shoes.

He stopped playing, head down, and reached for the open beer on the table in front of him. He toasted empty air. 'Happy birthday to you, man.' He tossed back three swallows, sighed, and put the bottle down. 'And here's to house arrest. What the hell. Own it or get owned.'

Claire coughed. He turned, startled, and saw her standing there on the stairs; his frown cleared after a second or two. 'Oh. You're the one Shane said wanted to talk about the room. Hey. Come on down.'

She did, trying not to limp, and when she got into the full light she saw his quick, intelligent blue eyes catalogue the bruises.

He didn't say a word about them. 'I'm Michael,' he said. 'And you're not eighteen, so this is going to be a real short conversation.'

She sat, fast, heart pounding. 'I'm in college,' she said. 'I'm a freshman. My name is—'

'Don't bullshit me, and I don't care what your name is. You're not eighteen. It's a good bet you're not even seventeen. We don't take anybody in this house who isn't legal.' He had a deep voice, warm but – at least right now – hard. 'Not that you'd be signing on to Orgy Central, but sorry, me and Shane have to worry about things like that. All it takes is you living here and somebody even hinting there's something going on—'

'Wait,' she blurted. 'I wouldn't do that. Or say that. I'm not looking to get you guys in trouble. I just need—'

'No,' he said. He put the guitar aside, in its case, and latched it shut. 'I'm sorry, but you can't stay here. House rules.'

She'd known it was coming, of course, but she'd let herself think – Eve had been nice, and Shane hadn't been horrible, and the room was so nice – but the look in Michael's eyes was as final as it got. Complete and utter rejection.

She felt her lips trembling, and hated herself for it. Why couldn't she be a badass, stone-cold bitch? Why couldn't she stand up for herself when she needed to, without breaking down into tears like a baby? *Monica* wouldn't be crying. Monica would be snapping some comeback at him, telling him that her stuff was already in the room. Monica would slap money down on the table and dare him to turn it down.

Claire reached in her back pocket and pulled out her wallet. 'How much?' she asked, and started counting out bills. She had twenties, so it looked like a lot. 'Three hundred enough? I can get more if I have to.'

Michael sat back, surprised, a little frown bracketing his forehead. He reached for his beer and took another sip while he thought about it. 'How?' he asked.

'What?'

'How would you get more?'

'Get a job. Sell stuff.' Not that she had much to sell, but in an emergency there was always the panicked call to Mom. 'I want to stay here, Michael. I really do.' She was surprised at the conviction in her voice. 'Yeah, I'm under eighteen, but I swear, you won't have any trouble from me. I'll stay out of your way. I go to school, and I study. That's all I do. I'm not a partyer, I'm not a slacker. I'm useful. I'll – I'll help clean and cook.'

He thought about it, staring at her; he was the kind of person you could actually see thinking. It was a little scary, although he probably didn't mean it to be. There was just something so...*adult* about him. So sure of himself.

'No,' he said. 'I'm sorry, kid. But it's just too much risk.'

'Eve's only a little bit older than I am!'

'Eve's eighteen. You're what, sixteen?'

'Almost seventeen!' If you were a little fluid on the definition of *almost*. 'I really am in college. I'm a freshman – look, here's my student ID...'

He ignored it. 'Come back in a year. We'll talk

about it,' he said. 'Look, I'm sorry. What about the dorm?'

'They'll kill me if I stay there,' she said, and looked down at her clasped hands. 'They tried to kill me today.'

'What?'

'The other girls. They punched me and shoved me down the stairs.'

Silence. A really long one. She heard the creak of leather, and then Michael was on one knee next to the chair. Before she could stop him, he was probing the bump on her head, tilting it back so he could get a good, impersonal look at the bruises and cuts.

'What else?' he asked.

'What?'

'Besides what I can see? You're not going to drop dead on me, are you?'

Wow, sensitive. 'I'm OK. I saw the doctor and everything. It's just – bruises. And a strained ankle. But they pushed me down the stairs, and they meant it, and she told me—' Suddenly, Eve's words about *vampires* came back to her and made her trip over her tongue. 'The girl in charge, she told me that tonight, I'd get what was coming to me. I *can't* go back to the dorm, Michael. If you send me out that door, they'll kill me, *because I don't have any friends and I don't have anyplace to go!*'

He stayed there for a few more seconds, looking her right in the eyes, and then retreated to the couch. He unlatched the guitar case again and cradled the instrument; she thought that was his comfort zone, right there, with the guitar in his arms. 'These girls. Do they go out in daylight?'

She blinked. 'You mean, outside? Sure. They go to classes. Well, sometimes.'

'Do they wear bracelets?'

She blinked. 'You mean, like—' Eve had left hers behind on the table, so she picked up the leather band with its red symbol. 'Like this? I never noticed. They wear a lot of stuff.' She thought hard, and maybe she did remember something after all. The bracelets didn't look like this, though. They were gold, and Monica and the Monickettes all had them on their right wrists. She'd never paid much attention. 'Maybe.'

'Bracelets with white symbols?' Michael made the question casual; in fact, he bent his head and concentrated on tuning his guitar, not that it needed it. Every note sounded perfect as it whispered out of the strings. 'Do you remember?'

'No.' She felt a pure burst of something that wasn't quite panic, wasn't quite excitement. 'Does that mean they have Protection?'

He hesitated for about a second, just long enough for her to know he was surprised. 'You mean condoms?' he asked. 'Doesn't everybody?'

'You know what I mean.' Her cheeks were burning. She hoped it wasn't as obvious as it felt.

'Don't think I do.'

'Eve said—'

He looked up sharply, and those blue eyes were suddenly angry. 'Eve needs to keep her mouth shut. She's in enough danger as it is, trolling around out there in Goth gear. They already think she's mocking them. If they hear she's talking...'

'They, who?' Claire asked. It was his turn to look away.

'People,' he said flatly. 'Look, I don't want your blood on my hands. You can stay for a couple of days. But only until you find a place, right? And make it fast – I'm not running a halfway house for battered girls. I've got enough to worry about trying to keep Eve and Shane out of trouble.'

For a guy who made such beautiful music, he was bitter, and a little scary. Claire put the money hesitantly on the table in front of him. He stared at it, jaw tense.

'The rent's a hundred a month,' he said. 'You buy groceries once a month, too. First month in advance. But you're not staying past that, so keep the rest.'

She swallowed and picked up two hundred of the three hundred she'd counted out. 'Thanks,' she said.

'Don't thank me,' he said. 'Just don't get us into trouble. I mean it.'

She got up, went into the kitchen, and spooned chilli into two bowls, added the bowls to trays along with spoons and Cokes, and brought it all back to set it on the coffee table. Michael stared at it, then her. She sat down on the floor – painfully – and began eating. After a pause, Michael took his bowl and tasted it.

'Shane made it,' Claire said. 'It's pretty good.'

'Yeah. Chilli and spaghetti, that's pretty much all Shane can cook. You know how to make anything?'

'Sure.'

'Like?'

'Lasagna,' she said. 'And, um, sort of a hamburger hash thing, with noodles. And tacos.'

Michael looked thoughtful. 'Could you make tacos tomorrow?'

'Sure,' she said. 'I have classes from eleven to five, but I'll stop and pick up the stuff.'

He nodded, eating steadily, glancing up at her once in a while. 'I'm sorry,' he finally said.

'About what?'

'Being an asshole. Look, it's just that I can't – I have to be careful. Really careful.'

'You weren't being an asshole,' she said. 'You're trying to protect yourself and your friends. That's OK. That's what you're supposed to do.'

Michael smiled, and it transformed his face, made it suddenly angelic and wonderful. *Dude*, she thought in amazement. *He's totally gorgeous*. No wonder he'd been worried about her being underage. A smile like that, he'd be peeling girls off of him right and left.

'If you're in this house, you're my friend,' he said. 'What's your name, by the way?'

'Claire. Claire Danvers.'

'Welcome to the Glass House, Claire Danvers.'

'But only temporarily.'

'Yeah, temporarily.'

They shared a smile, uneasily, and Michael cleared up the plates this time, and Claire went back up to her room, to spread out her books on the built-in desk and start the day's studying.

She listened to him playing downstairs, the soft and heartfelt accompaniment to the night, as she fell into the world she loved.

CHAPTER FOUR

Morning dawned bright and early, and Claire woke up to the smell of frying bacon. She stumbled to the bathroom down the hall, yawning, barely aware that she was scantily dressed in her extra-long T-shirt until she remembered, *Oh my God, boys live here, too.* Luckily, nobody saw, and the bathroom was free. Somebody had already been in it this morning; the mirrors were still frosted with steam, and the big black-and-white room glistened with drops of water. It smelt clean, though. And kind of fruity.

The fruity smell was the shampoo, she found, as she lathered and rinsed. When she wiped the mirror down and stared at herself, she saw the patterns of bruises up and down both sides of her pale skin. *I could have died.* She'd been lucky.

She tossed the T-shirt back on, then dashed back to her room to dig out the panties she'd rescued yesterday from the washer. They were still damp, but she put them on anyway, then dragged on blue jeans.

On impulse, she opened the closet, and found some old stuff pushed to the back. T-shirts, mostly, from bands she'd never heard of, and a few she remembered as ancient. A couple of sweaters, too. She stripped off her bloodstained shirt and dragged on a faded black one, and, after thinking about it, left her shoes on the floor.

Downstairs, Eve and Shane were arguing in the kitchen about the right way to make scrambled eggs. Eve said they needed milk. Shane said milk was for pussies. Claire padded silently past them, over to the refrigerator, and pulled out a carton of orange juice. She splashed some into a glass, then silently held the carton up for the other two. Eve took it and poured herself a glass, then handed it to Shane.

'So,' Shane asked, 'Michael didn't pitch you out.'

'No.'

Shane nodded slowly. He was even bigger and taller than she remembered, and his skin was a golden brown colour, like he'd spent a lot of time in the sun over the summer. His hair had that bronzy sheen, too. Sun-bleached where Michael was naturally blond. *OK, truthfully? They're both hotties.* She wished she hadn't really thought that, but at least she hadn't said it out loud.

'Something you should know about Michael,' he said. 'He doesn't like taking chances. I wasn't sure he'd let you stay. If he did, then he got a good vibe off of you. Don't disrespect that, because if you do – I won't be happy, either. Got it?'

Eve was silently watching the two of them, which Claire figured was a new experience for Eve, at least the not-talking part. 'He's your friend, right?'

'He saved my life,' Shane said. 'I'd die for him, but it'd be a dumbass thing to do to thank him for it. So yeah. He's been my friend all my life, and he's more like a brother. So don't get him in trouble.'

'I won't,' she said. 'No milk in the eggs.'

'See?' Shane turned back to the counter and started cracking eggs into a bowl. 'Told ya.'

'Traitor,' Eve sighed, and poked at the frying bacon with a fork. 'Fine. So. How was Linda last night?'

'Laura.'

'Whatever. Not like I have to remember a name for more than one date, anyway.'

'She bowled a one fifty.'

'God, you're *such* a disappointment. Share, already!'

Shane smiled tightly down at the eggs. 'Hey, not in front of the kid. You got the note.'

'Kid?' That hurt. Claire dropped plates on the counter with a little too much force. *'Note?'*

Shane handed over a folded piece of paper. It was short and sweet, and signed 'Michael'...and it told them that Claire was underage, and that the two of them were supposed to look out for her while she was in the house.

Cute. Claire didn't know whether to be pissed or flattered. On reflection…pissed. 'I'm not a kid!' she told Shane hotly. 'I'm only, like, a year younger than Eve!'

'And girls are much more mature.' Eve nodded wisely. 'So you're about ten years older than Shane, then.'

'Seriously,' Claire insisted. 'I'm not a kid!'

'Whatever you say, kid,' Shane said blandly. 'Cheer up. Just means you don't have to put up with me telling you how much sex I didn't get.'

'I'm telling Michael,' Eve warned.

'About how much sex I didn't get? Go ahead.'

'No bacon for you.'

'Then no eggs for you. Either of you.'

Eve glowered at him. 'Prisoner exchange?'

They glared at each other, then swapped pans and started scooping.

Claire was just about to join in when the front doorbell rang, a lilting silvery sound. It wasn't a scary sound, but Eve and Shane froze and looked at each other, and that was scary, somehow. Shane put his plate down on the granite countertop, licked bacon grease from his fingers, and said, 'Get her out of sight.'

Eve nodded. She dropped her own plate onto the counter, grabbed Claire's wrist, and hustled her to the pantry – a door half hidden in the shadow of the awkwardly placed refrigerator. It was big, dark, and dusty, shelves crowded with old cans of yams and asparagus and glass jars of ancient jellies. There was a light with a string pull above, but Eve didn't turn it on. She reached behind a row of murky-looking cans of fruit and hit some kind of a switch. There was a grating rumble, then a click, and part of the back wall swung open.

Eve pushed it back, reached in, and grabbed a flashlight that she handed to Claire. 'Inside,' she said. 'I'm going to turn the light on out here, but try to keep that flashlight off if you hear voices. It could show through the cracks.' Claire nodded, a little dazed, and crouched down to crawl through the small opening into…a big empty room, stone floored, no windows. A few spiderwebs in the corners, and loads of dust, but otherwise it didn't look too bad.

Until Eve shut the door, and then the darkness slammed down, and Claire hastily flicked on the flashlight, moved to the nearest corner, and knelt down there, breathing fast and hard.

Just one minute ago, they'd been laughing about bacon and eggs, and all of a sudden…what the hell had just happened? And why was there a secret compartment in this house? One with – so far as she could tell – no other entrances or exits?

She heard distant voices, and hastily thumbed off the flashlight. That was bad. She'd never really been afraid of the dark, but dark wasn't really *dark* most of the time… There were stars, moonlight, distant streetlights.

This was pitch-black, take-no-prisoners dark, and she had the ice-cold thought that anything could be right next to her, reaching out for her, and she'd never see it coming.

Claire bit down hard on her lip, gripped the flashlight tightly, and slid down the wall until her searching hand found the rough wood of the door she'd come in through. A little light was leaking in around it, barely a glimmer but enough to ease the pounding in her chest.

Voices. Shane's, and someone else's. A man's voice, deeper than Shane's. '...standard inventory.'

'Sir, there's nobody living here but what's on the roster. Just the three of us.' Shane sounded subdued and respectful, which didn't seem like him. Not that she knew him that well, but he was kind of a smart-ass.

'Which one are you?' the voice asked.

'Shane Collins, sir.'

'Get your third in here,' the voice said.

'Well, I would, but – Michael's not here. He's out until tonight. You want to check back then...?'

'Never mind.' Claire, straining her ears, heard paper rustling. 'You're Eve Rosser?'

'Yes, sir.' Eve sounded respectful, but brisk.

'Moved out of your parents' house – eight months ago?'

'Yes, sir.'

'Employed?'

'At Common Grounds, you know, the coffee—'

The man, whoever he was, interrupted her. 'You. Collins. Any employment?' Clearly talking to Shane.

'I'm between jobs, sir. You know how it is.'

'Keep looking. We don't like slackers in Morganville. Everybody contributes.'

'Yes, sir. I'll keep it in mind, sir.'

A brief pause. Maybe there had been a little bit more smart-ass in Shane's response than there should have been. Claire deliberately slowed her breathing, trying to hear more.

'You left town for a couple of years, boy. What brings you back?'

'Homesick, sir.' Yes, it was definitely back in his voice, and even *Claire* knew that was a bad thing. 'Missed all my old friends.'

She heard Eve clear her throat. 'Sir, I'm sorry, but I've got work in a half hour…?'

More paper shuffling. 'One other thing. Here's a picture of a girl that disappeared from her dorm last night. You haven't seen her?'

They both chorused a 'No.'

He must not have believed them, because he didn't sound convinced. 'What's in here?' He didn't wait to hear a response; he just opened the outer door of the pantry. Claire flinched and held her breath. 'You always leave the light on?'

'I was getting some jam when you rang, sir. I probably forgot to turn it off,' Eve said. She sounded nervous. 'Sorry.'

Click. The light in the pantry went out, taking what little there was seeping through the door with it. Claire barely controlled a gasp. *Don't move. Don't move.* She just knew he – whoever he was – was standing there in the dark, looking and listening.

And then, finally, she heard him say, 'You ring the station if you see that girl. She's got herself in some trouble. We're supposed to help her get straightened out.'

'Yes, sir,' Eve said, and the pantry door shut. The conversation moved away, became softer and softer until it faded into nothing.

Claire switched on the flashlight, covered it with her hand, and pointed it at the corner – only a little light escaped, just enough to convince her that no evil zombie was sneaking up on her in the dark. And then she waited. It seemed like a long time before there were two sharp raps on the door, and it swung open in a blaze of electric light. Eve's stark white make-up and black eyeliner looked even scarier than before.

'It's OK,' she said, and helped Claire out of the hidden room. 'He's gone.'

'Oh, the hell it's OK,' Shane said behind her. He had his arms folded across his chest, and rocked back and forth, frowning. 'Those assholes have her picture. They're *looking* for her. What'd you do, Claire? Knife the mayor or something?'

'Nothing!' she blurted. 'I – I don't know why –

maybe it's that they're just worried because I didn't show up last night?'

'Worried?' Shane laughed bitterly. 'Yeah, that's it. They're *worried* about you. Right. I'm going to have to talk this over with Michael. If they're going to turn the town upside down looking for you, either you're too hot to stay in Morganville, or we need to get you under some kind of Protection, fast.'

He said it the same way Eve had. 'But – maybe the police—?'

'That was the police,' Eve said. 'Told you. They run the town. These guys work for the vamps – they're not vamps themselves, but they're scary enough without the fangs. Look, can you call your parents? Get them to pull you out of school and take you home or something?'

Sure. That would be the easiest thing in the world, only it would mean failure, and they'd never believe a word of this stuff, ever, and if she tried to explain it, she'd end up drugged and in therapy for the rest of her life. And any chance – *any* chance – of making it to Yale or MIT or Caltech would be blown completely. She supposed it was kind of dumb to be thinking of it that way, but those things were *real* to her.

Vampires? Not so much.

'But – I haven't done anything!' she said, and looked from Shane to Eve, and back again. 'How can they be after me if I didn't do anything?'

'Life ain't fair,' Shane said, with all the certainty of two more years of experience at it. 'You must have pissed off the wrong people, is all I know. What's the girl's name? The one who smacked you around?'

'M-Monica.'

They both stared at her.

'Oh, crap,' Eve said, horrified. 'Monica *Morrell*?'

Shane's face went...blank. Completely blank, except for his eyes, and there was something pretty scary going on behind them. 'Monica,' he repeated. 'How come nobody told me?'

Eve was watching him, biting her lip. 'Sorry, Shane. We would have – I swear, I thought she left town. Went off to college somewhere else.'

Shane shook it off, whatever it was, and shrugged, trying to look like he didn't care. It was obvious to Claire that he did, though. 'She probably couldn't stand not being the queen bee, and had to come begging back to Daddy to buy her some grades.'

'Shane—'

'I'm fine. Don't worry about me.'

'She probably doesn't even remember you,' Eve blurted, and then looked as if she wished she hadn't said it. 'I – that's not what I meant. I'm sorry.'

He laughed, and it sounded wrong and a little bit shaky. There was a short, odd silence, and then Eve changed the subject by resolutely picking up her plate of cooling bacon and eggs.

And then went still and round-eyed. 'Oh, shit,' she said, and then covered her mouth.

'What?'

She pointed at the plates on the counter. Shane's, hers...and Claire's. 'Three plates. He knew something was up. We told him Michael wasn't around. No wonder he kept poking.'

Shane said nothing, but Claire could see he was – if possible – even more upset. He didn't show it much, but he picked up his plate and walked away, out into the living room, then up the steps two at a time.

His upstairs door slammed.

Eve bit her lip, watching after him.

'So... Shane and Monica...?' Claire guessed.

Eve kept staring at the doorway. 'Not like you're thinking,' she said. 'He wouldn't touch that skank in a million years. But they were in high school together, and Shane – got on her bad side. Just like you did.'

Claire's appetite for breakfast was suddenly gone. 'What happened?'

'He stood up to her, and his house burnt. He nearly died,' she said. 'His – his sister wasn't so lucky. Michael got him out of town, off on his own, before he did something crazy. He's been gone a couple of years. Just came back right before I moved in here.' Eve forced a bright smile. 'Let's eat, yeah? I'm starving.'

They sat out in the living room, chatting about

nothing, not talking about the thing that was most important: what to do.

Because, Claire sensed, neither one of them had a clue.

CHAPTER FIVE

Claire watched the clock – some old-style wall clock, with hands – crawl slowly up to, and past, eleven o'clock. *Professor Hamms is starting the lecture*, she thought, and felt a nauseating twist in her stomach. This was the second day in a row she'd missed school. In her whole life she'd never missed two days of school back-to-back. Sure, she'd read the textbook already – twice – but lectures were important. That was how you found out the good stuff, especially in classes like physics, where they did practical demonstrations. Lectures were the fun part.

It was Thursday. That meant she had a lab class later, too. You couldn't make up lab class, no matter how good your excuse.

She sighed, forced herself to look away from the time, and opened up her Calc II book – she'd tested out of Calc I, could have tested out of Calc II, but she'd thought maybe she might learn something new about solving linear inequalities, which had always been a problem for her.

'What the hell are you doing?' Shane. He was on the stairs, staring at her. She hadn't heard him coming, but that was probably because he was barefoot. His hair was a mess, too. Maybe he'd been asleep.

'Studying,' she said.

'Huh,' he said, like he'd never actually seen it done before. 'Interesting.' He vaulted over the railing three steps from the bottom and flopped down on the leather couch next to her, flicking the TV on with the remote next to him, then changing inputs. 'This going to bother you?'

'No,' she said politely. It was a lie, but she wasn't quite ready to be, you know, blunt. It was her first day.

'Great. Want to take a break?'

'A break?'

'That's when you stop studying' – he tilted his head to the side to look at the book – 'OK, whatever the hell that is, and actually do something fun. It's a custom where I come from.' He dumped something in the centre of her open book with a plastic *thump*. She flinched and picked up the wireless game controller with two fingers. 'Oh, come on. You can't tell me you've never played a video game.'

Truthfully, she had. Once. She hadn't liked it very much. He must have read that in her expression, because he shook his head. 'This is just sad. Now you *have* to take a break. OK, you've got a choice: horror, action, driving, or war.'

She blurted, 'Those are my *choices*?'

He looked offended. 'What, you want *girl games*? Not in my house. Never mind, I'll pick for you. Here. First-person shooter.' He yanked a box from a stack next to the couch and loaded a disc into the machine. 'Easy. All you have to do is pull the trigger. Trust me. Nothing like a little virtual violence to make you feel better.'

'You're crazy.'

'Hey, prove me wrong. Unless you think you can't.' He didn't look at her as he said it, but she felt it sting, anyway. 'Maybe you're just not up to it.'

She shut her Calc II book, picked up the controller, and watched the colourful graphics load up on the screen. 'Show me what to do.'

He smiled slowly. 'Point. Shoot. Try not to get in my way.'

He was right. She'd always thought it was kind of creepy, hanging out in front of a TV and killing virtual monsters, but damn if it wasn't...*fun*. Before too long, she was flinching when things lunged out of the corners of the screen, and whooping just like Shane when some monster got put down for the count.

When it ended for her, and the screen suddenly showed a snarling zombie face and splashes of red, she felt it like an ice cube down her back.

'Oops,' Shane said, and kept on firing. 'Sorry. Some days you're the zombie, some days you're the meal. Good try, kiddo.'

She put the controller on the couch cushions, and watched him play for a while. 'Shane?' she finally asked.

'Hang on – damn, that was close. What?'

'How did you get on Monica's—'

'Shit list?' he supplied, and drilled a few dozen bullets into a lunging zombie in a prom dress. 'You don't have to do much, just not crawl on your belly every time she walks in a room.' Which, she noticed, wasn't exactly an answer. Exactly. 'What'd you do?'

'I, uh… I made her look stupid.'

He hit some control and froze the game in mid-scream, and turned to look at her. 'You what?'

'Well, she said this thing about World War II being about the Chinese, and—'

Shane laughed. He had a good laugh, loud and full of raw energy, and she smiled nervously in return. 'You're feistier than you look, C. Good one.' He held up a hand. She awkwardly smacked it. 'Oh, man, that's sadder than the video game thing. Again.'

Five hand smacks later, she had mastered the high five to his satisfaction, and he unfroze the video game.

'Shane?' she asked.

This time, he sighed. 'Yeah?'

'Sorry, but – about your sister—'

Silence. He didn't look at her, didn't give any indication he'd heard a word. He just kept on killing things.

He was good at it.

Claire's nerve failed. She went back to her textbook. It didn't seem quite as exciting, somehow. After half an hour, she bagged it, stood, stretched, and asked, 'When does Michael get up?'

'When he wants to.' Shane shrugged. 'Why?' He made a face and narrowly avoided getting his arm clawed off on-screen.

'I – I figured I might go back to the dorm and get my things.'

He hit a button, and the screen paused in mid-shot again. 'What?' He gave her his full attention, which made her heart stutter, then pound harder. Guys like Shane did not give mousy little bookworms like her their full attention. Not like that.

'My stuff. From my dorm room.'

'Yeah, that's what I thought you said. Did you miss the part where the cops are looking for you?'

'Well, if I check in,' she said reasonably, 'I won't be missing anymore. I can say I slept over somewhere. Then they'll stop looking for me.'

'That's the dumbest thing I've ever heard.'

'No, it isn't. If they think I'm back in the dorm, they'll leave me to Monica, right? It could be a few days before she figures out I'm not coming back.

She could forget about me by then.'

'Claire—' He frowned at her for a second or two, then shook his head. 'No way are you going over there by yourself.'

'But – they don't know where I am. If you go with me, they'll know.'

'And if you don't come back from the dorm, I'm the one who has to explain to Michael how I let you go off and get yourself killed like a dumbass. First rule of horror movies, C. – never split up.'

'I can't just hide here. I have classes!'

'Drop 'em.'

'No way!' The whole thought horrified her. Nearly as much as *failing* them.

'Claire! Maybe you're not getting this, but *you're in trouble*! Monica wasn't kidding when she pushed you down the stairs. That was light exercise for her. Next time, she might actually get mad.'

She stood up and hoisted her backpack. 'I'm going.'

'Then you're stupid. Can't save an idiot,' Shane said flatly, and turned back to his game. He didn't look at her again as he started working the controls, firing with a vengeance. 'Don't tell them where you were last night. We don't need the hassle.'

Claire set her jaw angrily, chewed up some words, and swallowed them. Then she went into the kitchen to grab some trash bags. As she was stuffing them into her backpack, she heard the front door open and close.

'A plague upon all our houses!' Eve yelled, and Claire heard the silver jingle of her keys hitting the hall table. 'Anybody alive in here?'

'Yes!' Shane snapped. He sounded as mad as Claire felt.

'Damn,' Eve replied cheerfully. 'I was so hoping.'

Claire came out of the kitchen and met Eve on her way up the hall. She was in plaid today – a red and black tartan skirt, black fishnet hose, clunky patent leather shoes with skulls on the toes, a white men's shirt, suspenders. And a floor-length black leather coat. Her hair was up in two pigtails, fastened with skull-themed bands. She smelt like...coffee. Fresh ground. There were some brown splatters on her shirtfront.

'Oh, hey, Claire,' she said, and blinked. 'Where are you going?'

'Funeral,' Shane said. On-screen, a zombie shrieked and died gruesomely.

'Yeah? Cool! Whose?'

'Hers.' Shane said.

Eve's eyes widened. 'Claire – you're going back?'

'Just for some of my stuff. I figure if I show up every couple of days, let people see me, they'll think I still live there...'

'Whoa, whoa, whoa, bad idea. *Bad*. No cookie. You can't go back. Not by yourself.'

'Why not?'

'They're looking for you!'

Shane put the game on pause again. 'You think I

didn't already tell her that? She's not listening.'

'And you were going to let her just *go*?'

'I'm not her mom.'

'How about just her *friend*!'

He gave her a look that pretty clearly said, *Shut up*. Eve glared back, then looked at Claire. 'Seriously. You can't just... It's dangerous. You have no idea. If Monica's really gone to her Patron and tagged you, you can't just, you know, wander around.'

'I'm not wandering,' Claire pointed out. 'I'm going to my dorm, picking up some clothes, going to class, and coming home.'

'Going to *class*!' Eve made helpless little flapping motions with her black-fingernailed hands. 'No no no! No class, are you kidding?'

Shane raised his arm. 'Hello? Pointed it out already.'

'Whatever,' Claire said, and stepped around Eve to walk down the hall to the front door. She heard Shane and Eve whispering fiercely behind her, but didn't wait.

If she waited, she was going to lose her nerve.

It was only a little after noon. Plenty of time to get to school, do the rest of her classes, stuff some clothes in a garbage bag, say enough hellos to make everything OK, and get home before dark. And it was after dark that was dangerous, right? If they were serious about the vampire thing.

Which she was starting to believe, just a teeny little bit.

She opened the front door, stepped out, closed it, and walked out onto the porch. The air smelt sharp and crisp with heat. Eve must have been cooking in that coat; there were ripples of hot air rising up from the concrete sidewalk, and the sun was a pale white dot in a washed-denim sky.

She was halfway to the sidewalk, where Eve's big car lurked, when the door slammed behind her. 'Wait!' Eve blurted, and came hurrying after with the leather coat flapping in the hot wind. 'I can't let you do this.'

Claire kept walking. The sun burnt on the sore spot on her head, and on her bruises. Her ankle was still sore, but not enough to bother her that much. She'd just have to be careful.

Eve darted around her to face her, then danced backward when Claire kept walking. 'Seriously. This is dumb, Claire, and you don't strike me as somebody with a death wish. I mean, *I* have a death wish – it takes one to know one – OK, *stop*! Just *stop*!' She put out a hand, palm out, and Claire stopped short just a few inches away. 'You're going. I get that. At least let me drive you. You shouldn't be walking. This way I can call Shane if – if anything happens. And at least you'll have somebody standing by.'

'I don't want to get you guys into any trouble.' Michael had been pretty specific about that. 'That's why Shane's not coming. He's – well, he attracts trouble like TV screens attract dust. Besides, it's better not to put him anywhere near Monica. Bad things happen.' Eve unlocked the car doors. 'You have to call shotgun.'

'What?'

'You have to call shotgun to get the passenger seat.'

'But nobody else is—'

'I'm just telling you, get used to the idea, because if Shane was here? He'd already have it and you'd be in the back.'

'Um...' Claire felt stupid even trying to say it. 'Shotgun?'

'Keep practicing. Got to be fast on the trigger around here.'

The car had slick vinyl seats, cracked and peeling, and aftermarket seat belts that didn't feel any too safe. Claire tried not to slide around on the upholstery too much as the big car jolted down the narrow, bumpy road. The shops looked as dim and uninviting as Claire remembered, and the pedestrians just as hunched in on themselves.

'Eve?' she asked. 'Why do people stay here? Why don't they leave? If, you know...vampires.'

'Good question,' Eve said. 'People are funny that way. Adults, anyway. Kids pick up and leave all the time, but adults get all bogged down. Houses. Cars. Jobs. Kids. Once you have stuff, it's easy enough for the vamps to keep you on a leash. It takes a lot to make people just leave everything behind and run. Especially when they know they might not live long if they do. *Oh crap, get down*!'

Claire unhooked her seat belt and slithered down into the dark space under the dash. She didn't hesitate, because Eve hadn't been kidding – that had been pure panic in her voice. 'What is it?' She barely dared to whisper.

'Cop car,' Eve said, and didn't move her lips. 'Coming right toward us. Stay down.'

She did. Eve nervously tapped fingernails on the hard plastic steering wheel, and then let out a sigh. 'OK, he went past. Just stay down, though. He might come back.'

Claire did, bracing herself against the bumps in the road as Eve turned toward the campus. Another minute or two passed before Eve gave her the all clear, and she flopped back into the seat and strapped in.

'That was close,' Eve said.

'What if they'd seen me?'

'Well, for starters, they'd have hauled me in to the station for interfering, confiscated my car...' Eve patted the steering wheel apologetically. 'And you'd have just...disappeared.'

'But—'

'Trust me. They're not exactly amateurs around here at making that happen. So let's just get this done and hope like hell your plan works, OK?'

Eve steered slowly through crowds of lunchtime students walking across the streets, hit the turnaround, and followed Claire's pointed directions toward the dorm.

Howard Hall didn't look any prettier today than it had yesterday. The parking lot was only half-full, and Eve cruised the big Caddy into a parking space near the back. She clicked off the ignition and squinted at the sunlight glaring off the hood. 'Right,' she said.

'You go in, get your stuff, be back here in fifteen minutes, or I start launching Operation Get Claire.'

Claire nodded. She wasn't feeling so good about this idea, now that she was staring at the door's entrance.

'Here.' Eve was holding something out. A cell phone, thin and sleek. 'Shane's on speed dial – just hit star two. And remember, fifteen minutes, and then I freak out and start acting like your mom. OK?'

Claire took the phone and slipped it in her pocket. 'Be right back.'

She hoped she didn't sound scared. Not too scared, anyway. There was something about having friends – even brand-new ones – that helped keep the tremors out of her voice, and shakes out of her hands. *I'm not alone. I have back-up.* It was kind of a new sensation. Kind of nice, too.

She got out of the car, waved awkwardly to Eve, who waved in reply, and turned to walk back into hell.

CHAPTER SIX

The cold air of the lobby felt dry and lifeless, after the heat outside; Claire shivered and blinked fast to adjust her eyes to the relative dimness. A few girls were in the lobby with books propped up on tables; the TV was running, but nobody was watching it.

Nobody looked at her as she walked by. She went to the glassed-in attendant booth, and the student assistant sitting inside looked up from her magazine, saw her bruises, and made a silent O with her mouth.

'Hi,' Claire said. Her voice sounded thin and dry, and she had to swallow twice. 'I'm Claire, up on four? Um, I had an accident yesterday. But I'm OK. Everything's fine.'

'You're the – they were looking for you, right?'

'Yeah. Just tell everybody I'm OK. I've got to get to class.'

'But—'

'Sorry, I'm late!' Claire hurried to the stairs and

went up as fast as her sore ankle would allow. She passed a couple of girls, who gave her wide-eyed looks, but nobody said anything.

She didn't see Monica. Not on the stairs, not at the top. The hallway was empty, and all the doors were shut. Music pounded from three or four different rooms. She hurried down to the end, where her own room was, and started to unlock it.

The knob turned limply in her fingers. *Great.* That, more than any graffiti, said *Monica wuz here*.

Sure enough, the room was a wreck. What wasn't broken was dumped in piles. Books were defaced, which really hurt. Her meagre clothes had been dragged out of the closet and scattered over the floor. Some of the blouses had been ripped, but she seriously didn't care that much; she sorted through, found two or three that were intact, and stuffed them in the garbage bag. One pair of sweatpants was fine, and she added that, too. She had a lucky find of a couple of ratty old pairs of underwear that hadn't been discovered, shoved in the corner of the drawer, and added those to the sack.

The rest was another pair of shoes, what books she could salvage, and the little bag of make-up and toiletries she kept on the shelf next to the bed. Her iPod was gone. So were her CDs. No telling if that had been Monica's doing, or the work of some other dorm rat who'd scavenged later.

She looked around, swept the worst of the mess into a corner, and grabbed the photo of her mom and dad off of the dresser to take with her.

And then she left, not bothering to try to lock the door.

Well, she thought shakily. That went OK, after all.

She was halfway down the steps when she heard voices on the second-floor landing. '—swear, it's her! You should see the black eye. Unbelievable. You really clocked her one.'

'Where the hell is she?' Monica's voice, hard-edged. 'And how come nobody came to get me?'

'We – we did!' someone protested. Someone who sounded as scared as Claire suddenly felt. She reached in her pocket, grabbed the phone, and held on to it for security. *Star two. Just press star two – Shane's not far away, and Eve's right downstairs...* 'She was up in her room. Maybe she's still there?'

Crap. There was nobody in the dorm she could trust, not now. Nobody who'd hide her, or who'd stand up for her. Claire retreated back up the steps to the third-floor landing and went to the fire stairs, flung open the door, and hurried down the concrete steps as fast as she dared, ducking to avoid the glass window at the second-floor exit. She made it to the lobby exit door sweating and trembling from the effort, with her backpack and the garbage bag dragging painfully on her sore muscles, and risked a quick look out the window to the lobby itself.

Monica-groupie Jennifer was on guard, watching the stairs. She looked tense and focused, and –

Claire thought – a little bit scared, too. She kept fooling with the bracelet around her right wrist, turning it over and over. One thing was certain: Jennifer would see her the second she opened the door. And sure, maybe that wouldn't matter; maybe she could get by Jen and out the door and they wouldn't be attacking her in *public*, would they?

Watching Jennifer's face, she wasn't so sure. Not so sure at all.

The fire door a couple of floors up boomed open, and Claire flinched and looked for a place to hide. The only possible spot was under the concrete stairs. There was some kind of storage closet crammed under there, but when she tried the knob it was locked, and she didn't have Monica's lock-smashing superpowers.

And she didn't have time, anyway. There were footsteps coming down. Either she could hope the person didn't look back in the corner, or she could make a break for the door. Once again, Claire touched the phone in her pocket. *One phone call away. It's OK.* And once again, she left the phone where it was, took a deep breath, and waited.

It wasn't Monica; it was Kim Valdez, a freshman like Claire. A band geek, which put her only a tiny step higher than Claire's status as resident freak of nature. Kim kept to herself, and she didn't seem to be all that afraid of Monica or her girls; Kim didn't seem afraid of much. Not friendly, though. Just…solitary.

Kim looked back at her, blinked once or twice, then stopped before putting her hand on the door to exit. 'Hey,' she said. She pushed back the hood of her knit shirt, revealing short, shiny black hair. 'They're looking for you.'

'Yeah, I know.'

Kim was holding her instrument case. Claire wasn't exactly clear on which instrument it was, but it was big and bulky in its scuffed black case. Kim set it down. 'Monica do that?' She gestured at Claire's bruises. Claire nodded wordlessly. 'I always knew she was a bitch. So. You need to get out of here?'

Claire nodded again, and swallowed hard. 'Will you help me?'

'Nope.' Kim flashed her a sudden, vivid grin. 'Not officially. Wouldn't be too smart.'

They had it worked out in a matter of frantic seconds: Claire zipped up in the shirt, pulled the hood down around her face, and held the instrument case by the handle.

'Higher,' Kim advised. 'Tilt it so it covers your face. Yeah, like that. Keep your head down.'

'What about my bags?'

'I'll wait a couple of minutes, then come out with 'em. Wait outside. And don't go nowhere with my cello, and I mean it. I'll kick your ass.'

'I won't,' she swore. Kim opened the door for her, and she took a gasping breath and barged out, head down, trying to look like she was late for a rehearsal.

As she passed Jennifer, the girl gave her a reflexive glance, then dismissed her to focus back on the stairs. Claire felt a hot rush of adrenaline that felt like it might set her face on fire, and resisted the urge to run the rest of the way for the door. It seemed to take forever, her crossing the lobby to the glass doors.

She was swinging the door open when she heard Monica say, 'That freak couldn't get out of here! Check the basement. Maybe she went down the trash chute, like her stupid laundry.'

'But—' Jen's feeble protest. 'I don't want to go down to the—'

She would, though. Claire suppressed a wild grin – mostly because it still hurt too much to do that – and made it out of the dorm.

The sunlight felt amazing. It felt like...safety.

Claire took a deep breath of hot afternoon air, and walked around the corner to wait for Kim. The heat was brutal out against the sunbaked walls – suffocating. She squinted against the sun and saw the distant glitter of Eve's car, parked all the way at the back. Even hotter in there, she guessed, and wondered if Eve had gotten out of that Goth-required leather coat yet.

And just as she was thinking that, she saw a shadow fall across hers from behind, and half turned, but it was too late. Something soft and dark muffled her vision and clogged her mouth and nose, and pressure around her head yanked her off-balance.

She screamed, or tried to, but somebody punched her in the stomach, which took care of the screaming and most of the breathing, and Claire saw a weak, watery sunshine through the weave of the cloth over her face, and shadows, and then everything got dark. Not that she fainted, or anything like that, although she was wanting to, badly.

The hot pressure of the sun went away, and then she was being dragged and carried into someplace dark and quiet.

Then down a flight of stairs.

When the moving stopped, she heard breathing and whispers, sounds of more than a few people, and then she was shoved backward, hard, and fell off-balance onto a cold concrete floor. The impact stunned her, and by the time she clawed her way out of the bag that had been jammed onto her head – a black backpack, apparently – she found there was a whole circle of girls standing around her.

She had no idea where this room was. Some kind of storage room, maybe, in the basement. It was crammed with stuff – suitcases, boxes labelled with names, all kinds of things. Some of the boxes had collapsed and spilt out pale guts of old clothes. It smelt like moulding paper, and she sneezed helplessly when her frantic gasps filled her mouth and nose with dust.

A couple of girls giggled. Most didn't do anything, and didn't look very happy to be there, either. Resigned, Claire guessed. Glad it wasn't them lying on the floor.

Monica stepped out of the corner.

'Well,' she said, and put her hands on her hips. 'Look what the cats dragged in.' She flashed Claire a cold toothpaste-ad smile, as if the rest of them weren't even here. 'You ran away, little mouse. And just when we were starting to have *fun*.'

Claire faked more sneezing, lots of it, and Monica backed away in distaste. Faking sneezing, Claire discovered, wasn't as easy as she'd thought. It hurt. But it provided time and cover for her to pull the phone out of her pocket, cover it with her body, and frantically punch 2.

She pressed SEND and shoved it between two boxes, hoping the blue glow of the buttons wouldn't attract Monica's attention. Hoping Shane wouldn't be iPoding or Xboxing and ignoring the phone. Hoping...

Just hoping.

'Oh, for God's sake. Get her up!' Monica ordered. Her Monickettes sprang forward, Jen taking one of Claire's arms, Gina the other. They hauled her up to her feet and held her there.

Monica pulled the hood back from Claire's bruised face and smiled again, taking in the damage. 'Damn, freak, you look like hell. Does it hurt?'

'What did I ever do to you?' Claire blurted. She was scared, but she was angry, too. Furious. There were seven girls standing around doing *nothing* because they were scared, and of what? *Monica*?

What the hell gave the Monicas the right to run the world?

'You know exactly what you did. You tried to make me look stupid,' Monica said.

'*Tried*?' Claire shot back, which was dumb, but she couldn't stop the impulse. It got her hit in the face. Hard. Right on top of the first bruise, which took away her breath in slow throbs of white-hot agony. Everything felt funny, rattled by the impact of Monica's jab. Claire felt pressure on her arms, and realised that the Monickettes were holding her up. She put some stiffness back into her legs, opened her eyes, and glared at Monica.

'How come you live in Howard?' she asked.

Monica, inspecting her knuckles for signs of bruising, looked up in honest surprise.

'What?'

'Your family's rich, right? You could be living in an apartment. Or in a sorority house. How come you live in Howard Hall with the rest of us freaks?' She caught her breath at the sudden cold blaze in Monica's eyes. 'Unless you're a freak, too. A freak who gets off on hurting somebody weaker than you. A freak your family's ashamed of. Somebody they hide here where they don't have to look at you.'

'Shut up,' Jennifer hissed, low in her ear. 'Don't be stupid! She'll kill you – don't you get it?'

She jerked her head away. 'I heard you went away to college,' Claire continued. Her stomach was rolling, she felt like she was going to puke and die, but all she had to do was stall for time. Shane would come. Eve would come. Maybe Michael. She could imagine Michael standing in the doorway, with those ice-cold eyes and that angel's face, staring holes through Monica. Yeah, that would *rock*. Monica wouldn't look so big then. 'What's the matter? Couldn't you cut it? I'm not surprised – anybody who thinks World War Two was in China isn't exactly going to impress—'

She saw the punch coming this time, and ducked as best she could. Monica's fist smashed into her forehead, which hurt, but it must have hurt Monica a whole lot more, because she let out a shrill little scream and backed off, clutching her right hand in her left. That made the horrible throbbing in Claire's head almost OK.

'Careful,' Claire gasped, nearly giggling. The scab on her lip had broken open, and she licked blood from her lips. 'Don't break a nail! I'm not worth it, remember?'

'Got *that* right!' Monica snarled. 'Let that bitch go. What are you waiting for? Go on, do it! Do you think that wimp's going to *hurt* me?'

The Monickettes looked at each other, clearly wondering if their queen bee had lost her mind, then let go of Claire's arms and stepped back. Jennifer bumped into the towering column of boxes, spilling an avalanche of dust and old papers, but when Claire looked at her, Jennifer was staring at a spot between the boxes.

The spot where Claire had hidden the phone. Jen had to have seen it, and Claire gasped out loud, suddenly a whole lot more afraid than she'd thought she was.

'What the hell are *you* looking at?' Monica snarled at Jen, and Jen very deliberately turned her back on the incriminating phone, folded her arms, and stood there blocking it from view. Not looking at Claire at all. *Wow. That's*...what? Not lucky, exactly. Jennifer had shown some cracks already. And maybe she wasn't a complete convert to the First Church of Monica.

Maybe Monica had just pissed her off one too many times. Not that she would be stepping in on Claire's side anytime soon.

Claire wiped the blood from her lip and looked at the other girls. The ones who were standing, uneasy and indecisive. Monica had been challenged and, so far, hadn't exactly delivered the smackdown everybody – Claire included – had expected. Kind of weird, really. Unless Claire really struck some nerve besides the ones running through Monica's knuckles.

Monica was rubbing her hand, looking at Claire as if she'd never seen her before. Assessing her. She said, 'Nobody's told you the facts of life, *Claire*. The fact is, if you suddenly just up and disappear...?' She jerked her pretty, pointed chin at the dusty towers of boxes. 'Nobody but the janitor's ever going to know or care. You think Mommy and Daddy are going to get all upset? Maybe they would, but by the time they spend their last dime putting your picture on milk cartons and chasing down rumours of how you ran off with somebody else's boyfriend? They're going to hate to even think about you. Morganville's got it down to a science, making people disappear. They never disappear *here*. Always somewhere else.'

Monica wasn't taunting her. That was the scary part. She was talking evenly, quietly, as if they were two equals having a friendly conversation.

'You want to know why I live in Howard?' she continued. 'Because in this town, I can live anywhere I want. Any way I want. And you – you're just a walking organ donor. So take my advice, Claire. Don't get in my face, because if you do, you won't have one for long. Are we clear?'

Claire nodded slowly. She didn't dare look away. Monica reminded her of a feral dog, one that would jump for your throat the second you showed weakness. 'We're clear,' she said. 'You're kind of a psycho. I get that.'

'I might be,' Monica agreed, and gave her a slow, strange smile. 'You're one smart little freak. Now run away, smart little freak, before I change my mind and stick you in one of these old suitcases for some architect to find a hundred years from now.'

Claire blinked. 'Archaeologist.'

Monica's eyes turned winter cold. 'Oh, you'd *better* start running away now.'

Claire went back to where Jennifer was standing, and reached behind her to drag the phone out from between the boxes. She held it up to Monica. 'Speak clearly for the microphone. I want to make sure my friends get every word.'

For a second, nobody moved, and then Monica laughed. 'Damn, freak. You're going to be fun.' She glanced away from Claire, behind her. 'Not until I say so.'

Claire looked over her shoulder. Gina was standing there, *right there*, and she had some kind of metal bar in her hand.

Oh my God. There was something awful and cold in Gina's eyes.

'She'll get hers,' Monica said. 'And we'll get to watch. But hey, why hurry? I haven't had this much fun in years.'

Claire's legs felt like they'd suddenly turned into overcooked spaghetti. She wanted to throw up, wanted to cry, and didn't dare do anything but pretend to be brave. They'd kill her down here if they thought she was bluffing.

She walked past Gina, between two girls who wouldn't meet her eyes at all, and put her hand on the doorknob. As she did, she glanced down at the phone's display.

No signal.

She opened the door, walked outside, and found

her bags dumped on the grass where she'd been abducted. She pocketed the phone, picked up the bags, and walked across the parking lot to Eve's car. Eve was still sitting in the driver's seat, looking clown-pale and scared.

Claire tossed her bag in the back as Eve asked, 'What happened? Did they see you?'

'No,' Claire said. 'No problems. I've got class. I'll see you later. Thanks, Eve. Um – here's your phone.' She passed it over. Eve took it, still frowning. 'I'll be home before dark.'

'Better be,' Eve said. 'Seriously, Claire. You look – weird.'

Claire laughed. 'Me? Check the mirror.'

Eve flipped her off, but the same way she'd have flipped off Shane. Claire grabbed her backpack, closed the door, and watched Eve's big black car cruise away. Heading back to work, she guessed.

She got halfway to her chem lab when her reaction hit her, and she sat down on a bench and cried silently into her hands.

Oh my God. Oh my God, I want to go home! She wasn't sure if that meant back to Michael's house, or all the way home, back in her room with her parents watching over her.

I can't quit. She really couldn't. She never in her life had been able to, even when it might have been the smart thing to do.

She wiped her swollen eyes and went to class.

✕ ✕ ✕

Nobody killed her that afternoon.

After the first couple of hours, she quit expecting it to happen, and focused on class. Her back-to-back labs weren't too much of a disaster, and she actually knew the answers in history. *Bet Monica wouldn't*, she thought, and looked guiltily around the classroom to see if Monica was there, or one of her crew. It wasn't a big class. She didn't see anybody who'd been in the basement.

She made it to the grocery store after class without getting killed, too. Nobody jumped her while she was picking out lettuce and tomatoes, or while she was in line for checkout. She thought the guy at the meat counter had looked suspicious, though.

She walked back to the Glass House, watching for vampires in the fading afternoon and feeling pretty stupid for even thinking about it. She didn't see anybody except other college students, strolling along with bulging backpacks. Most of them travelled in bunches. Once she got past the area that catered to students, the stores were closed, lights off, and what few people were walking were hurrying.

At the corner of *Gone with the Wind* and *The Munsters*, the front gate was open. She closed it behind her, unlocked the door with the shiny new key that she'd found on her dresser that morning, and slammed the door behind her.

There was a shadow standing at the end of the

hallway. A tall, broad shadow in a grungy yellow T-shirt and low-slung, faded jeans frayed at the bottom. A shadow in bare feet.

Shane.

He just looked at her for a few seconds, then said, 'Eve put your crap up in your room.'

'Thanks.'

'What's that?'

'Stuff for dinner.'

He cocked his head slightly, still staring at her. 'For a smart girl, you do some stupid things. You know that?'

'I know.' She walked toward him. He didn't move.

'Eve says you never saw Monica.'

'That's what I said.'

'You know what? I'm not buying it.'

'You know what?' she shot back. 'I don't care. Excuse me.' She ducked past him, into the kitchen, and set her bags down. Her hands were shaking. She balled them into fists and started setting out things on the counter. Ground beef. Lettuce. Tomatoes. Onions. Refried beans. Hot sauce, the kind she liked, anyway. Cheese. Sour cream. Taco shells.

'Let me guess,' Shane said from the doorway. 'You're making Chinese.'

She didn't answer. She was still too pissed and – all of a sudden – too scared. Scared of what, she didn't know. Everything. Nothing. Herself.

'Anything I can do?' His voice sounded different. Quieter, gentler, almost kind.

'Chop onions,' she said, although she knew that wasn't exactly what he meant. Still, he came over, picked up the onions, and grabbed a huge scary-looking knife from a drawer. 'You have to peel it first.'

He shot her a dirty look, just like he would have Eve, and got to work.

'Um – I should probably call my mom,' Claire said. 'Can I use the phone?'

'You pay for long distance.'

'Sure.'

He shrugged, reached over, and grabbed the cordless phone, then pitched it underhanded to her. She nearly dropped it, but was kind of proud she didn't. She got out a big iron skillet from under the cabinet and put it on the counter, heated up the burner, and found some oil. As it was warming, she read over the thin little recipe book she'd bought at the store one more time, then dialled the phone.

Her mom answered on the second ring. 'Yes?' It was never *hello* with her mother.

'Mom, it's Claire.'

'Claire! Baby, where have you been? I've been trying to call you for days!'

'Classes,' she said. 'Sorry. I'm not home that much.'

'Are you sleeping enough? If you don't get

enough rest, you'll get sick – you know how you are—'

'Mom, I'm fine.' Claire frowned down at the recipe on the counter in front of her. What did *sauté* mean, exactly? Was it like frying? *Diced*, she understood. That was just cutting things into cubes, and Shane was doing that already. 'Really. It's all OK now.'

'Claire, I know it's hard. We really didn't want you to go even just the few hundred miles to TPU, honey. If you want to come back home, your dad and I would be so glad to have you back!'

'Honestly, Mom, I don't – I'm fine. It's OK. Classes are really good' – that was stretching the truth – 'and I've made friends here. They're looking out for me.'

'You're sure.'

'Yes, Mom.'

'Because I worry. I know you're very mature for your age but—'

Shane opened his mouth to say something. Claire made frantic *NO NO NO* motions at him, pointing at the phone. *Mom!* she mouthed. Shane held up both hands in surrender and kept chopping. Mom was still talking. Claire had missed some of it, but she didn't think it really mattered exactly. '—boys, right?'

Wow. Mom radar worked even at this distance. 'What, Mom?'

'Your dorm doesn't allow boys to come up to the

rooms, does it? There's someone on duty at the desk to make sure?'

'Yes, Mom. Howard Hall has somebody on duty twenty-four/seven to keep the nasty evil boys out of our rooms.' She hadn't actually lied, Claire decided. That was completely true. The fact that she wasn't actually *living* in Howard Hall...well, that wasn't really something she needed to throw in, right?

'It's not a laughing matter. You've been very sheltered, Claire, and I don't want you to—'

'Mom, I have to go. I need to eat dinner and I have a ton of studying to do. How's Dad?'

'Dad's just fine, honey. He says hello. Oh, come on, Les, get up and say hello to your very smart daughter. It won't break your back.'

Shane handed her a bowl full of diced onions. Claire cradled the phone against her ear and dropped a handful of them into the pan. They started sizzling immediately, much to her panic; she lifted the pan off the burner and almost dropped the phone.

'Hi, kiddo. How are classes?' That was Dad. Not *How was your day?* or *Have you made any friends?* No, his philosophy had always been, *Eyes on the prize; the other stuff just gets in your way.*

And she loved him anyway. 'Classes are great, Daddy.'

'Are you frying something? Do they let you have hot plates in the dorm? Didn't in my day, I can tell you...'

'Um…no, I just opened a Coke.' OK, that was a straight-up lie. She hastily put the pan down, walked to the fridge, and pulled out a cold Coke so she could open it. There. Retroactively truthful. 'How are you feeling?'

'Feel fine. Wish everybody would stop worrying about me, not like I'm the first man in history to have a little surgery.'

'I know, Daddy.'

'Doctors say I'm fine.'

'That's great.'

'Gonna have to go, Claire, the game's on. You're OK down there, aren't you?'

'Yes. I'm just fine. Daddy—'

'What is it, honey?'

Claire bit her lip and sipped Coke, indecisive. 'Um…do you know anything about Morganville? History, that kind of thing?'

'Doing research, eh? Some kind of report? No, I don't know much. The university's been there for nearly a hundred years – that's all I know about it. I know you're on fire to get to the bigger schools, but I think you need to spend a couple of years close to home. We talked about all that.'

'I know. I was just wondering… It's an interesting town, that's all.'

'OK, then. You let us know what you find out. Your mother wants to say goodbye.' Dad never did. By the time Claire got out 'Bye, Dad!' he was already gone, and Mom was back on the line.

'Honey, you call us if you get worried about anything, OK? Oh, call us whatever happens. We love you!'

'Love you, too, Mom. Bye.'

She put the phone down and stared at the sizzling onions, then the recipe. When the onions turned transparent, she dumped in the ground beef.

'So, finished lying to the folks?' Shane asked, and reached around Claire to snag a bite of grated cheese from the bowl on the counter. 'Tacos. Brilliant. Damn, I'm glad I voted somebody in with skills.'

'I heard that, Shane!' Eve yelled from the living room, just as the door slammed. Shane winced. 'Do your own bathroom cleaning this weekend!'

Shane winced. 'Truce!'

'Thought so.'

Eve came in, still flushed from the heat outside. She'd sweated off most of her make-up, and underneath it, she looked surprisingly young and sweet. 'Oh my God, that looks like real food!'

'Tacos,' Shane said proudly, as if it were his idea. Claire elbowed him in the ribs, or tried to. His ribs were a lot more solid than her elbow. 'Ow,' he said. Not as if it hurt.

Claire glanced out the window. Night was falling fast, the way it did in Texas at the end of the day – furious burning sun all of a sudden giving way to a warm, sticky twilight. 'Is Michael here?' she asked.

'Guess so.' Shane shrugged. 'He's always here for dinner.'

The three of them got everything ready, and sometime midway through the assembly-line process they'd developed – Claire putting meat in taco shells, Eve adding toppings, Shane spooning beans onto the plates – a fourth pair of hands added itself to the line. Michael looked as if he'd just gotten up and showered – wet hair, sleepy eyes, beads of water still sliding down to soak the collar of his black knit shirt. Like Shane, he was wearing jeans, but he'd gone formal, with actual shoes.

'Hey,' he greeted them. 'This looks good.'

'Claire did it,' Eve jumped in as Shane opened his mouth. 'Don't *even* let Shane take credit.'

'Wasn't going to!' Shane looked offended.

'Riiiiiight.'

'I chopped. What did you do?'

'Cleaned up after you, like always.'

Michael looked over at Claire and made a face. She laughed and picked up her plate; Michael picked up his, and followed her out into the living room.

Someone – Michael, she guessed – had cleared the big wood table next to the bookcases, and set up four chairs around it. The stuff that had been piled there – video game cases, books, sheet music – had been dumped in other places, with a cheerful disregard for order. (Maybe, she amended, that had been Shane's idea.) She set her plate down, and Eve promptly slapped her own down next to Claire's and slid a cold Coke across to her, along with a fork and napkin. Michael and Shane strolled back in, took seats, and began shovelling in food like – well, like boys. Eve nibbled. Claire, who was surprisingly hungry, found herself on her second taco before Eve had gotten through her first one.

Shane was already headed back for more.

'Hey, dude,' he said as he returned with a reloaded plate, 'when are you going to get a gig again?'

Michael stopped chewing, flashed a look at Eve, then Claire, and then finished the bite before saying, 'When I'm ready.'

'Pussy. You had a bad night, Mike. Get back on the horse, or whatever.' Eve frowned at Shane, and shook her head. Shane ignored her. 'Seriously, man. You can't let them get you down.'

'I'm not,' Michael said. 'Not everything is about beating your head against the wall until it breaks.'

'Just most things.' Shane sighed. 'Whatever. You let me know when you want to stop hermitting.'

'I'm not hermitting. I'm practising.'

'Like you don't play good enough. Please.'

'I get no respect,' Michael said. Shane, busy taking another crunchy bite, rubbed his thumb and forefinger together. 'Yeah, I know, world's smallest violin playing just for me. Change the subject. How was that hot date with Lisa, anyway? Rented shoes turn her on or what?'

'It's Laura,' Shane said. 'Yeah, she was hot, all right, but I think she had the hots for you – kept saying how she saw you over at the Waterhouse last year and you were all, like, wow, amazing. It was like a *ménage a trois*, only you weren't there, thank God.'

Michael looked smug. 'Shut up and eat.'

Shane shot him the finger.

All in all, it was a pretty good time.

Michael and Eve washed dishes, having lost out on the coin toss, and Claire hovered in the living room, not sure what she wanted to do. Studying sounded ...boring, which surprised her. Shane was concentrating on the video game selection, bare feet propped up on the coffee table. Without looking directly at Claire, he asked, 'You want to see something cool?'

'Sure,' she said. She expected him to put a game in, but he dumped it back in the pile, got up off the couch, and padded up the stairs. She stood at the bottom, staring up, wondering what to do. Shane appeared at the top of the stairs again and gestured, and she followed.

The second floor was quiet, of course, and dimly lit; she blinked and saw Shane already halfway down the hall. Was he heading for her room? Not that she didn't have a crazy hot picture in her head of sitting on the bed with him, making out...and she had no idea why that popped into her head, except that, well, he was just...yeah.

Shane moved aside a picture hanging on the wall

between her room and Eve's, and pressed a button underneath.

And a door opened on the other side of the wall. It was built into the panelling, and she'd never have even known it was there. She gasped, and Shane beamed like he'd invented the wheel. 'Cool, huh? This damn house is full of crap like that. Trust me, in Morganville it pays to be up on the hiding places.' He pushed open the door, revealed another set of stairs, and padded up them. She expected them to be dusty, but they weren't; the wood was clean and polished. Shane's feet left prints of the ball of his foot and his toes.

It was a narrow pitch of just eight steps, half a story, really, and there was another door at the top. Shane opened it and flipped on a switch just inside. 'First time I saw this, and the room back of the pantry, I figured, yep. Vampire house. What do you think?'

If she believed in vampires, he might have been right. It was a small room, no windows, and it was...old. It wasn't just the stuff in it, which was antique and dark; it had this sense of...something ancient, something not quite right. And it was cold. Cold, in the middle of a Texas heat wave.

She shivered. 'Does everybody know about this room?'

'Oh yeah. Eve says it's haunted. Can't really blame her. It creeps me the hell out, too. Cool, though. We'd have stuck you in here when the cops came, only they'd have seen you through the windows coming out of the kitchen. They're nosy bastards.' Shane wandered across the thick Persian carpet to flop on the dark red Victorian couch. Dust rose in a cloud, and he waved it off, coughing. 'So what do you think? Think Michael sleeps off his evil-undead days in here, or what?'

She blinked. 'What?'

'Oh, come on. You think he's one of them, right? 'Cause he doesn't show up during the day?'

'I – I don't think anything!'

Shane nodded, eyes downcast. 'Right. You weren't sent here.'

'Sent – sent here by *who*?'

'I got to thinking… The cops were looking for you, but maybe they were looking for you to make us want to keep you here, instead of pitch you out. So which is it? Are you working for them?'

'Them?' she echoed thinly. 'Them, who?' Shane suddenly looked at her, and she shivered again. He wasn't like Monica, not at all, but he wasn't playing around, either. 'Shane, I don't know what you mean. I came to Morganville to go to school, and got beaten up, and I came here because I was scared. If you don't believe me – well, then I guess I'll go. Hope you liked the tacos.'

She went to the door, and stopped, confused.

There wasn't a doorknob.

Behind her, Shane said quietly, 'The reason I think this is a vampire's room? You can't get out of it unless you know the secret. That's real convenient, if you like to bring victims up here for a little munch session.'

She whirled around, expecting to see him standing there with that huge knife he'd used on the onions, and she'd broken the first rule of horror movies, hadn't she, or was it the second one? She'd trusted someone she shouldn't have...

But he was still sitting on the couch, slumped at ease, arms flung over the back on both sides.

Not even looking at her.

'Let me out,' she said. Her heart was hammering.

'In a minute. First, you tell me the truth.'

'I *have*!' And, to her fury and humiliation, she started to cry. Again. 'Dammit! You think I'm trying to hurt you? Hurt Michael? How could I? *I'm the one everybody hurts!*'

He looked at her then, and she saw the hardness melt away. His voice was a lot gentler when he spoke. 'And if I was somebody who wanted to kill Michael, I'd put somebody like you in to do it. Be real easy for you to kill somebody, Claire. Poison some food, slip a knife in his back...and I have to look out for Michael.'

'I thought he looked out for you.' She swiped angrily at her eyes. 'Why do you think somebody wants to kill him?'

Shane raised his eyebrows. 'Always somebody wanting to kill a vampire.'

'But – he's not. Eve said—'

'Yeah, I know he's not a vampire, but he doesn't

get up during the day, he doesn't go out of the house, and I can't get him to tell me what happened, so he might as well be. And somebody's going to think so, sooner or later. Most people in Morganville are either Protected or clueless – kind of like you can raise rabbits for either pets or meat. But some of them fight back.'

She blinked the last of the brief storm of tears away. 'Like you?'

He cocked his head to one side. 'Maybe. How about you? You a fighter, Claire?'

'I'm not working for anybody. And I wouldn't kill Michael even if he was a vampire.'

Shane laughed. 'Why not? Besides the fact that he'd snap you in two like a twig if he was.'

'Because – because—' She couldn't put it into words, exactly. 'Because I like him.'

Shane watched her for another few, long seconds, and then pressed a raised spot on the head of the lion-carving armrest of the couch.

The door clicked and popped open half an inch.

'Good enough for me,' he said. 'So. Dessert?'

CHAPTER SEVEN

She couldn't sleep.

Maybe it was the memory of that creepy little Gothic room – which she suspected Eve really, deeply loved – but all of a sudden, her lovely cosy room seemed full of shadows, and the creaks of old wood in the wind sounded...stealthy. *Maybe the house eats people*, Claire thought, lying there alone in the dark, watching the bone-thin shadows of branches shudder on the far wall. The wind made twigs tap her window, like something trying to get in. Eve had said vampires couldn't get in, but what if they could? What if they were already inside? What if Michael...?

She heard a soft, silvery note, and knew that Michael was playing downstairs. Something about that helped – pushed the shadows back, turned the sounds into something normal and soothing. It was just a house, and they were just kids sharing it, and if there was anything wrong, well, it was outside.

She must have slept then, but it didn't feel like it; some noise startled her awake, and when Claire checked the clock next to her bed it was close to five thirty. The sky wasn't light outside, but it wasn't totally dark, either; the stars were faded, soft sparkles in a sky gradually turning dark blue.

Michael's guitar was still going, very quietly. Didn't he ever sleep? Claire slid out of bed, tossed a blanket over her shoulders over the T-shirt she wore to bed, and shuffled out and into the still-dark hallway. As she passed the hidden door she glanced at it and shivered, then continued on to the bathroom. Once she'd gotten that out of the way – and brushed her hair – she crept quietly down the steps and sat down, blanket around her, listening to Michael play.

His head was down, and he was deep into it; she watched his fingers move light and quick on the strings, his body rock slowly with the rhythm, and felt a deep sense of...safety. Nothing bad could happen around Michael. She just knew it.

Next to him, a clock beeped an alarm. He looked up, startled, and slapped it off, then got up and put his guitar away. She watched, puzzled... Did he have someplace to be? Or did he actually have to set an alarm to go to bed? Wow, that was obsession...

Michael stood, watching the clock as if it were his personal enemy, and then he turned and walked over to the window.

The sky was the colour of dark turquoise now, all

but the strongest stars faded. Michael, holding a beer in his hand, drank the rest of the bottle and put it down on the table, crossed his arms, and waited.

Claire was about to ask him what he was waiting for when the first ray of sun crept up in a blinding orange knife, and Michael gasped and hunched over, pressing on his stomach.

Claire lunged to her feet, startled and afraid for the look of sheer agony on his face. The movement caught his attention, and he jerked his head toward her, blue eyes wide.

'No,' he moaned, and pitched forward to his hands and knees, gasping. 'Don't.'

She ignored that and jumped down the stairs to run to his side, but once she was there she didn't know what to do, didn't have any idea how to help him. Michael was breathing in deep, aching gasps, in terrible pain.

She put her hand on his back, felt his fever-hot skin burning through the thin cloth, and heard him make a sound like nothing she'd ever heard in her life.

Like someone dying, she thought in panic, and opened her mouth to scream for Shane, Eve, *anybody*.

Her hand suddenly went right through him. The scream, for whatever reason, locked tight in her throat as Michael – *transparent* Michael – looked up at her with despair and desperation in his eyes.

'Oh, God, don't tell them.' His voice came from a long, long way off, a whisper that faded on the shafts of morning sun.

And so did he.

Claire, mouth still open, utterly unable to speak, waved her hand slowly through the thin air where Michael Glass had been standing. Slowly, then faster. The air felt cold around her, like she was standing in a blast from an air conditioner, and the chill slowly faded.

Like Michael.

'Oh my God,' she whispered, and clapped both hands over her mouth.

And muffled the scream that she had to let out or explode.

She might have blacked out a little, because next thing she knew, she was sitting on the couch, next to Michael's guitar case, and she felt kind of funny. Bad funny, as if her brain had turned liquid and sloshed around in her head.

Weirdly calm, though. She reached over and touched the leather cover of his guitar case. It felt real. When she flipped up the latches and pulled her shaking fingers across the strings, they made a wistful sort of whisper.

He's a ghost. Michael's a ghost.

He wasn't a ghost. How could he be a ghost, if he sat here – right here! – at the table and ate dinner? Tacos! What kind of ghost ate tacos? What kind of...?

Her hand went right through him. *Right through him.*

But he was real. She'd touched him. She'd—

Her hand went right through him.

'Don't panic,' she said numbly, out loud. 'Just...don't panic. There's some explanation...' Yeah, right. She'd stumble over to Professor Wu's physics class and ask. She could just imagine how *that* would go over. They'd toss a net over her and pump her full of Prozac or whatever.

He'd said, *Oh, God, don't tell them.* Tell who? Tell...? Was he gone? Was he *dead*?

She was about carried away by panic again, and then something stopped it cold. Something silly, really.

The alarm clock sitting on the table next to the sofa. The one that had gone off just a few minutes ago.

The one that had warned Michael that sunrise was coming.

This happens...every day. He hadn't acted like it was odd, just painful.

Shane and Eve had both said that Michael slept days. They were both night owls; they were sound asleep right now, and wouldn't be up for hours yet. Michael could have...disappeared...daily like this with nobody paying attention.

Until she came along, and got nosy.

Don't tell them. Why not? What was so secret?

She was crazy. That was the only rational

explanation. But if she was crazy, she wasn't rational...

Claire curled up on the sofa, shivering, and felt cold air brush over her again. Ice-cold. She sat up. 'Michael?' she blurted, and sat very still. The chill went away, then brushed over her again. 'I – I think I can feel you. Are you still here?' Another second or two without the icy draft, and then it drifted across her skin. 'So – you can see us?' Yes, she figured, since the warm-cold cycle repeated. 'You don't go away during the day? Oh – um, stay where you are if it's no, OK?' The chill stayed steady. 'Wow. That's – harsh.' A yes, and weirdly, she felt a little cheered. OK, she was having a conversation with a *breeze*, but at least she didn't feel alone. 'You don't want me to tell Shane and Eve?' Clearly, a no. If anything, it got colder. 'Is there anything – anything I can do?' Also a no. 'Michael – will you come back?' Yes. 'Tonight?' Yes, again. 'We are *so* going to talk.'

The chill withdrew completely. *Yes.*

She collapsed back on the sofa, feeling giddy and strange and exhausted. There was a ratty old blanket piled near the guitar case; she carefully moved the instrument over to the table (and imagined an invisible Michael following her anxiously the whole way), then wrapped herself in the blanket and let herself drift off into sleep, with the ticking of the grandfather clock and memories of Michael's guitar as a soundtrack.

◁ ◁ ◁

That day, Claire went to class. Eve argued with her; Shane didn't. Nothing much happened, although Claire spotted Monica twice on campus. Monica was surrounded by admirers, both male and female, and didn't have time for grudges. Claire kept her head down and stayed out of any deserted areas. It was an early afternoon for her – no labs – and although she wanted to get home and wait around for Michael to show up (and boy, she wanted to see how that happened!) she knew she'd drive herself crazy, and make Shane suspicious.

As she walked in that general direction, she spotted the small coffee shop, wedged in between the skateboard shop and a used-book store. Common Grounds. That was where Eve worked, and she'd said to stop by...

The bell rang with a silvery tinkle as Claire pushed open the door, and it was like walking into the living room of the Glass House, only a little more Gothic. Black leather sofas and chairs, thick colourful rugs, accent walls in beige and blood red, lots of nooks and crannies. There were five or six students scattered at café tables and built-in desks. None looked up from their books or computers. The whole place smelt like coffee, a constant simmering warmth.

Claire stood for a second, indecisive, and then walked over to an empty desk and dumped her backpack before going to the counter. There were two people behind the waist-high barrier. One was

Eve, of course, looking perky and doll-like with her dye-dark hair in two pigtails, eyes rimmed with liner, and lipstick a dramatic Goth black. She was wearing a black mesh shirt over a red camisole, and she grinned when she spotted Claire.

The other was an older man, tall, thin, with greying curly hair that fell nearly to his shoulders. He had a nice, square face, wide dark eyes, and a ruby earring in his left ear. Hippie to the core, Claire guessed. He smiled, too.

'Hey, it's Claire!' Eve said, and hurried around the counter to slip her arm around Claire's shoulders.

'Claire, this is Oliver. My boss.'

Claire nodded hesitantly. He looked nice, but hey, a boss. Bosses made her nervous, like parents. 'Hello, sir.'

'Sir?' Oliver had a deep voice, and an even deeper laugh. 'Claire, you've got to learn about me. I'm not a *sir*. Believe me.'

'That's true.' Eve nodded wisely. 'He's a *dude*. You'll like him. Hey, want a coffee? My treat?'

'I – uh—'

'Don't touch the stuff, right?' Eve rolled her eyes. 'One non-coffee drink, coming up. How about hot cocoa? Chai? Tea?'

'Tea, I guess.'

Eve went back behind the counter and did some stuff, and within a couple of minutes, a big white cup and saucer appeared in front of Claire, with a tea bag steeping in the steaming water. 'On the house. Well, actually, on me, because, yikes, boss is right here.'

Oliver, who was working on some complicated machine that Claire guessed was something that made cappuccino, shook his head and grinned to himself. Claire watched him curiously. He looked a little bit like a distant cousin she'd met from France the same kind of hook nose, anyway. She wondered if he'd been a professor at the university, or just a perpetual student. Either looked possible.

'I heard you had some trouble,' Oliver said, still concentrating on unscrewing parts on the machine. 'Girls in the dorm.'

'Yeah,' she admitted, and felt her cheeks burn. 'Everything's OK, though.'

'I'm sure it is. Listen, though: if you have trouble like that, you come here and tell me about it. I'll make sure it stops.' He said it with absolute assurance. She blinked, and his dark eyes moved to rest on hers for a few seconds. 'I'm not without influence around here. Eve tells me that you're very gifted. We can't have some bad apples driving you off.'

'Um...thanks?' She didn't mean to make it a question; it just came out that way. 'Thanks. I will.'

Oliver nodded and went back to his work dissecting the coffeemaker. Claire found a seat not far away. Eve slipped out from behind the counter and pulled up a chair next to her, leaning forward, all restless energy. 'Isn't he *great*?' she asked. 'He means it, you know. He's got some kind of pipeline to—' She made a V sign with her fingers. V, for *vampires*. 'They listen to him. He's good to have on your side.'

Claire nodded, dunking the tea bag and watching the dark stains spread through the water. 'You talk about me to everybody?'

Eve looked stricken. 'No! Of course I don't! I just – well, I was worried. I thought maybe Oliver knew something that... Claire, you said it yourself – they tried to kill you. Somebody ought to be doing something about that.'

'Him?'

'Why not him?' Eve jittered her leg, tapping the thick heel on her black Mary Janes. Her hose had green and black horizontal stripes. 'I mean, I get that you're all about being self-sufficient, but come on. A little help never hurts.'

She wasn't wrong. Claire sighed, took the tea bag out, and sipped the hot drink. Not bad, even on a blazing-hot day.

'Stay,' Eve said. 'Study. It's a really good place for that. I'll drive you home, OK?'

Claire nodded, suddenly grateful; there were too many places to get lost on the way home, if Monica had noticed her after all. She didn't like the idea of walking three blocks between the student streets, where things were bright and busy, and the colourless hush of the rest of the town, where the

Glass House lived. She put the tea to one side and unpacked books. Eve went back to take orders from three chattering girls wearing sorority T-shirts. They were rude to her, and giggled behind her back. Eve didn't seem to notice – or if she did, she didn't care.

Oliver did. He put down the tools he was using, as Eve bustled around getting drinks, and stared steadily at the girls. One by one, they went quiet. It wasn't anything he did, exactly, just the steadiness of the way he watched them.

When Eve took their money, each one of the girls meekly thanked her and took her change.

They didn't stay.

Oliver smiled slightly, picked up a piece of the disassembled machine, and polished it before reattaching it. He must have known Claire was watching, because he said, in a very low voice, 'I don't tolerate rudeness. Not in my place.'

She wasn't sure if he was talking about the girls, or her staring at him, so she hurriedly went back to her books.

Quadratic equations were a great way to pass the afternoon.

Eve's shift ended at nine, just as the nightlife at Common Grounds picked up; Claire, not used to the babble, chatter, and music, couldn't keep her mind on her books anyway. She was glad of an excuse to go when Eve's replacement – a surly-looking pimpled boy about Shane's age – took her place behind the counter. Eve went in the back to get her stuff, and Claire packed up her backpack.

'Claire.' She looked up, startled that somebody remembered her name other than, well, people who wanted to kill her, and saw Kim Valdez, from the dorm.

'Hey, Kim,' she said. 'Thanks for helping me out—'

Kim looked mad. Really mad. 'Don't even start! You left my cello just laying around out there! Do you have any idea how hard I worked for that thing? Way to be an asshole!'

'But – I didn't—'

'Don't lie. You bugged out somewhere. Hope you got your bags and crap. I left them out there just like you left my stuff.' Kim jammed her hands in her pockets and glared at her. '*Don't* ask me for any favours again. Right?'

She didn't wait for an answer, just moved off toward the counter. Claire sighed. 'I won't,' she said, and zipped the backpack. She waited for a few minutes, but the crowd was getting thicker, and Eve was nowhere in sight. She stood up, stepped out of the way of a group of boys, and backed into a table in the shadowy corner.

'Hey,' a voice said softly. She looked back and saw a coffee cup tipping over, and a pale, long-fingered hand catching it before it did. The hand belonged to a young man – she couldn't really call him a boy – with thick dark hair and light-coloured eyes, who'd claimed the table when she wasn't looking.

'Sorry,' she said. He smiled at her and licked a couple of drops of coffee from the back of his hand with a pale tongue.

She felt something streak hot down her backbone, and shivered. He smiled wider.

'Sit,' he said. 'I'm Brandon. You?'

'Claire,' she heard herself say, and even though she didn't intend to, she sat, backpack thumping on the floor beside her. 'Um, hi.'

'Hello.' His eyes weren't just light; they were – pale a shade of blue so faint it was almost silver. Scary-cool. 'Are you here alone, Claire?'

'I – no, I – ah—' She was babbling like an idiot, and didn't know what was wrong with her. The way he was looking at her made her feel naked. Not in a secretly cool, wow-I-think-he-likes-me way, but in a way that made her want to hide and cover herself. 'I'm here with a friend.'

'A friend,' he said, and reached across to take her hand. She wanted to pull it back – she *did* – but somehow she couldn't get control of herself. All she could do was watch as he turned her hand palm down, and brought it to his mouth to kiss. The warm, damp pressure of his lips on her fingers made her shiver all over.

Then he brushed his thumb across her wrist. 'Where is your bracelet, little Claire? Good girls wear their bracelets. Don't you have one?'

'I—' There was something sick and terrible happening in her head, something that made her tell the truth. 'No. I don't have one.' Because she knew now what Brandon was, and she was sorry she'd laughed at Eve, sorry she'd ever doubted any of it.

You'll get yours, Monica had promised.

Well, here it was.

'I see.' Brandon's eyes seemed to get even paler, until they were pure white with tiny black dots for pupils. She couldn't breathe. Couldn't scream. 'The only question is who will have you, then. And since I'm here first—'

He let go of her, both her hand and her mind, and she fell backward with a breathless little gasp. Somebody was standing behind her chair, a solid warmth, and Brandon was frowning and staring past her.

'You offend my hospitality,' Oliver said, and put his hand on Claire's shoulder. 'You ever bother my friend Claire in here again, Brandon, and I'll have to revoke the privileges for everyone. Understand? I don't think you want to be explaining that.'

Brandon looked furious. His eyes were blue again, but as Claire watched, he snarled at Oliver, and revealed fangs. Real, genuine fangs, like a snake's, that snapped down into place from some hidden spot inside of his mouth, and then back up again, quick as a scorpion's sting.

'None of that,' Oliver said calmly. 'I'm not

impressed. Off with you. Don't make me have a conversation with Amelie about you.'

Brandon slid out of his chair and slouched away through the crowd, toward the exit. It was dark outside now, Claire noticed. He went out into the night and disappeared from sight.

Oliver still had his hand on her shoulder, and now he squeezed it gently. 'That was unfortunate,' he said. 'You need to be careful, Claire. Stay with Eve. Watch out for each other. I'd hate to see anything happen to you.'

She nodded, gulping. Eve came hurrying out of the back, leather coat flapping around her ankles. Her smile died at the sight of Claire's face. 'What happened?'

'Brandon came in,' Oliver said. 'Trolling. Claire happened to run into him.'

'Oh,' Eve said in a small voice. 'Are you OK?'

'She's fine. I spotted him before any permanent damage was done. Take her home, Eve. And keep a sharp eye out for that one; he doesn't take being ordered off very well.'

Eve nodded and helped Claire to her feet, picked up the backpack, and got her outside. The big black Caddy was parked at the curb, and Eve unlocked it and thoroughly checked it over, backseat and trunk, before putting Claire inside of it. When Claire was fastening the seat belt, she noticed two things: first, Oliver was standing in the doorway of Common Grounds, watching them.

Second, Brandon was standing at the corner, in the very edge of the glow of the streetlamp. And he was watching them, too.

Eve saw, too. 'Son of a bitch,' she said furiously, and shot him the finger. Which might not have been too smart, but it made Claire feel better. Eve cranked the engine and squealed out of her parking space, driving like she was breaking the record at a NASCAR race, and screeched to a halt in front of the house just a couple of minutes later. 'OK, you go first,' she said. 'Run for the door, bang on it while you're opening it. *Go, Claire!*'

Claire bailed out breathlessly and slammed the gate back, pounded up the paved walk and up the stairs as she was digging her key out of her pocket. Her hands were shaking, and she missed the keyhole on the first try. She kicked the door and yelled, 'Shane! Michael!' as she tried again.

Behind her, she heard the car door slam, and Eve's shoes clatter on the sidewalk…and stop.

'Now,' said Brandon's low, cold voice, 'let's not be rude, Eve.'

Claire whirled, and saw Eve standing absolutely still ten steps from the porch, her back to the house. Hot wind whipped her leather coat behind her with a dry snapping sound.

Brandon was facing her, his eyes completely white in the pale starlight.

'Who's your sweet little friend?' he asked.

'Leave her alone.' Eve's voice was faint and shaking. 'She's just a kid.'

'You're all just kids.' He shrugged. 'Nobody asks the age of the cow that gave you hamburger.'

Claire, purely terrified now, concentrated, turned back to the door, and rammed the key into the lock...

...just as Shane whipped it open.

'Eve!' she gasped, and Shane pushed her out of the way, jumped down the steps, and got between Eve and Brandon.

'Inside,' Michael said. Claire hadn't heard him, hadn't seen him coming, but he was in the doorway, gesturing her in. As soon as she was over the threshold he grabbed her arm and pushed her out of sight behind him. She peeked around him to see what was happening.

Shane was talking, but whatever he was saying, she couldn't hear it. Eve was backing up, slowly, and when the back of her heels touched the porch steps she whirled and ran up, diving into the doorway and Michael's arms.

'Shane!' Michael shouted.

Brandon lunged at Shane. Shane dodged, yelled, and kicked the vampire with all his weight. Brandon flew backward into the fence, broke through, and rolled into the street.

Shane fell flat on the ground, scrambled up, and ran for the door. It was impossible for Brandon to move that fast, but the vampire seemed to *flash* from lying in the street to reaching for Shane's back...

...and grabbed hold of Shane's T-shirt, yanking him to a sudden stop. But Shane was reaching, too, for Michael's hand, and Michael pulled him forward.

The shirt ripped, Shane stumbled in over the threshold, and Brandon tried to follow. He bounced off an invisible barrier, and for the second time Claire saw his fangs snap down, deadly sharp.

Michael didn't even flinch. 'Try it again, and we'll come stake you in your sleep,' he said. 'Count on it. Tell your friends.'

He slammed the door. Eve collapsed against the wall, panting and trembling; Claire couldn't stop shaking, either. Shane looked flushed and more worried about the damage to his T-shirt than anything else.

Michael grabbed Eve by the shoulders. 'You OK?'

'Yeah. Yeah, he never – wow. That was close.'

'No kidding. Claire?'

She waved, unable to summon up a word.

'Where the hell did he come from?' Shane asked.

'He picked up Claire's scent at the coffee shop,' Eve said. 'I couldn't shake him. Sorry.'

'Damn. That's not good.'

'I know.'

Michael clicked the locks on the front door. 'Check the back. Make sure we're secure, Shane. Upstairs, too.'

'Check.' Shane moved off. 'Dammit, this was my last Killers T-shirt. Somebody's paying for this…'

'Sorry, Michael,' Eve said. 'I tried, I really did.'

'I know. Had to happen sooner or later, with four of us here. You did OK. Don't worry about it.'

'I'm glad you and Shane were here.'

Michael started to say something, then stopped, looking at Claire. Eve didn't seem to notice. She stripped off her leather coat and hung it on a peg by the door, and clumped off in the direction of the living room.

'We were just *attacked*,' Claire finally managed to say. 'By a *vampire*.'

'Yeah, I saw,' Michael said.

'No, you don't understand. We were *attacked*. By a *vampire*. Do you know how impossible that is?'

Michael sighed. 'Truthfully? No. I grew up here, and so did Eve and Shane. We're just kind of used to it.'

'That's crazy!'

'Absolutely.'

It hit her then that there was another impossible thing she'd nearly forgotten about, in the press of panic, and she started to blurt it out, then looked around to be sure Shane and Eve were nowhere in sight. 'What about, you know? You?' She pointed at him.

'Me?' He raised his eyebrows. 'Oh. Right. Upstairs.'

She expected him to take her to the secret room

Shane had shown her, but he didn't; instead, he took her to his own room, the big one on the corner. It was about twice the size of her own room, but didn't have much more furniture; it did have a fireplace – empty this time of year – and a couple of chairs and a reading lamp. Michael settled in one. Claire took the other, feeling small and cold in the heavy leather seat. The wing chair was about twice her size.

'Right,' Michael said, and leant forward, resting his elbows on his knees. 'Let's talk about this morning.' But having said that, he didn't seem to know how to start. He fidgeted, staring at the carpet.

'You died,' Claire said. 'You vanished.'

He seemed glad to have something to respond to.

'Not exactly, but – yeah. Close enough. You know I used to be a musician?'

'You still are!'

'Musicians play someplace besides their own houses. You heard Shane at dinner. He's pushing to find out why I'm not playing gigs. Truth is, I can't. I can't go outside of this house.'

She remembered him standing in the doorway, white-faced, watching Shane face off with Brandon. That hadn't been caution; he wanted to be out there, fighting next to his friend. But he couldn't.

'What happened?' she asked softly. She could tell it wasn't going to be an easy story.

'Vampire,' he said. 'Mostly they just feed, and

eventually they kill you if they feed hard enough. Some of them like that kind of thing, not all of them. But – this one was different. He followed me back from a gig and tried – tried to make me—'

She felt her face burn, and dropped her gaze. 'Oh. Oh God.'

'Not that,' he said. 'Not exactly. He tried to make me a vampire. But he couldn't. I guess he – killed me. Or nearly, anyway. But he couldn't make me into what he was, and he was trying. It nearly killed us both. When I woke up later, it was daylight, he was gone, and I was a ghost. Wasn't until night came that I realised I could make myself real again. But only at night.' He shook his head slowly, rubbing his hands together as if trying to wash off a stain. 'I think the house keeps me alive.'

'The house?' she echoed.

'It's old. And it has a kind of—' He shrugged. 'A kind of power. I don't know what it is, exactly. When my parents traded up to this house, they only lived here for a couple of months, then moved away to New York. Didn't like the vibes. I liked it fine. I think it liked me, too. But anyway, I can't leave it. I've tried.'

'Even during the day? When you're not, you know, here?'

'Doesn't matter,' he said. 'Can't go out any door, window, or crack. I'm trapped here.'

He looked oddly relieved to be telling her. If he hadn't told Shane or Eve, he probably hadn't told anybody. That felt odd, being the keeper of that secret, because it was a big one. Attacked by a vampire, left for dead, turned into a ghost, trapped in the house? How many secrets *was* that, anyway?

Something occurred to her. 'You said the vampire, did he…drink your blood?'

Michael nodded. He didn't meet her eyes.

'And you – died?'

Another silent nod.

'What happened to your – you know – body?'

'I'm still kind of using it.' He gestured at himself. Claire, unable to stop herself, reached out and touched him. He felt real and warm and alive. 'I don't know how it works, Claire, I really don't. Except I do think it's the house, not me.'

She took a deep breath. 'Do you drink blood?'

He looked up this time, surprised, lips parted. 'No. Of course I don't. I told you, he couldn't – make me what he was.'

'You're sure.'

'I eat Shane's garlic chilli. Does that sound like a vampire to you?'

She shrugged thoughtfully. 'Until today, I thought I knew what a vampire was, all capes and fake Romanian accents and stuff. What about crosses? Do crosses work?'

'Sometimes. Don't rely on them, though. The older ones aren't stopped by things like that.'

'How about Brandon?' Since he was her main concern right now.

Michael's lip curled. 'Brandon's a punk. You could melt him with a Super Soaker full of tap water, so long as you told him it was blessed. He's dangerous, but so far as vampires go, he's at the bottom of the food chain. It's the ones who *don't* go around flashing fangs and trying to grab you off the street you need to worry about. And yeah, wear a cross – but keep it under your clothes. You'll have to make one if you don't already have one – they don't sell them anywhere in town. And if you can find things like holy water and Eucharist, keep them on hand, but the vampires in this town closed down most of the churches fifty years ago. There's still a few operating underground. Be careful, though. Don't believe everything you hear, and never, ever go by yourself.'

That was the longest speech she'd ever heard from Michael. It tumbled out in a flood, driven with intensity and frustration. *He can't do anything. He can't do anything to help us when we go outside the door.*

'Why did you let us move in?' she asked. 'After – what happened to you?'

He smiled. It didn't look quite right somehow. 'I got lonely,' he said. 'And since I can't leave the house, there's too much I can't do. I needed somebody to help with groceries and stuff. And...being a ghost doesn't exactly pay the bills. Shane – Shane was looking for a place to stay, and he said he'd pitch in for rent. It was perfect. Then

Eve...we were friends back in high school. I couldn't just let her wander around out there after her parents threw her out.'

Claire tried to remember what Eve had said. Nothing, really. 'Why did they do that?'

'She wouldn't take Protection from their Patron when she turned eighteen. Plus, she started dressing Goth when she was about your age. Said she was never going to kiss any vampire ass, no matter what.' Michael made a helpless gesture with his hands. 'At eighteen, they threw her out. Had to, or it would have cost the whole family their Protection. So she's on her own. She's done OK – she's safe here, and she's safe at the coffee shop. It's only the rest of the time she has to be careful.'

Claire couldn't think of anything to say. She looked away from Michael, around the room. His bed was made. *Oh my God, that's his bed.* She tried to imagine Michael sleeping there, and couldn't. Although she could imagine some other things, and shouldn't have because it made her feel hot and embarrassed.

'Claire,' he said quietly. She looked back at him. 'Brandon's too young to be out before dark, so you're safe in the daytime, but *don't* stay out after dark. Got it?'

She nodded.

'About the other thing...'

'I won't tell,' she said. 'I won't, Michael. Not if you don't want me to.'

He let out his breath in a long, slow sigh. 'Thanks. I know it sounds stupid, but...I just don't want them to know yet. I need to figure out how to tell them.'

'It's your business,' Claire said. 'And Michael? If you start, you know, getting this craving for red stuff...?'

'You'll be the first to know,' he said. His eyes were steady and cool. 'And I expect you to do whatever you have to do to stop me.'

She shivered and said yes, OK, she'd stake him if she had to, but she didn't mean it.

She hoped she didn't, anyway.

CHAPTER EIGHT

Shane's turn for cooking dinner, and he came up with chilli dogs – more chilli, but at least he did a good job with it. Claire had two, watching in amazement as Michael and Shane downed four each, and Eve nibbled one. She smiled at Shane, and shot back barbs whenever he sent one sailing her way, but Claire noticed something else.

Eve couldn't keep her eyes off of Michael. At first, Claire thought, *She knows something*, but then she saw the flush in Eve's cheeks showing through the pale make-up, and the glitter in her eyes.

Oh. Well, she guessed Michael had looked pretty hot, grabbing her out of danger like that and dragging her out of harm's way. And now that she thought about it, Eve had been making little glances his direction every time they'd been together.

Eve finally shoved her plate away and claimed

dibs on the bathroom for a long, hot, soaking bubble bath. Which Claire wished she'd thought of first. She and Michael did the dishes while Shane practiced his zombie-fighting skills on Xbox.

'Eve likes you, you know,' she said casually as she was rinsing off the last plate. He nearly dropped the one he was drying.

'What?'

'She does.'

'Did she tell you that?'

'No.'

'I don't think you understand Eve, then.'

'Don't you like her?'

'Of course I like her!'

'Enough to...?'

'I am *not* talking about this.' He put the plate into the drainer. 'Jesus, Claire!'

'Oh, come on. You like her, don't you?'

'Even if I did—' He stopped short, glancing toward the doorway and lowering his voice. 'Even if I did, there are a few *problems*, don't you think?'

'Everybody's got problems,' she said. 'Especially in this town. I've only been here six weeks, and I already know that.'

Whatever he thought about that, he dried his hands and walked out. She heard him talking to Shane, and when she went out the two of them were deep into the video game, elbowing each other and fighting for every point.

Boys. Sheesh.

She was on her way to her room, passing the bathroom, when she heard Eve crying. She knocked quietly, and looked in when Eve muffled her sobs. The door wasn't locked.

Eve was dressed in a black fluffy robe, sitting on the toilet; she'd stripped off her make-up and let her hair down, and she looked like a little girl in a too-large adult outfit. Fragile. She gave Claire a shaky grin and wiped tear tracks from her face. 'Sorry,' she said, and cleared her throat. 'Kind of a suck-ass day, you know?'

'That guy. That vampire. He acted like he knew you,' Claire said.

'Yeah. He – he's the one who gives my family Protection. I turned him down. He's not too happy.' She gave a hollow little laugh. 'Guess nobody likes rejection.'

Claire studied her. 'You OK, though?'

'Sure. Peachy.' Eve waved her out. 'Go study. Get smart enough to blow this town. I'm just a little bit down. Don't worry about it.'

Later, when Michael started playing, Claire heard Eve crying through the wall again.

She didn't go investigate, and she didn't watch Michael vanish. She didn't think she had the courage.

Shane went with her the next day to buy some clothes. It was only three blocks to the colourless retail section of town, with all its dingy-looking thrift stores; she didn't want his company, but he wasn't letting her go alone.

'You let Eve go alone,' she pointed out as he sat on the couch putting on his shoes.

'Yeah, well, Eve has a car,' he said. 'Besides, I wasn't up. You get escorted. Live with it.'

She felt secretly pleased about it. A little. It was another typically sunny day, the sidewalks almost vibrating with heat. Not a lot of pedestrians, but then, there rarely were. Shane walked with a long, loping stride, hands in his pockets; she had to hurry to keep up. She kept waiting for him to say something, but he didn't. After a while, she just started talking. 'Did you have a lot of friends, growing up here?'

'Friends? Yeah, I guess. A few. Michael. I kind of knew Eve back then, but we hung with different crowds. Couple of other kids.'

'What – what happened to them?'

'Nothing,' Shane said. 'They grew up, got jobs, claimed Protection, kept right on going. That's how it works in Morganville. You either stay in, or you run.'

'Do you ever see them?' Because she'd been amazed how much she'd missed her friends back home, especially Elizabeth. She'd always thought she was a loner, but…maybe she wasn't. Maybe nobody really was.

'No,' he said. 'Nothing in common these days. They don't want to hang with somebody like me.'

'Somebody who doesn't want to fit in.' Shane glanced at her and nodded. 'Sorry.'

He shrugged. 'Nobody's fault. So what about you? Any friends back home?'

'Yeah. Elizabeth, she's my best friend. We talked all the time, you know? But...when she found out I was going away to school, she just...' Claire decided a shrug was about the best opinion she could offer about it.

'Ever call her?'

'Yeah,' she said. 'But it's like we don't know each other anymore. You know? We have to think about what to say. It's weird.'

'God, I know what you mean.' Shane suddenly stopped and took his hands out of his pockets. They were in the middle of the block, in between two stores, and at first she thought he was going to look in a window, but then he said tensely, 'Turn around and walk away. Just go into the first store you see, and hide.'

'But—'

'Do it, Claire. Now.'

She backed away and turned, walked as fast as she dared to the store they'd already passed. It was a skanky-looking used-clothing store, nowhere she'd willingly shop, but she pushed open the door and looked back over her shoulder as she did.

A cop car was gliding to the curb next to Shane. He was standing there, hands at his sides, looking bland and respectful, and the cop who was driving leant out of the window to say something to him.

Claire nearly fell forward as the door was jerked open, and stumbled over the threshold into a darkened, musty-smelling interior.

'Hey there,' the uniformed cop who'd opened the door said to her. He was an older man, blond, with thinning hair and a thick moustache. Cold blue eyes and crooked teeth. 'Claire, right?'

'I—' She couldn't think what to say to that. All her life she'd been told not to lie to the police, but... 'Yes, sir.' She could tell he already knew, anyway.

'My name's Gerald. Gerald Bradfield. Pleased to meet you.' He held out his hand. She swallowed hard, wiped her sweaty palm, and shook. She half expected that he'd click handcuffs around her wrists, but he just half crushed her hand as he pumped it twice, up and down, and let go. 'People been looking for you, you know.'

'I – didn't know that, sir.'

'Didn't you?' Cold, cold eyes, no matter what the smile said. 'Can't imagine that, little girl. Fact is, the mayor's daughter was worried about where you might have got off to. Asked us to find you. Make sure you were all right.'

'I'm fine, sir.' She could barely talk. Her mouth had gone dry. 'I'm not in trouble, am I?'

He laughed. 'Why would you be in trouble,

Claire? No, you don't have to worry about that. Fact is, we already know where you are. And who you're running with. You should be more careful, honey. You're brand-new here, but you already know a hell of a lot more than you ought. And your friends aren't exactly the kind that guarantee a peaceful life in this town. Troublemakers. You don't look like a troublemaker to me. Tell you what, you move back into the dorm, be a good girl, go to classes, I'll personally make sure nothing happens to you.'

Claire wanted to nod, wanted to agree, wanted to do *anything* to get away from this man. She looked around the store. There were other people in there, but she couldn't get any of them to look at her. It was like she didn't even exist.

'You don't think I can do it,' he said. 'I can. Count on it.'

She looked back at him, and his eyes had gone white, with little dots of pupils in the middle. When he smiled, she saw a flash of fangs.

She gasped, backed away, and grabbed for the door handle. She lunged out into the street, running, and saw Shane standing right where he'd been, watching the police car pull away from the curb. He turned and grabbed her as she practically crashed into him.

'Vampire!' she gasped. 'V-vampire cop. In the store!'

'Must have been Bradfield,' Shane said. 'Tall

guy? Kind of bald, with a moustache?'

She nodded, shaking all over. Shane didn't even look surprised, much less alarmed. 'Bradfield's OK,' he said. 'Not the worst guy in town, that's for sure. He hurt you?'

'He – he just shook my hand. But he said he knew! He knew where I was living!'

Again, Shane didn't look surprised. 'Yeah, well, that was just a matter of time. They pulled over to ask me your full name. They added it to inventory.'

'*Inventory?*'

'That's what they call it. It's like a census. They always know how many are living in a place. Look, just walk, OK? And don't look so scared. They aren't going to jump us in broad daylight.'

Shane had a lot more confidence in that than she did, but she got control of her shaking and nodded, and followed him up another block to a thrift shop that looked brighter, friendlier, and less likely to have vampires lurking inside. 'This is Mrs Lawson's place. She used to be a friend of my mom's. It's OK.' Shane held open the door for her, like a gentleman. She supposed his mom had taught him that. Inside, the place smelt nice – incense, Claire thought – and there were lots of lights burning. No dark corners here, and a bell rang with a pleasant little tinkling sound when Shane let the door shut behind them.

'Shane!' A large woman in a brightly coloured tie-dyed shirt and big, swirly skirt hustled over from behind the counter at the back, gathered Shane up in a hug, and beamed at him when she stepped back. 'Boy, what the hell are you doing back here? Up to no good?'

'Up to no good, ma'am. Just like always.'

'Thought so. Good for you.' The woman's dark eyes landed on Claire. 'Who's your little friend?'

'This is Claire. Claire Danvers. She's – she's a student at the college.'

'Nice to meet you, Claire. Now. I'll bet you didn't come in here just to say "hey", boy, so what can I do for you?'

'Clothes,' Claire said. 'I'm looking for some clothes.'

'Those we got. You're about a size four, right? Come with me, honey. I've got some really nice things just your size. Shane, you look like you could use some new clothes, too. Those jeans are raggedy.'

'Supposed to be.'

'Lord. Fashion. I just don't understand it anymore.'

Maybe she didn't, but Mrs Lawson had all kinds of cute tops and jeans and things, and cheap, too. Claire picked an armload and followed her to the counter, where she counted out a grand total of twenty-two dollars, including tax. As Mrs Lawson was ringing it up, Claire looked behind her to the things on the wall. There was some kind of official-looking certificate hanging there, framed, with an embossed seal... No, that wasn't a seal. That was a symbol. The same symbol as the one on the bracelet Mrs Lawson wore.

'You take care,' Mrs Lawson said as she handed over the bag with the clothes. 'Both of you. Tell Shane he needs to get himself right, and he needs to do it quick. They've been cutting him some slack, given what he went through, but that won't last. He needs to be thinking about his future.'

Claire looked over her shoulder to where Shane was staring out the window, looking bored. Eyes half-closed.

'I'll tell him,' she said doubtfully.

She couldn't imagine Shane was thinking about anything else.

Days slipped away, and Claire just let them go. She was worried about class, but she was tired and her bruises had turned Technicolor, and the last thing she wanted to do was be the centre of attention. It was better – Shane had convinced her – to do some home study and get back to class when she was better, and Monica had had some time to let things blow over.

The week slipped away. She fell into a regular routine – up late with Michael and Shane and Eve, sleep until noon, argue over bathroom rights, cook, clean, study, do it all again. It felt...good. Real, somehow, in a way that dorm life didn't, exactly.

The following Monday, when she got up and

made breakfast, she had to make it for two: Shane was awake, looking grumpy and groggy. He silently grabbed the bacon and fried some up while she did the eggs; there wasn't any banter, as there had been between him and Eve a couple of mornings back. She tried a little conversation, but he wasn't in the mood. He just grunted replies. She waited until he was done with his breakfast – which included a cup of coffee, brewed in the tiny little coffeemaker on the corner of the counter – before she asked, 'What are you doing up so early?'

Shane leant his chair back on two legs, balancing as he chewed. 'Ask Michael.'

Can't exactly do that... 'You doing something for him?'

'Yeah.' He thumped his chair back down and brushed his hand over his hair, which still looked like a mess. 'Don't expect me to dress up or anything.'

'What?'

'What you see is what you get.' She just looked at him, frowning, trying to figure out what he was saying. 'I'm taking you to class. You were going back today, right?'

'You're kidding,' she said flatly. He shrugged. 'You're *kidding*. I'm not some six-year-old who needs her big brother to walk her to school! No way, Shane!'

'Michael thinks you should have an escort. Brandon was pretty pissed. He could find a way to take it out on you, even if he can't do it himself. He's got plenty of people who'd kick your ass on his say-so.' Shane's eyes slid away from hers. 'Like Monica.'

Oh, crap. 'Monica belongs to Brandon?'

'The whole Morrell family does, far as I know. He's their own personal badass. So.' He rubbed his hands together. 'What exciting classes do we have today?'

'You can't go to *class* with me!'

'Hey, you're welcome to knock me out and stop me, but until you do, I'm your date for the day. So. What classes?'

'Calculus II, Physics of Sound, Chemistry III, chem lab, and Biochemistry.'

'Holy crap. You really *are* smart. Right, I'll take some comics or something. Maybe my iPod.'

She kept glaring at him. It didn't seem to do any good – if anything, it just made him more cheerful.

'I always wanted to be a big man on campus,' Shane said. 'Guess this is my chance.'

'I'm dead,' she moaned, and rested her forehead on her hands.

'Not yet. And that's kind of the point.'

She was afraid Shane would make a big deal out of it, but he didn't. He even combed his hair, which turned out to make him look totally hot in ways that she was afraid to notice. Especially if she had to spend the whole day with him. He'd picked a plain white shirt and his best pair of blue jeans, which were still out at the knees and frayed at the hems. And plain running shoes. 'In case we have to do any retreating,' he said. 'Plus, kicking somebody when you're wearing flip-flops hurts.'

'But you're not kicking anybody,' she said quickly. 'Right?'

'Nobody who doesn't deserve it,' he said. 'What else do I need to fit in?'

'Backpack.' She found her spare – she'd brought two – and tossed it to him. He stuck in some paperbacks, a PSP, and his iPod and headphones, then raided the cabinets for Twinkies and bottled water. 'We're not exactly going to the wilderness, Shane. You don't have to take *everything*. There are vending machines.'

'Yeah? I didn't see any lunch in that schedule. You'll thank me later.'

In fact, she did feel better with Shane loping along beside her; he was watching the shadows, the dark alleys, the empty buildings. Watching everything. Even though he'd packed the iPod, he wasn't listening to it. She missed hers, all of a sudden, and wondered if Monica had it.

They made it to campus without incident, and they were halfway across it, heading for her first class, when Claire suddenly thought of something and came to a full stop. Shane kept going for a couple of paces, then looked back.

'Monica,' she said. 'Monica's going to be

hanging around. She usually is. She'll see you.'

'I know.' Shane hitched his backpack to a more comfortable spot. 'Let's go.'

'But – *Monica*!'

He just looked at her, and started walking. She stayed where she was. 'Hey! You're supposed to be *with* me, not leaving me!'

'Monica's my business,' he said. 'Drop it.' He waited for her, and she reluctantly caught up. 'She doesn't mess with us, I won't mess with her. How's that?'

Wishful thinking, to Claire's mind. If Monica really had gotten it in for Shane, even a year or two ago, and gone far enough to *kill his sister*, she couldn't imagine any situation where Shane just walked away. Shane wasn't a walking-away kind of guy.

The square concrete courtyard between the Architecture Building and the Math Sciences Building was packed with students crossing between classes. Now that Claire knew what to look for, she couldn't help but notice how many of them had bracelets – leather, metal, even braided cloth – with symbols on them.

And how many students *didn't*.

The ones who wore the symbols were the shiny, confident ones. Sorority girls. Frat guys. Athletes. Popular kids. The loners, the sideliners, the dull and average and strange...they were the ones who weren't Protected.

They were the cattle.

Shane was scanning the crowd. Claire kept walking quickly toward the Math Building; she knew for a fact that Monica wouldn't be caught dead – or killing anybody – in a place that geeky. The only problem was that the third building on the Quad was the Business Administration Building, and that was, of course, where Monica liked to spend her time hanging out, looking for rich boys.

Almost there...

She was actually on the steps leading up to the Math Building when she heard Shane stop behind her. He was staring off into the Quad, and as Claire turned, she saw Monica, surrounded by a clique of admirers, staring right back at him. The two of them might as well have been alone. It was the kind of look that people in love exchanged, or people who were about to kill each other.

'Son of a bitch,' Shane breathed. He sounded shaken.

'Come on,' Claire said, and grabbed his elbow. She was afraid he wouldn't let her pull him on, but he did, as if his mind was somewhere else. When he finally glanced at her, his eyes were dark and hard.

'Not here,' she said. 'She won't come in.'

'Why not?'

'It would embarrass her.'

He nodded slowly, as if that made sense to him, and followed her to class.

Claire had a hard time keeping her mind on the

droning lecture, which was familiar anyway, and she'd read far ahead of where the professor was teaching…but mostly, she kept thinking about Shane, sitting motionless next to her, hands on the desk, staring blankly into space. He wasn't even listening to his iPod. She could sense the tenseness in his body, like he was just waiting for the chance to hit something.

I knew this was a bad idea.

It was an hour-and-a-half lecture with a fifteen-minute break in the middle; when Shane got up and walked out, she hastily followed him. He went up to the glass doors and looked out over the Quad.

'She's gone,' he said, without looking at Claire. 'Quit worrying about me. I'm OK.'

'She – Eve said she burnt your house.' No reply. 'And – your sister—?'

'I couldn't get her out,' Shane said. 'She was twelve, and I couldn't get her out of the house. That was my job. Watch out for her.'

He still didn't look at her. She couldn't think of anything to say. After a while, he walked away, into the boys' bathroom; she dashed into the girls', waiting impatiently for the line to clear, and came back out to find him nowhere in sight.

Oh, crap.

But when she went back to the lecture hall he was sitting right where he'd been, this time with his iPod earbuds in place.

She didn't say anything. Neither did he.

It was the longest lecture, and the least enjoyable, that Claire could remember.

Physics was in the same building; if Monica was waiting out in the wilting sun on the Quad, she'd be getting a really good tan. Shane sat like a statue, if a statue wore headphones and radiated angry coiled tension that made hair stand up on a person's arms. She felt like she was sitting next to an unexploded bomb, and given all of the physics she'd had, she understood exactly what that meant. Talk about potential energy...

Physics crawled slowly by. Shane broke out water and Twinkies, and shared. Chemistry was in the next building, but Claire made sure that they went out the side entrance, not through the Quad. No sign of Monica. She suffered through another hour and a half of chemistry and tension. Shane gradually unwound to the point that her nerves didn't jangle like sleigh bells every time he moved, and ended up playing on his PSP through most of the class. Killing zombies, she hoped. That seemed to put him in a good mood.

In fact, he was positively cheerful during chem lab, interested in the experiment and asking so many questions that the teaching assistant, who'd never had to come to Claire's table before, wandered over and stared at Shane as if trying to figure out what he was doing there.

'Hey, man,' Shane said, and stuck out his hand. 'Shane Collins. I'm – what's the word I'm looking for? Auditing. Auditing the class. With my friend here. Claire.'

'Oh,' said the TA, whose name Claire had never learnt. 'Right. OK, then. Just – follow along.'

Shane gave him a thumbs-up and a goofy grin. 'Hey,' he said in an undertone, leaning close to Claire. 'Any of this stuff blow up?'

'What? Um…yeah, if you do it wrong, I guess.'

'I'm thinking about practical applications. Bombs. Things like that.'

'Shane!' He really was distracting. And he smelt good. Guy good, which was different from girl good – darker, spicier, a smell that made her go all fluttery inside. *Oh, come on, it's* Shane! she told herself. That didn't help, especially when he shot her that crooked smile and a look that probably would kill most girls at ten feet. *He's a slacker. And he's – not that smart.*

Maybe he was, though. Just in different places than she was. It was a new idea to her, but she kind of liked it.

She slapped his hand when he reached for the re-agents, and concentrated on the details of the experiment.

She was concentrating so hard, in fact, and Shane had gotten so engrossed in watching what she was doing, that neither of them heard footsteps behind them. The first Claire knew about it was a searing, burning sensation down the right side of her back. She dropped the beaker she was holding and screamed – couldn't help it, because *God*, that hurt – and Shane whirled around and grabbed somebody by the collar who was backing away.

Gina, the Monickette. She snarled and slapped at him, but he didn't let go; Claire, gasping in pain and trying to twist to see what was happening on her back, could see that it was taking everything Shane had not to deck his prisoner then and there. The TA came rushing over and other students started realising there was something wrong, or at least more interesting than lab work; Claire slipped off the stool at the table and tried to look at what was happening to her back, because it *hurt*. She smelt something terrible.

'Oh my God!' the TA blurted. He grabbed the bottled water out of Shane's backpack, opened it, and dumped the contents over Claire's back, then dashed to a cupboard on the side and came back with a box of baking soda. She heard it sizzle when it hit her back, and nearly passed out. 'Here. Sit. Sit down. You, call an ambulance. Go!' As Claire sank down breathlessly again on another, lower stool, the TA grabbed a pair of scissors and cut her shirt up the back, and folded it aside. He cut her bra strap, too, and she just barely had the presence of mind to grab hold before the whole thing slid down her arms. *God, it hurts, it hurts...* She tried not to cry. The burn was easing up a little as the baking soda did its work. *Acid has a low pH; baking soda has a high one…* Well, at least she'd retained some grasp of chemistry, even now.

She looked up and saw that Shane still had hold of Gina. He'd twisted her arm behind her back and made her let go of the beaker; what remained of the acid she'd splashed on Claire was still in the glass, looking as innocent as water.

'It was an accident!' she yelped, and stood on her tiptoes as Shane twisted harder. 'I tripped! I'm sorry! Look, I didn't mean it…'

'We're not working with H_2SO_4 today,' the TA said grimly. 'You've got no reason to be walking around with it. Claire? Claire, how bad is the pain?'

'I – it's OK. I'm OK,' she said, though truthfully she had no idea if she was or not. She felt light-headed, sick, and cold. Shock, probably. And embarrassment, because *God*, she was half naked in front of the entire chem lab, and… Shane… 'Can I put something on?'

'No, you can't let anything touch that. The burn's through several layers of skin. It'll need treatment, and antibiotics. You just sit still.' The TA turned to Shane and Gina, and levelled a finger at her. '*You*, you're talking to the campus police. I will not tolerate this kind of attack in my classroom. I don't care *who* your friends are!'

So he knew her. Or at least he knew enough. Shane was whispering something in Gina's ear, something too low for Claire to hear, but it couldn't be good, by the expression on the girl's face.

'Sir?' Claire asked faintly. 'Sir, can I have a make-up on the lab work and—'

And she passed out before she finished saying, *and I'm sorry for the mess.*

CHAPTER NINE

When she woke up, she was on her side, and she felt warm all over. Sleepy. There was someone sitting next to her, a boy, and she blinked twice and realised that it was Shane. Shane was in her bedroom. No, wait, this wasn't her bedroom; it was somewhere else...

'Emergency room,' he said. She must have looked confused. 'Damn, Claire. Warn a guy before you do a face-plant on the floor next time. I could have looked all heroic and caught you or something.'

She smiled. Her voice came out sounding lazy and slow. 'You caught Gina.' That was funny, so she said it again. 'You caught Geeeeeeeeeena.'

'Yeah, ha-ha, you're high as a kite, you know? And they called your parents.'

It took her a little while to realise what he'd just said. 'Parents?' she repeated, and tried to lift her head. 'Oh. Ow. Not good.'

'Not so much. Mom and Dad were pretty freaked to hear you became a lab accident. The campus cops forgot to mention the part where Gina deliberately threw acid on your back. They seem to think it was just one of those funky accidents.'

'Was it?' she asked. 'Accident?'

'No way. She meant to hurt you.'

Claire plucked at the ugly blue hospital gown she was wearing. 'Killed my shirt.'

'Yeah, pretty much.' Shane looked pale and tense. 'I've been trying to call Michael. I don't know where he is. I don't want to leave you alone here, but—'

'He's OK,' she said softly, and closed her eyes. 'I'm OK, too.'

She thought she felt his hand on her hair, a second of light, sweet pressure. 'Yeah,' Shane said. 'You're OK. I'll be here when you wake up.'

She nodded sleepily, and then everything faded into a lemon yellow haze, like she was lying in the sunlight.

Ouch.

Waking up was *not fun*. No hazy druggy lemon sunlight; this was more like a blowtorch burning on her back right on the shoulder blade. Claire whimpered and burrowed into her pillow, trying to get away from the pain, but it followed close behind.

The drugs had worn off.

She blinked and whimpered and slowly sat up; a passing nurse stopped and came in to check her over. 'Congratulations,' she said. 'You're doing well. That burn is going to hurt for a while, but if you take the antibiotics and keep the wound clean, you'll be fine. You're lucky somebody was there to wash it off and neutralise the reaction. I've seen battery acid burns down to the bone.'

Claire nodded, not sure she could actually speak without throwing up. Her whole side felt hot and bruised.

'Do you want to get down?'

She nodded again. The nurse helped her down, and gave her what was left of her clothes when she asked. The bra, cut through, was a total loss. The shirt – not much left of that, either. The nurse came up with a loose black T-shirt from lost and found and got her presentable, and the doctor came around to give her a quick once-over. From the brisk way they dispensed with her, a little sulphuric acid burn was barely worth working up a sweat about, at least in Morganville.

'How bad is it?' she asked Shane as he wheeled her through the halls to the exit. 'I mean, is it, like, really gross?'

'Unbelievably gross,' he said. 'Horror movie gruesome.'

'Oh God.'

He relented. 'It's not so bad. It's about the size of

a quarter. Your teacher guy did a good job chopping up your clothes and getting it away from your skin. I know it hurt like hell, but it could have been a lot worse.'

There had been a lot more in the beaker in Gina's hand. 'Do you – do you think she was going to—?'

'Pour it all on you? Hell yeah. She just didn't have time.'

Wow. That was...unpleasant. She felt hot and cold and a little sick, and it had nothing to do with shock this time. 'I guess that was Monica's payback.'

'Some of it, anyway. She'll be really pissed now that it didn't go over the way she thought it would.'

The idea of Monica being really pissed wasn't the best way to end the day – and it *was* the end of the day, she realised as Shane rolled her up to the automatic glass double doors.

It was dark.

'Oh,' she said, and covered her mouth. 'Oh no.'

'Yeah, well, we've got transpo covered, at least. Ready?'

She nodded, and Shane suddenly accelerated her chair into a flat-out run. Claire yelped and grabbed for the handles, feeling utterly out of control as the chair bounced its way down the ramp and skidded to a halt just inches from the shiny black side of Eve's car. Eve threw open the passenger door, and Claire tried to get up on her own, but Shane grabbed her around the waist and lifted her straight into the seat. It took seconds, and then he was kicking the wheelchair back toward the ramp, where it bumped into the railing and sat there, looking lost.

Shane dived into the back. 'Punch it!' he said. Eve did, as Claire struggled to find some kind of seat belt setting that wouldn't reduce her to gasps and tears of pain. She settled for hunching forward, bracing herself on the massive dashboard, as Eve peeled out of the parking lot and raced down the dark street. The street-lights looked eerie and too far apart – was that deliberate? Did the vampires control even how far apart they built the lights? Or was she just freaked beyond belief?

'Is he there?' Shane asked, leaning over the seat back. Eve shot him a look.

'Yeah,' she said. 'He's there. But don't put me in the middle of it. I have to work there, you know.'

'I promise, I won't tick off your boss.'

She didn't believe him – that much was clear – but Eve turned right instead of left at the next light, and in about two minutes pulled up at the curb in front of Common Grounds, which was ablaze with light. Crowded, too. Claire frowned, but before she could even ask, Shane was out of the car and heading inside the coffee shop.

'What's he doing?' she asked.

'Something stupid,' Eve said. 'How's the burn? Hurts, huh?'

Claire would have shrugged, but when she even *thought* about it the imagined pain made her flinch.

'Not so bad,' she said bravely, and tried a smile. 'Could have been a lot worse, I guess.'

'I guess,' Eve agreed. 'Told you classes were dangerous. We need to get this under control. You can't go back if this kind of thing happens.'

'I can't *quit*!'

'Sure you can,' Eve said cheerfully. 'People do it all the time. Just not people like you – oh, damn.'

Eve bit her black-painted lip, eyes wide and worried as she stared through the window at the brightly lit interior of the shop. And after a few seconds, Claire saw what she was worried about: the hippie manager, Oliver, was standing at the window watching them right back, and behind him, Shane was pulling up a chair to the far-corner table, where a dark shape was sitting.

'Tell me he's not talking to Brandon,' Claire said.

'Um… OK. He's not talking to Brandon.'

'You're lying.'

'Yeah. He's talking to Brandon. Look, let Shane do his thing, OK? He's not as stupid as he looks, mostly.'

'But he's not – Protected, right?'

'That's why he's talking in Common Grounds. It's sort of a truce spot. Vampires don't hunt there, or they're not supposed to, anyway. And it's where all kinds of deals and treaties and stuff get made. So Shane's safe enough in there.'

But she was still biting her lip and looking worried. 'Unless?' Claire guessed.

'Unless Shane attacks first. Self-defence doesn't count.'

Shane was being good, as far as Claire could see... His hands were on the table, and although he was bent over saying something, he wasn't slugging anybody. That was good, right? Although she had no idea what he could be saying to Brandon, anyway. Brandon wasn't the one who had poured acid on her back.

Whatever Shane said, it didn't seem to go down too hard; eventually, Shane just shoved his chair back and walked out, nodding to Oliver on the way out. Brandon slid out from behind the table, dark and sleek, to follow Shane to the doorway, close enough to reach out and grab him. But that was just a mind game, Claire realised as she started to yell a warning. Brandon wanted to freak him out, not hurt him.

Shane just looked over his shoulder, shrugged, and exited the coffee shop. When Brandon started to follow, Oliver reached across and put his arm in the way. By the time Brandon had snarled something at him, Shane was in the car, and Eve was already gunning it away from the curb.

'Do we need to be afraid now?' she asked. 'Because I'd like a head start before the official terror alert goes up.'

'Nope. We're clear,' Shane said. He sounded tired, and a little strange. 'Claire's got a free pass.

Nobody's going to come after her. Including Monica and her sock puppets.'

'But – what? Why?' Claire asked. Eve evidently didn't have to ask. She just looked grim and angry.

'We did a trade,' Shane said. 'Vampires are all about the one-up.'

'You're such an *idiot*!' Eve hissed.

'I did what I had to do! I couldn't ask Michael. He wasn't—' Shane bit off whatever he was about to say, violently, and got the anger in his voice under tight control. 'He wasn't around. Again. I had to do something. Claire wasn't kidding. They'll kill her, or at least, they'll hurt her so bad she'll wish they'd finish it up. I can't let that happen.'

There was, Claire thought, a silent *not again* at the end of that. She wanted to turn and look at him, but it hurt too much to try. She tried to meet his eyes in the mirror instead.

'Shane,' she said. 'What did you promise?'

'Nothing I can't afford to lose.'

'Shane!'

But Shane didn't answer. Neither did Eve, although she parted her lips a couple of times, then shut them without making a sound. The rest of the drive was done in silence, and once they'd pulled in at the curb, Eve got out and hurried up the walk to unlock the door. Claire opened the passenger door and started to get out, but again, Shane was there ahead of her, helping her up. Man, he was...strong. And he had big, warm hands. She shivered, and he immediately asked, 'Cold?' but it wasn't that. Not that at all.

'Shane, what did you promise?' she blurted, and grabbed his forearm. Not that he couldn't have pulled free, but...he didn't. He just looked down at her. They were standing really close together, close enough she felt every nerve in her body fizz like a shaken can of Coke. 'You didn't – do something—'.

'Stupid?' he asked. He looked down at her hand, and after a second, he touched it with his own. Just for a second, and then yanked away from her like she'd burnt him. She'd been right; he could break free without even thinking about it. 'Yeah. That's what I'm good at. The stupid stuff. Probably for the best; having two big brains in the house might get kinda crowded.' When she tried to say something, he motioned her toward the house. 'Unless you want to hang a This Vein for Rent sign around your neck, *move* already!'

She moved. The front door was open, and Shane followed behind her, close behind, until she was going up the steps.

She didn't hear his footsteps anymore, and turned to look. He was standing at the bottom of the stairs, watching the street.

There was a vampire standing at the corner, under the glow of a streetlight. Brandon. Just standing there, arms folded, he was leaning against the lamppost like he had all the time in the world.

He blew them a kiss, turned, and walked away.

Shane shot him the finger and practically shoved Claire across the threshold. 'Don't you ever stop out there!'

'You said I got a free pass!'

'It doesn't come with a written guarantee!'

'What did you promise him?' she yelled.

Shane slammed the door, hard, and started to push past her to go down the hall, but just as he got there, Michael stepped into his path. And Michael looked pissed.

'Answer her,' he said. 'What the hell did you do, Shane?'

'Oh, *now* you care? Where the hell were you, man? I called! I came and looked for you. Hell, I even picked the lock to your room!'

Michael's blue eyes flickered from Shane to Claire and back. 'I had things to do.'

'Dude, today you had things to do? Whatever, man. You weren't around, and I had to make the call. So I made it.'

'Shane.' Michael reached out and grabbed him by the arm, dragging him to a stop. 'It sounds like she deserves an answer. We all do.' Behind him, Eve stepped around the corner, arms folded.

Shane let out a short, harsh laugh. 'Ganging up on me with the girls? Low blow, man. Low blow. What happened to male bonding?'

'Eve says you talked to Brandon.'

Claire watched the fight go out of Shane's

shoulders. 'Yeah. I did. I had to. I mean – look, they *threw acid on her* and the damn cops wouldn't even – I had to go to the source. You taught me that.'

'You made a deal with Brandon,' Michael said, and Claire heard the sick tremor in his voice. 'Oh, dammit to hell, Shane. You didn't.'

Shane shrugged. He wasn't meeting Michael's eyes. 'Dude, it's done. Don't make a thing out of it. It's only twice. And he can't drain me or anything.'

'Shit!' Michael turned and slammed his hand hard into the wooden doorframe. 'You don't even know her, man! You can't make a crusade out of this!'

'I'm not!'

'She's not Alyssa!' Michael yelled, and that was the loudest shout she'd ever heard in her life. Claire flinched and stepped back, and saw Eve do the same behind him.

Shane didn't move. It was like he couldn't. He just stood there, head down.

And then he took a deep breath, raised his head, and met Michael's furious eyes.

'I know she's not Alyssa,' he said, and his tone was still, quiet, and completely cold. 'You need to back the hell off, Michael, and you need to stop thinking I'm the screwed-up kid you knew back then. I know what I'm doing, and you're not my dad.'

'I'm the closest thing you have to family around

here!' Michael came off of the yelling, but Claire could hear the anger bubbling in his voice. 'And I'm *not* letting you play the hero. Not now.'

'I wouldn't have to if you'd step up and watch my back!'

Shane shoved past him this time, pounded up the stairs, and slammed the door to his room. Michael stood there, staring after him until Claire took a step forward. She froze when he looked at her, afraid he'd be angrier at her than he had been at Shane. After all, it had been her fault...

'Come sit down,' Michael said. 'I'll get you something to eat.'

'I don't—'

'Yes, you do. Sit. Eve, hold her down if you have to.' He took her hand for a second, squeezed it, and stood aside for her to move to the couch. She sank onto it with a sigh of relief and rested her forehead on her hands. God, what a miserable day. It had started out so – and Shane – but—

'You understand what Shane did, right?' Eve asked, plopping next to her. 'How he, you know, made the deal?'

'No.' She felt hot, and miserable, and she definitely didn't want food. But Michael wasn't exactly in the mood to take no for an answer. 'I have no idea what's going on.'

'Shane traded two sessions to Brandon in exchange for him leaving you alone.'

'He – what?' Claire looked up, mortally

confused. Was Shane gay? She hadn't even thought about the possibility...

'Sessions. You know, bites.' Eve mimed fangs. 'The agreement is that Brandon can fang him twice. He just can't, you know, kill him. It's not about food, it's pleasure. And power.' Eve smoothed her pleated skirt and frowned down at her short, black fingernails. 'Michael's right to be angry about it. Not killing somebody is a hell of a long way from not hurting them. And Brandon's got a lot of experience at making deals. Shane doesn't.'

Somehow, she'd known that – from the way Shane had acted, the way Brandon had been watching them, the way Michael had been so angry. It wasn't just that Shane had told Brandon to back off, or made some dumbass promise. Shane had traded his life for hers – or at least, he was risking it.

Claire gasped, and fear prickled her skin so hard it was like rolling in needles. 'But if he gets bitten, is he – won't he—?'

'Turn into a vampire?' Eve shook her head. 'It can't work that way, or Morganville'd be the Undead Metroplex by now for sure. All my life, I've never seen or heard of anybody turned into a vampire from a bite. The suckers around here are really old. Not that Shane wouldn't look completely hot with a nice set of fangs, but...' She fiddled with the pleats on her skirt. 'Shit. This is stupid. Why not me? I mean, not that I exactly *want* to – not anymore but…it's worse for guys.'

'Worse? Why?'

Eve shrugged, but Claire could see she was avoiding the question. 'Shane's *definitely* not going to be able to handle it. Boy can't even let somebody else have the last corn dog, and he doesn't even like corn dogs. He's a total control freak.' She fidgeted for a few more seconds, then added, softly, 'And I'm afraid for him.'

As Michael came back into the room, Eve jumped up and ran around moving things, stacking things, until Michael gave her a none-too-subtle signal to leave. Which she did, making some excuse Claire didn't hear, and clattered upstairs to her room.

Michael handed Claire a bowl. 'Chilli. Sorry. It's what we've got.'

She nodded and took a spoonful, because she'd always pretty much done what she was told…and the second the chilli hit her tongue, she realised that she was starving. She swallowed it almost without chewing, and was scooping up the next bite before she knew what she was doing. Shane needed to go into the chilli business.

Michael slipped into the leather armchair to the left and picked up the guitar he'd laid aside. He started tuning it as if the whole scene with Shane hadn't even happened. She ate, stealing glances at him as he bent over the instrument, drawing soft, resonant notes.

'You're not mad?' she finally asked, or mumbled.

'Mad?' He didn't raise his curly blond head. 'Mad is what you get when somebody flips you the finger on the freeway, Claire. No. I'm scared. And I'm trying to think what to do about it.'

She stopped chewing for a few seconds, then realised that choking on her food wasn't likely to make things any better.

'Shane's hotheaded,' Michael said. 'He's a good guy, but he doesn't think. I should have thought for him, before I brought you in here.'

Claire swallowed. The food had suddenly gone a little sour in her mouth, so she put the spoon down. 'Me?'

Michael's fingers stilled on the guitar strings. 'You know about his sister, right?'

Alyssa. That was the name Michael had thrown out. The one that had hurt Shane. 'She's dead.'

'Shane's not a complicated guy. If he cares about somebody, he fights for them. Simple. Lyssa – Lyssa was a sweet kid. And he had that whole big-brother thing working. He'd have died for her.' Michael slowly shook his head. 'Nearly did. Anyway, the point is that Lyssa would have been your age by now, and here you are getting hurt by the same bitches who killed his sister, trying to get him. So yeah. He'd do anything – *anything* – not to have to live through that again. You may not be Lyssa, but he likes you, and more than that, he *hates* Monica Morrell. So much he—' Michael couldn't seem to say it. He stared off into space for a few seconds, then went on. 'Making deals with the vampires in this town will keep you alive on the outside, but it eats you on the inside. I watched it happen to my folks, before they got out of here. Eve's parents, too. Her sisters. If Shane goes through with this, it'll kill him.'

Claire stood up. 'He's not going through with it,' she said. 'I'm not letting him.'

'How exactly are you going to stop him? Hell, I can't stop him, and he listens to me. Mostly.'

'Look, Eve said – Eve said vampires own this town. Is that true? Really?'

'Yes. They've been here as long as anybody can remember. If you live here, you learn to live with them. If you can't, then you go.'

'They don't just run around biting people, though.'

'That would be rude,' he said gravely. 'They don't need to. Everybody in town – everybody who's a resident – pays taxes. Blood tax. Two pints a month, down at the hospital.'

She stared. 'I didn't have to!'

'College kids don't. They get taxed a different way.' He looked grim, and with a sick, twisting sense of horror she realised what he was going to say right before he made it real. 'Vamps have a deal with the school. They get to take two percent a year, right off the top. Used to be more, but I think they got worried. Couple of close calls with the media.

There's nothing TV stations like more than a pretty young college girl gone missing. Claire, what are you thinking?'

She took a deep breath. 'If the vamps have this all planned out, then they've got, you know, structure. Right? They can't all just be running their own shows. Not if there are a lot of them. There's got to be somebody in charge.'

'True. Brandon's got a boss. And his boss probably has a boss.'

'So all we have to do is make a deal with his boss,' she said. 'For something other than Shane getting bit.'

'All?'

'They have to want something. Something more than what they already have. We just need to find out what it is.'

There was a creak on the stairs. Michael turned to look, and so did Claire. Eve was standing there.

'Didn't hear you coming,' Michael said. She shrugged and padded down the steps; she'd taken off her shoes. Even her black-and-white hose had little skulls on the toes.

'I know what they want,' she said. 'Not that we're going to be able to find it.'

Michael looked at her for a long time. Eve didn't look away; she walked right up to him, and Claire suddenly felt like she was in the middle of something personal. Maybe it was the way he was looking at her, or how she was smiling at him, but it made Claire fidget and closely examine a stack of books on the end table.

'I don't want you in this,' Michael said. Out of the corner of her eye, she saw him reach out and take Eve's hand.

'Shane's in it. Claire's in it. Hey, even *you're* in it.' Eve shrugged. 'You know how much I hate being left out. Besides, if there's a way to stick it to Brandon, I'm all for it. That guy needs a poke in the eye with a nice, sharp stake.'

They were still holding hands. Claire cleared her throat, and Michael let go first. 'What is it? What do they want?'

Eve grinned. 'Oh, you're gonna *love* this,' she said. 'They want a book. And I can't think of anybody who'd have a better shot at finding it than you, book girl.'

There were a lot of rules to Morganville Claire hadn't even thought about. The blood donation, that was one – and she was starting to wonder how Michael was getting away with not paying his taxes. He couldn't, right? If he couldn't leave the house?

She sat down cross-legged on the floor with a ledger notebook, turned to a fresh sheet of paper, and made a heading that read *Pluses for Vampires*. Under that column, she wrote down *blood donation, Protection, favours, deals.*

'Oh, put down *curfew,*' Eve said.

'There's a curfew?'

'Well, yeah, of course. Except for the school. They don't care if the students roam around all night, because, you know—' Eve mimed fangs in the neck. Claire swallowed and nodded. 'But for locals? Oh yeah.'

'How is that a plus for them?'

'They don't have to worry about who's safe to bite and who's not. If you're out running around, you're lunch.'

She wrote down *curfew*. Then she turned the page and wrote down *Minuses for Vampires*.

'What are they afraid of?' she asked.

'I don't think we were done with the pluses,' Michael said. He sat down on the floor next to the two girls – well, closer to Eve, Claire noticed. 'Probably a lot you didn't write down.'

'Oh, let the girl feel better about it,' Eve said. 'It's not all gloomy. Obviously, they don't like daytime—'

Claire wrote it down.

'And garlic...silver...um, holy water—'

'You sure about those?' Michael asked. 'I always thought they pretended on a lot of that, just in case.'

'Why would they do that?'

Claire answered without looking up. 'Because it makes it easier to hide what really can hurt them. I'm writing it down anyway, but it may not be right.'

'Fire is for real,' Michael said. 'I saw a vampire die once, when I was just a kid. One of those revenge deals.'

Eve pulled in a deep breath. 'Oh, yeah. I remember hearing about it. Tom Sullivan.'

Claire asked, wide-eyed, 'The vampire was named—?'

'Not the vampire,' Michael said. 'The guy who killed him. Tommy Sullivan. He was kind of a screw-up, drank a lot, which isn't too unusual around here. He had a kid. She died. He blamed the vampires, so he doused one with gas and set him on fire, sitting right in the middle of the restaurant.'

'You saw that?' Claire asked. 'How old were you?'

'You grow up fast in Morganville. The point is, there was a trial the next night. Not much chance for Tommy. He was dead before morning. But…fire works. Just don't get caught.'

Claire wrote down *fire*. 'What about stakes?'

'You've seen Brandon,' Eve said. 'You want to try to get close enough to stake him? Yeah, me neither.'

'But do they *work*?'

'Guess so. You have to fill out a form when you buy wood.'

Claire wrote it down. 'Crosses?'

'Definitely.'

'Why?'

'Because they're evil, soulless, bloodsucking fiends?'

'So was my sixth-grade gym teacher, but *he* wasn't afraid of a cross.'

'Funny,' Eve said, in the way that meant *not*. 'Because there are hardly any churches, and so far as I know, crosses are impossible to come by unless you make 'em yourself. Also, all these guys grew up – isn't that weird, thinking of them growing up? – when religion wasn't just something you did on Sundays. It was something you *were*, every minute, every day, and God was always up for a little recreational smiting of the wicked.'

'Don't,' Michael murmured. 'God's scarce enough around here.'

'No offence to the Big Guy, Michael, but he made himself scarce,' Eve shot back. 'You know how many nights I spent in bed praying, *Dear God, please take away all the bad people*? Yeah, that really worked.' Michael opened his mouth to say something. 'And please don't tell me God loves me. If God loved me, he'd drop a bus ticket to Austin in my lap so I could blow this town once and for all.'

Eve sounded – well, *angry*. Claire tapped her pencil against the pad, not making eye contact.

'How do they keep people from leaving?' she asked.

'They don't. Some people leave. I mean, Shane did,' Michael said. 'I think the question you're looking for is, how do they keep them from *talking*? And that's where it gets weird.'

'*That's* where?' Claire murmured. Eve laughed.

'I don't know myself, because I never got out of town, but Shane says that once you get about ten miles outside of Morganville, you get this terrible headache, and then you just…start to forget. First you can't remember what the name of the town was, and then you can't remember how to get there, and then you don't remember that the town had vampires. Or the rules. It just – doesn't exist anymore for you. It comes back if you return to town, but when you're out, you can't run around telling all about Morganville because you just don't remember.'

'I heard rumours,' Eve said. 'Some people start remembering, but they get—' She made a graphic throat-cutting gesture. 'Hit squads.'

Claire tried to think of things that would cause that kind of memory loss. Drugs, maybe? Or…some kind of local energy field? Or… OK, she had no idea. But it sounded like magic, and magic made her nervous. She supposed vampires were magic, too, when you got right down to it, and that made her even more nervous. Magic didn't exist. Shouldn't exist. It was just…*wrong*. It offended her scientific training.

'So where does all that leave us?' Michael asked. It was a reasonable question.

Claire flipped another page, wrote down *memory loss aft. depart,* and said, 'I'm not sure. I mean, if we're going to put together any kind of a plan, we have to basically know as much as we can to make sure it's a good enough approach. So keep talking. What else?'

It went on for hours. The grandfather clock solemnly announced the arrival and departure of nine o'clock, then ten, then eleven. It was nearly midnight, and Claire had scribbled up most of the ledger pages, when she looked at Michael and Eve and asked, 'Anything else?' and got negative shakes of their heads in reply. 'OK, then. Tell me about the book.'

'I don't know a lot,' Eve said. 'They just put out a notice about ten years ago that they were looking for it. I heard they have people all over town going through libraries, bookstores, anyplace it could be hidden. But the weird thing is that vamps can't actually read it.'

'You mean it's in some other language?'

Michael raised his eyebrows. 'I don't think it's that easy. I mean, every one of these suckers has got to speak a dozen languages, at least.'

'*Dead* languages,' Eve said. When they looked at her, she grinned. 'What? Come on. Funny!'

'Maybe they can't read it for the same reason people can't remember anything outside of town,' Claire said slowly. 'Because something doesn't want them to.'

'That's kind of a leap, but the Russian judge gave you a nine point five for style, so OK,' Eve said. 'The important thing is that *we* know what it looks like.'

'Which is?' Claire put her pencil to paper.

'A book with a brown leather cover. Some kind of symbol on the front.'

'What kind?' Because *brown leather cover* didn't exactly narrow things down when it came to books.

Eve pushed up the sleeve of her skin-tight black mesh top, and held out her forearm. There, tattooed in plain blue, was a symbol that looked kind of like an omega, only with some extra waves in it. Simple, but definitely nothing Claire could remember seeing before. 'They've been searching for it. They gave everybody growing up in a Protected family the tattoo so that we remember what to look for.'

Claire stared for a couple of seconds, wanting to ask how old Eve was when she got the tattoo, but she didn't quite dare. She dutifully marked the symbol down in her notebook. 'And nobody's found it. Are they sure it's here?'

'They seem to think so. But I'll bet they've got their sources searching all over the world for it. Seems pretty important to them.'

'Any idea why?'

'Nobody knows,' Michael said. 'I grew up asking, believe me. Nobody has a clue. Not even the vampires.'

'How can they be looking for something and not even know why?'

'I'm not saying *somebody* doesn't know why. But the vampires have ranks, and the only ones I've ever really talked to aren't exactly in charge. Point is, we can't find out, so we shouldn't waste time worrying about it.'

'Good to know.' Claire put *contents unknown* next to the symbol of the book, then *valuable!!!!!* underneath, underscored with three dark lines. 'So if we can find this book, we can trade it to get Monica off my back, and make sure Shane's deal is called off.'

Michael and Eve looked at each other. 'Did you miss the part where the vamps have been turning Morganville upside down trying to find it?' Eve asked.

Claire sighed, flipped back a page, and pointed at a note she'd made. Eve and Michael both craned over to read it.

Vampires can't read it.

They looked blank.

'I'm going to need to spend some time at the library,' Claire said. 'And we're going to need some supplies.'

'To do what?' Eve still wasn't catching on, but Michael was.

'Fake the book?' he asked. 'You really think that'll work? What do you think happens when they figure out we cheated?'

'Bad idea,' Eve said. 'Very bad idea. Honest.'

'Guys,' Claire said patiently. 'If we're careful, they'll never suspect we're smart enough to do something like that. Not to mention brave enough. So we give them a fake – it's still more than anybody else has. They may be pissed, but they'll be pissed that *somebody* faked it. We just found it.'

They were both looking at her now like they'd never seen her before. Michael shook his head.

'Bad idea,' he said.

Maybe so. But she was going to try it anyway.

CHAPTER TEN

She was too wired to sleep, and besides, her back hurt, and she couldn't stand the thought of waiting even one more night to get started. Brandon hadn't seemed like the kind of guy to wait for his revenge, and Shane – Shane wasn't the kind of guy to not hold up his end of a deal, either.

If he's stupid enough to want to get bitten, fine, but he's not using me for an excuse.

Shane hadn't come out of his room all night. She hadn't heard a thing when she'd listened – carefully – at his door. Eve had mimed headphones and turning up an invisible stereo. Claire could understand that; she'd spent lots of hours trying to blow out her own eardrums to avoid the world.

Eve lent her a laptop – a retro thing, big and black and clunky, with a biohazard-symbol sticker on the front. When Claire plugged it into the broadband connection and booted it up, the desktop graphic was a cartoon Grim Reaper holding a road sign instead of a scythe – a road sign that read MORGANVILLE, with an arrow pointing down.

Claire clicked on a couple of folders – guiltily, but she was curious – and found they were full of poetry. Eve liked death, or at least, she liked to write about it. Florid romantic stuff, all angst and blood and moonlit marble…and then Claire noticed the dates. The last of the poetry had been done three years ago. Eve would have been, what, fifteen? She'd been starry-eyed about vampires back then, but something had changed. No poetry at all for the past three years…

Eve walked in the open door. 'Working OK?' she asked. Claire jumped, guilty, and gave her the thumbs-up as she clicked open the Internet connection. 'OK, I called my cousin in Illinois. She's going to let us use her PayPal account, but I have to send her cash, like, tomorrow. Here's the account.' She handed over a slip of paper. 'We're not going to get her killed, right?'

'Nope. I'm not buying much from any one place. A lot of people buy leather and tools and stuff. And paper – how old is this book supposed to be?'

'Old.'

'Was it on vellum?'

'Is that paper?'

'Vellum is the oldest kind of paper they used in books,' Claire said. 'It's sheepskin.'

'Oh. I guess that, then. It's really old.'

Vellum would be hard. You could get it, but it was easy to trace. But it wasn't any good being freak smart if you couldn't get around things like that... Oh, yeah, she needed to think about using somebody else to do the research, too. Too dangerous having tracks that led right back here to the Glass House...

Claire went to work. She didn't even notice Eve going and shutting the door behind her.

For four days, Claire studied. Four *solid* days. Eve brought her up soup and bread and sandwiches, and Shane dropped by once or twice to tell her she was crazy and he wanted her to stay the hell out of his business; Claire didn't pay any attention. She got like that when she was completely inside of something. She heard him, and she said something back, but no way was she listening. Like her parents, Shane eventually gave up and went away.

Michael came to her room just a little before dawn. That one surprised her long enough to drag her out of her trance for a while. 'How's it going?' he asked.

'Mission Save Shane? Yeah, it's going,' she said. 'I have to work the long way around. No traces. Don't worry – even if the vamps get angry, they won't be able to prove we did anything but bring them what we thought they were looking for.'

Michael looked pleased, but worried. He worried a lot. She supposed that being trapped the way he was, that was really all he could do – fight anything that got inside to hurt them, and worry about everything else. Frustrating, she guessed.

'Hey,' she said, 'when does Eve go to work?'

'Four o'clock.'

'But that's—'

'The night shift. I know. She's safe enough there, though, and I don't think any vamp is stupid enough to try to get in the way of that damn car. It's like being run over by a Hummer. I made her promise that Oliver would walk her to the car, and Shane's going to get her from the sidewalk inside.'

Claire nodded. 'I'm going with her.'

'To the coffee shop? Why?'

'Because it's anonymous,' she said. 'Every college student in there has a laptop, and the place has free wireless. If I'm careful, they won't be able to trace who's looking up how to fake-age a book.'

He gave her an exasperated look. On him, it looked cute. *God.* She was still noticing. She really needed to stop that, but hey. Sweet sixteen and never been kissed...

'I don't like *Eve* out there at night. You're *definitely* not going.'

'If I do it here, everybody could be in danger. Including Eve.'

Oh, low blow – she saw his eyes shift, but he toughed it out. 'So your answer is that I let you go out there, risk your life, sit in a coffee shop with

Brandon, and pretend like that's safer? Claire. In no way does that equal safer.'

'Safer than the vampires deciding that everybody in this house deliberately set out to cheat them out of the thing they want most,' Claire said. 'We're not playing, are we? I mean, I can stop if you want, but we don't have anything else we can trade for Shane's deal. Nothing big enough. I'd let Brandon – you know – but somehow I don't think—'

'Over my—' Michael stopped and laughed. 'I was going to say, "Over my dead body" but—'

Claire winced.

'No,' he said.

'You're not my dad,' she pointed out, and all of a sudden...*remembered.*

Shane, at the hospital, when she'd been drugged up, had said, *They called your parents.* Also, she distinctly remembered the words *freaked out.*

Oh, *crap*!

'Dad,' she said aloud. 'Oh no...um, I need to use the phone. Can I?'

'Calling your parents? Sure. Long distance—'

'Yeah, I know. I pay for it. Thanks.'

She picked up the cordless phone and dialled her home number. It rang five times, then flipped over to the machine. 'Hello, you've reached Les and Katharine Danvers and their daughter, Claire. Leave us a message!' It was her mom's bright, businesslike voice.

When the beep sounded, Claire had a second of

blind panic. Maybe they were just out shopping. Or...

'Hi, Mom and Dad, it's Claire. I just wanted to – um – say hi. I should have called you, I guess. That lab accident thing, that was nothing, really. I don't want you to be worried about me – everything's just fine. Really.'

Michael, leaning against the doorframe, was making funny faces at her. That seemed like Shane's job, somehow. She stuck her tongue out at him.

'I just – I just wanted to say that. Love you. Bye.'

She hung up. Michael said, 'You ought to get them to come and take you home.'

'And leave you guys in this mess? You're in it because of me. *Shane's* in it because of me. Now that Monica knows he's back...'

'Oh, believe me, I'm not underestimating how much trouble we're in, but you can still go. And you should. I'm going to try to convince Shane to get out, too. Eve – Eve won't go, but she should.'

'But—' *That leaves you alone*, she thought. *Really alone*. There was no getting out for Michael. Not ever.

Michael looked up and out the window, where the sky was gradually washing from midnight blue to a paler dawn. 'My time's up,' he said. 'Promise me you won't go with Eve tonight.'

'I can't.'

'Claire.'

'I can't,' she said. 'I'm sorry.'

He didn't have time to argue, though she could see he wanted to. He walked down the hall; she heard his bedroom door close, and thought about what she'd seen downstairs in the living room. She wasn't sure how she'd handle that if she had to face it every day – it looked really painful. She supposed the worst of it, though, was his knowing that if he'd been alive, been able to walk around in the daylight, he'd have been able to stop Shane from doing what he'd done.

I wouldn't have to if you'd step up and watch my back! Shane had yelled at him, and yeah, that must have hurt just about worse than dying.

Claire went back to work. Her eyes burnt, her muscles ached, but in some strange and secret place, she was *happy* to finally be doing something that wasn't just protecting herself, but protecting other people, too.

If it worked.

The strange thing was, she just knew it would. She knew.

She really was a freak, she decided.

Claire woke up at three thirty, bleary-eyed and aching, and struggled into a fresh T-shirt and a pair of jeans that badly needed washing. One more day, she decided, and then she'd brave the washing machine in the basement. She had monster bed-head, even though she'd barely slept for three hours, and had to stick her head under the faucet and finger fluff her hair back to something that wasn't too puke-worthy.

She stuck the laptop into the messenger-bag case and dashed downstairs; she could hear Eve's shoes clumping through the house, heading for the door.

'Wait up!' she yelled, and pelted down the stairs and through the living room just as the front door slammed. 'Crap...'

She opened it just before Eve succeeded in locking it. Eve looked guilty. 'You were going to leave me,' Claire said. 'I told you I wanted to go!'

'Yeah, well...you shouldn't.'

'Michael talked to you last night.'

Eve sighed and fidgeted one black patent leather shoe. 'Little bit, yeah. Before he went to bed.'

'I don't need everybody protecting me. I'm trying to help!'

'I get it,' Eve said. 'If I say no and drive off, what are you going to do?'

'Walk.'

'That's what I was afraid of.' Eve shrugged. 'Get in the car.'

Common Grounds was packed with students reading, chatting, drinking chai and mochas and lattes. And, Claire was gratified to see, working on laptops. There must have been a dozen going at once. She gave Eve a thumbs-up, ordered a cup of tea, and went in search of a decent spot to work. Something with her back to the wall.

Oliver brought her tea himself. She smiled uncertainly at him and minimised the browser window; she was reading up on famous forgeries and techniques. Dead giveaway, with emphasis on *dead*. Not that she disliked Oliver, but any guy who seemed to be able to enforce rules on the vampires was somebody she couldn't trust real far.

'Hello, Claire,' he said. 'May I sit?'

'Sure,' she said, surprised. Also, uncomfortable. He was old enough to be her dad, not to mention kind of hippie-dippie. Though, being a fringer herself, she didn't mind that part so much. 'Um, how's it going?'

'Busy today,' he said, and settled into the chair with a sigh of what sounded like gratitude. 'I wanted to talk to you about Eve.'

'OK,' she said slowly.

'I'm concerned about her,' Oliver said. He leant forward, elbows on the table; she hastily closed the cover of the laptop and rested her hands protectively on top of it. 'Eve seems distracted. That's very dangerous, and I'm quite sure that by now you understand why.'

'It's—'

'Shane?' he asked. 'Yes. I thought that was probably the case. The boy's gotten himself into a great deal of trouble. But he did it with a pure heart, I believe.'

Her pulse was hammering faster, and her mouth

felt dry. Boy, she really didn't like talking to authority figures. Michael was one thing – Michael was like a big brother. But Oliver was…different.

'I might be able to help,' Oliver said, 'if I had something to trade. The problem is, what does Brandon want that you, or Shane, can give? Other than the obvious.' Oliver looked thoughtful, and tapped his lips with a fingertip. 'You are a very bright girl, Claire, or so Eve tells me. Morganville can use bright girls. We might be able to bypass Brandon altogether, perhaps, and find a way to make a deal with someone…else.'

Which was pretty much exactly what they'd already talked about, only without the Oliver part. Claire tried not to look horribly guilty and transparent. 'Who?' she asked. It was a reasonable question. Oliver smiled, and his dark eyes looked sharp and cool.

'Claire. Do you really expect me to tell you? The more you know about this town, the less safety there is for you. Do you understand that? I've had to create my own peace here, and it only works because I know exactly what I'm doing, and how far I can go. You – I'm afraid your first mistake might be your last.'

Her mouth wasn't dry anymore; it was mummified. She tried to swallow, but got nothing but a dry click at the back of her throat. She hastily picked up her tea and sipped it, tasting nothing but glad of the moisture.

'I wasn't going to—'

'Don't,' he cut her off, and his voice wasn't so kind this time. 'Why else would you be here today, when you know Brandon is likely to show up any time after dark? You want to make a deal with him to save Shane. That much is obvious.'

Well, it wasn't why she was here, but still, she tried to look guilty about that, too. Just in case. It must have worked, because Oliver sat back in his chair, looking more relaxed.

'You're clever,' he said. 'So is Shane. But don't let it go to your heads. Let me help.'

She nodded, not trusting her voice not to quiver or break or – worse – betray how relieved she was.

'That's settled, then,' Oliver said. 'Let me talk to Brandon and a few others, and see what I can do to make this problem go away.'

'Thanks,' she said faintly. Oliver got up and left, looking like any skinny ex-hippie who hadn't quite let go of the good old days. Inoffensive. Ineffective, maybe.

She couldn't rely on adults. Not for this. Not in Morganville.

She opened up the laptop, maximised the browser window, and went back to work.

Like always, time slipped away; when she looked up next, it was night outside the windows, and the crowd in the coffee shop had switched over from studious to chatty. Eve was busy at the bar, talking and smiling and generally being about as cheerful as a Goth chick could be.

She went quiet, though, when Brandon slouched in from the back room and took his accustomed seat at the table in the darkest corner. Oliver brought him some kind of drink – *God*, she hoped it wasn't blood or anything! – and sat down to have some intense and quiet conversation. Claire tried to look like she wasn't there. She and Eve exchanged a few glances between customers at the bar.

Putting together the book, Claire had learnt during the long research marathon, was work for experts, not sixteen-year-old (nearly seventeen) wannabes. She could put *something* together, but – to her vast disappointment – anybody with an eye for rare books could spot a fake pretty easily, unless it was expertly done. She suspected that her leatherworking and bookbinding skills needed work.

All of which brought her back to square one, Shane Gets Bitten. Not acceptable.

A line in one of the dozens of windows she'd opened caught her eye. *Nearly anything can be created for the movies, including reproductions of ancient books, because the reproduction only has to fool one of the senses: vision...*

She didn't have time – or cash – to get some Hollywood prop house to make a book for her, but it gave her an idea.

A really good idea.

Or a really bad one, if it didn't work.

Nearly anything can be created for the movies.

She didn't need the book. She just needed a picture.

By the time midnight rolled around – and Common Grounds ushered the last caffeine addict out into the night – Claire was reasonably sure she could pull it off, and she was too tired to care if she couldn't. She packed up the laptop and leant her head on her hand, watching while Eve cleaned up cups and glasses, loaded the dishwasher, chatted with Oliver, and deliberately ignored the dark shadow sitting in the corner.

Brandon hadn't taken off after his walking snacks. Instead, he kept sitting there, nursing a fresh cup of whatever it was he was drinking, smiling that cruel, weird little smile at Eve, then Claire, then Eve.

Oliver, drying ceramic cups, had been watching the watcher. 'Brandon,' he said, and tossed the towel across his shoulder as he began slotting cups into their pull racks. 'Closing time.'

'You didn't even call last round, old man,' Brandon said, and turned that smile on Oliver.

Where it died, fast. After a moment of silence, Brandon stood up to stalk away.

'Wait,' Oliver said, very quietly. 'Cup.'

Brandon looked at him in utter disbelief, then picked up the cup – disposable paper – and dumped it in the trash can. First time he'd bused his own table in a few dozen years, Claire guessed. If ever. She hid a nervous grin, because he didn't seem like the kind of guy – much less vamp – who'd appreciate her sense of humour.

'Anything else?' Brandon asked acidly. Not as if he actually cared.

'Actually, yes. If you wouldn't mind, I'd like the ladies to leave first.'

Even in the shadows, Claire saw the gleam of sharp teeth when Brandon silently opened his mouth – flashing his fangs. Showing off. Oliver didn't seem impressed.

'If you wouldn't mind,' he repeated. Brandon shrugged and leant against the wall, arms folded. He was wearing a black leather jacket that drank in light, a black knit shirt, dark jeans. Dressed to kill, Claire thought, and wished she hadn't.

'I'll wait,' he said. 'But they don't need to worry about me, old man. The boy made a deal. I'll stick to it.'

'That's what I'm worried about,' Oliver said. 'Eve, Claire, get home safe. Go.'

Eve slammed the door on the dishwasher and turned it on; she grabbed her purse from behind the counter and ducked out to take Claire's hand and pull her toward the door. She flipped the front sign from OPEN to CLOSED and unlocked the door to let Claire out. She locked it back behind them with a set of keys, then hustled Claire quickly to the car, which sat in the warm glow of the streetlight. The street looked deserted; wind whipped trash and dust into clattering ghosts, and the blinking red stoplights danced and swayed along. Eve unlocked the car in record time, and both of them slammed down the locks once they were inside. Eve started up the Caddy and motored away from the curb; only then did she sigh a little in relief.

And then she gasped, because another car turned the corner and whipped past them in a black blur, stopping at the curb where they'd been parked. 'What the hell?' Eve blurted, and slowed down. Claire turned to look back.

'It's a limo,' she said. She didn't even think Morganville *had* a limo, but then she thought about funeral homes and funerals, and got chills. For all she knew, maybe Morganville had more limos than any city in Texas...

This one wasn't part of a procession, though. It was big and black and gleamed like the finish on a cockroach, and as the Caddy inched along, Claire saw a uniformed driver get out and walk around to the back.

'Who is it?' Eve asked. 'Can you see?'

The driver handed out a woman. Small – not much taller than Claire herself, she guessed. Pale, with hair that glowed white or blond in the streetlights. They were too far for Claire to get a really good look, but she thought the woman looked...sad. Sad, and cold.

'She's not very tall – white hair? And kind of elegant?'

Eve shrugged. 'Nobody I've met, but most of the vamps don't mingle with the little people. Kind of like the Hiltons don't shop at Wal-Mart.'

Claire snorted. As Eve turned the corner, she saw the woman standing in front of the door of Common Grounds, and saw Oliver opening it for her. No sign of Brandon. She wondered if Oliver had already sent him out, or if he was making the vamp give them a head start. 'How does Oliver do this?' she asked. 'I mean, why don't they just…?'

'Kill him? I wish I knew. He's got balls of platinum, for one thing,' Eve said. Passing streetlights strobed across her face. 'You saw how he did Brandon back there? Dissing him? Unbelievable. Anybody else would be dead by dawn. Oliver…just gets away with it.'

Which made Claire even more curious about the why. Or at least the how. If Oliver could get away with it, maybe other people could, too. Then again, maybe other people had already tried, and ended up as organ donors.

Claire turned back face forward, lost in thought, as Eve sped through the silent, watching streets for home. A police car prowled a side street, but somehow in Morganville she thought they weren't looking so much for criminals as potential victims.

At first, she thought she was so tired she was imagining things – that happened when you didn't sleep; you saw ghosts in mirrors and spooky faces at the window – but then she saw something moving fast through the glow of a streetlight. Something pale.

'They're following,' Eve said grimly. 'Damn.'

'Brandon?' Claire tried to scan the sides of the street, but Eve pressed the gas and went faster.

'Not Brandon. Then again, he doesn't have to get his fangs dirty personally—'

Fifty feet ahead, someone stepped in front of the car.

Claire and Eve screamed, and Eve stamped on the brakes. Claire pitched forward against the seat belt, which snapped tight and grabbed so hard she just knew she was going to pass out from pain as the acid burn on her back rubbed against the seat. But the pain flashed away, buried by fear, because the car was fishtailing to a stop on the dark street, and there was a vampire standing there, resting its hands on the hood.

Grinning with way, way too many teeth.

'Claire!' Eve yelled. 'Don't look at him! Don't look!'

Too late. Claire had, and she felt something going soft in her head. The fear went away. So did all her good sense. She reached for the lock on the door, but Eve lunged across and grabbed her arm. 'No!' she screamed, and held on as she slammed the car into reverse and burnt rubber backward. She didn't get far. Another vampire stepped out, blocking the street. This one was tall, ugly, and old. Same number of gleaming teeth. 'Oh, God...'

Claire kept fumbling for the lock on the door. Eve muttered something that would have definitely gotten Claire grounded at home, hit the brakes again, and said, 'Claire, honey, this is going to hurt,' and then she pushed Claire forward and slapped her on the burn. Hard.

Claire screeched loud enough to deafen dogs three counties away, nearly fainted, and quit trying to get out of the car. Even the two vampires outside the car – who were all of a sudden *right there at the doors* – flinched and stepped back.

Eve gunned the engine. Claire, half fainting from the red-hot throbbing agony in her back, heard noise like iron nails on a chalkboard, but then it stopped and they were moving, driving, flying through the night.

'Claire? Claire?' Eve was shaking her by the other shoulder, the one that didn't feel like she'd taken another acid bath. 'Oh, God, I'm sorry! It was just – he was going to get you to open the door, and I couldn't – I'm sorry!'

Panic was still a hot wire through her nerves, but Claire managed a nod and a weak, sick smile. She understood. She'd always wondered how in the hell anybody could be stupid enough to open up a door to the scary bad thing in the movies, but now she knew. She absolutely knew.

Sometimes, you just didn't have a choice.

Eve was gasping for breath and crying furiously in between. 'I hate this,' she said, and slammed her hand into the hard plastic steering wheel, over and over. 'I hate this town! I hate them!'

Claire got that. She was starting to really hate them, too.

CHAPTER ELEVEN

Shane was in the doorway, ready for action, when Eve screeched the car to a stop; if he was still mad, at least he wasn't letting it get in the way of a good fight. Eve frantically signalled for him to stay where he was, on safe ground, and checked the street on all sides.

'Do you see anything?' she asked Claire anxiously. Claire shook her head, still sick. 'Damn. *Damn!* OK...but you know the drill, right? Asses and elbows. Bail!'

Claire fumbled open the lock, bolted out of the car, and hit the sidewalk running. She heard Eve's door slam and running footsteps. Déja vu, she thought. Now all they needed was for Brandon to show up and act like a total asshole...

She nearly ran into Shane as she pelted across the threshold; he stepped out of the way in time, just far enough to let her pass, and grabbed Eve to pull her inside as he slammed the door and locked it.

'You have *got* to get a better job,' he said. Eve wiped at her ruined make-up with the back of one hand and threw him a filthy look.

'At least I *have* a job!'

'What, professional blood donor? Because that's all you're going to be if you—'

Claire turned, ran into a vampire, and screamed her lungs out.

OK, so she wasn't a vampire. That was established in about thirty more seconds by a combination of Shane doubling over with laughter, the vampire screaming in fright and cowering, and – last of all – Eve saying, in blank surprise, 'Miranda! Honey, what the hell are you doing here?'

The vamp – she *looked* like a vamp, Claire amended, but now that her heart rate was going down below race-car speeds she saw that it was make-up and drama, not nature – slowly lowered her arms, peered at Claire uncertainly through thick black mascaraed eyelashes, and made a little O with her ruby red lips. 'I had to come,' she said. She had a breathy, floaty voice, full of drama. 'Oh, Eve! I had such a terrible vision! There was blood and death, and it was all about *you*!'

Eve didn't seem impressed. She sighed, turned to Shane, and said, 'You let her in? I thought you hated her!'

'Couldn't leave her out there, could I? I mean, she's got a pulse. Besides, she's your friend.'

From the look Eve gave him, *friend* might have been stretching things.

Miranda gave Shane a loopy smile. *Great*, Claire thought, annoyed and disgusted and still trying to contain the aftermath of a nuclear terror explosion. The girl was tall and most of her was thin, storklike legs revealed by a black leather miniskirt. She had lots of make-up, the standard dyed-black hair, shag cut around a long white face. Ragged Magic Marker crosses drawn on her wrists and around her neck.

Miranda suddenly swung around and looked up at the ceiling. She raised her hands to her mouth in dread, but, Claire noticed, didn't smudge her lipstick. 'This house,' she said. 'Oh my. It's so…strange. Don't you feel it?'

'Mir, if you wanted to warn me about something, you could have called,' Eve said, and steered her into the living room. 'Now we've got to figure out how to get you home. Honestly, don't you have any sense? You know better than this!'

As Miranda sat down on the couch, Claire caught sight of something else on her neck…bruises. And in the centre of the bruises, two raw, red holes. Eve saw it, too, and blinked, looked at Shane, and then at Claire. 'Mir?' she asked gently, and turned the girl's chin to one side. 'What happened to you?'

'Nothing,' Miranda said. 'Everything. You've really got to try it. It's everything I dreamt it would be, and for a second I could see, I could really see—'

Eve let go of her like she'd caught on fire. 'You *let* somebody bite you?'

'Just Charles,' Miranda said. 'He loves me. But Eve, you have to listen – this is serious! I tried to call, but I couldn't get anyone, and I had this terrible dream—'

'Thought you said it was a vision,' Shane said. He'd followed Claire into the room and was standing near her, arms folded. She felt a little bit of the tight knot of anger and tension unravel at his closeness, even if he wasn't looking at her. *Yeah, Claire, way to go. He treats you like the furniture. Maybe you need some hooker lipstick and Kleenex in your bra, too.*

'Don't, Shane, she's been through hell—' Eve evidently remembered, too late, that whatever Miranda had been through, it waited for Shane, too, unless they could somehow negate his deal with Brandon. 'Um, right. Vision. What did you see, Mir?'

'Death.' Miranda said it with hushed relish, leaning forward and rocking gently back and forth. 'Oh, he fought, he didn't want it, didn't want the gift, but...and there was blood. Lots of blood. And he died...right...here.' She put out a hand and pointed to a spot on the floor covered by a throw rug.

Claire realised, with a sinking sense of horror, that she was probably talking about *Michael*.

'Is it – is it Shane? Are you seeing Shane's future?' Eve asked. She sounded spooked, but then, they'd had a spooky night all around. And worrying about Shane made sense.

'She can't see the future,' Shane said flatly. 'She makes crap up. Right, Mir?'

Miranda didn't answer. She craned her neck up and looked at the ceiling again. Claire realised, with a strange creepy sensation, that she was looking exactly at where the secret room would be. Did Miranda know? How?

'This house,' she said again. 'This house is so strange. It doesn't make sense, you know.'

There was a creak on the stairs, and Claire looked over to see Michael padding down to join them, barefoot as usual. 'Yeah,' he said. 'It's not the only one. Eve, what the hell is *she* doing here?'

'Don't ask me! Shane let her in!'

'Hello, Michael,' Miranda said absently. She was still staring at the ceiling. 'This one's new.' She waved at Claire.

'Yeah. That's Claire.' He hadn't exactly come bounding to the rescue when Claire had screamed, and she wondered why. Maybe he'd been trying to stay away from Miranda; she understood why he'd want to. Talk about freaky weird...even Eve seemed not quite sure what to do with her.

She realised he hadn't heard Miranda's eerie description of his death. Maybe that was for the best.

'Claire,' Miranda whispered, and suddenly looked directly at her. She had pale blue eyes, really strange. They seemed to look right through her. 'No, it's not her, not her. Something else. Something strange in this house. Something not right. I need to read the cards.'

'The hell?' Shane asked. Miranda grabbed Eve's hand and jumped up, and practically dragged her to the stairs. 'OK, now this is just too much. Eve?'

'Um...right, it's OK!' Eve called back, as Miranda practically yanked her arm out of its socket. 'She just wants to do some tarot or something. It's OK! I'll bring her back down! Just a sec!'

Shane, Michael, and Claire just looked at one another for a few seconds, and then Shane made a loopy gesture at his temple and whistled.

Michael nodded. 'She didn't use to be that bad,' he said.

'I guess it's this Charles guy she was talking about,' Shane said grimly. 'Should have known that if anybody would hook up with a bloodsucker for troo wuv' – Shane made it sound ridiculous – 'it'd be some ditz like Miranda. I should have made her walk home. She'd probably get off on another bite.'

'She's a kid, Shane,' Michael said. 'But the sooner we get her out of here, the better I'll feel. She gets Eve a little – nervous.'

Eve? But Eve didn't really believe all that crap, did she? Claire had become convinced that it was just costuming, that underneath, Eve was just a normal girl after all, all the Goth stuff just posturing. But did she really believe in visions and crystals and tarot cards? Magic was just science misunderstood, she reminded herself. Or, on the other hand, just crazy talk.

The two boys looked at Claire. 'What?' she asked. 'Oh, by the way, I'm fine, thanks for asking. Got chased by some vampires. Business as usual.'

'Told you not to go,' Shane said, and shrugged. 'So, who's going to get Miranda to leave?'

They kept looking at her, and Claire finally understood that somehow, it had become her job. Probably because she was new, and didn't know Miranda, and she was a girl. Michael was too polite to ask her to go. Shane – she couldn't tell what Shane felt about Miranda, except that he wanted her the hell out of the house.

'Fine,' Claire said. 'I'll go.'

'That girl's smart,' Shane said without smiling, to Michael, as she started up the steps.

'Yep,' Michael agreed. 'I like that about her.'

The bedroom doors were all closed except for Eve's, which was casting a flickering light out onto the polished wood floor. Claire smelt the bright flare of matches. They were lighting candles.

Oh, she *really* didn't want to do this. Maybe if she just kept walking, went to her room, and locked the door…?

She took a deep breath and looked around the doorway with a smile that felt totally forced. Eve was lighting the candles – and boy, she had a lot of them, sitting basically everywhere. Big tall black ones, purple ones, blue ones. Nothing in the pastel family. Her bed was black satin, and there was a pirate flag – skull and crossbones – hanging above it like a billowing headboard. Little Christmas lights strung everywhere – no, not Christmas lights after all. Halloween pumpkins and ghosts and skulls. Cheery and strange.

'Hey,' Eve said, not looking up from the black pillar candle she was lighting. 'Come on in, Claire. I guess you haven't really met Miranda exactly.'

Not unless screaming and fleeing counted. 'Hi,' she said awkwardly. She didn't know what to do with her hands. Miranda didn't seem to notice or care, and *her* hands were up and in the air, petting some invisible cat or something. Weird. The longer that Claire was around the girl, the younger she looked – younger than Eve, for sure. Maybe even younger than Claire herself. Maybe it was all make-believe for her...except the bite. That was deadly serious stuff.

'Um... Eve? Can I talk to you for a sec?' Claire asked. Eve nodded, opened a black-painted dresser, and took out a black lacquer box. When opened, it had a blood-red interior. There was a black silk package inside, which, as Eve unwrapped it, proved to be a deck of cards.

Tarot cards.

Eve held them between her two palms for a few seconds, then cut the deck several times and handed it to Miranda. 'I'll be right back,' she said, and went out into the hall with Claire, closing the door behind her. Before Claire could say anything, Eve held up her hand. She wouldn't meet Claire's eyes. 'The guys sent you up?' At Claire's nod, she muttered, 'Pansies, both of them. Fine. They want her out, right?'

'Um...yeah. I guess.' Claire rocked uncomfortably back and forth. 'She is a little...weird.'

'Miranda's – yeah, she's weird. But she's also kind of gifted,' Eve said. 'She sees things. Knows things. Shane ought to get that. She told him about the fire before—' Eve shook her head. 'Doesn't matter. If she came all the way over here in the dark, something's wrong. I should try to find out what.'

'Well...can't you just, you know, ask her?'

'Miranda's a psychic,' she said. 'It's not that simple – she can't just blurt it out. You have to *work* with her.'

'But she can't really see the future, right? You don't believe that?' *Because if you do,* Claire thought, *you're crazier than I thought you were when I first met you.*

Eve finally met her eyes. Angry. 'Yes. Yes, I do believe that, and for a smart kid you're pretty dumb if you don't understand that science isn't perfect.

Things happen. Things that physics and math and crap that gets measured in a lab can't explain. People aren't just laws and rules, Claire. They're…sparks. Sparks of something beautiful and huge. And some of the sparks glow brighter, like Miranda.' Eve looked away again, obviously uncomfortable now. But not half as uncomfortable as Claire felt, because this was…wow. Space cadet city. 'You guys just leave us alone for a little while. It'll be fine.'

She went back into the room and shut the door. It wasn't quite a slam. Claire swallowed hard, feeling hot all over and wishing she hadn't let the boys push her into that, and slowly went back down the stairs. Michael and Shane were sitting on the couch and playing a video game with open beers on the table in front of them. Elbowing each other as their on-screen cars raced around turns.

'Not exactly legal,' she said, and sat down on the steps. 'The beer. Nobody here's twenty-one.'

Michael and Shane clicked bottles. Honestly, it was *juvenile*. 'Here's to crime,' Shane said, and tipped his up. 'Hey, it was a birthday present. Two six-packs. We're only one down, so give us a break. Morganville's got the highest alcoholics per capita of any place in the world, I'll bet.'

Michael put the game on pause. 'Is she leaving yet?'

'No.'

'If she starts trying to tell me I'm going to meet a tall dark stranger, I'm leaving,' Shane said. 'I mean, the kid's a head case, and I don't want to be mean, but jeez. She really believes this stuff. And she's got Eve half-convinced, too.'

There was no *half* about it, but Claire wasn't going to say that. She just sat there, trying not to think too hard about anything...about her plans to get Shane free of his agreement, which had seemed really good back in the coffee shop and not so solid now. About the dull-knife scrape of pain in her back. About the desperation in Eve's eyes. Eve was *scared*. And Claire didn't know how to help that, because she was scared half to death herself.

'She was looking at the secret room,' Claire said. 'When she was standing down here. She was staring right at it.'

Michael and Shane looked at her. Two sets of eyes, both guilty and startled. And one by one, they shrugged and went for the beer. 'Coincidence,' Michael said.

'Total coincidence,' Shane agreed.

'Eve said that Miranda had some kind of vision about you, Shane, when—'

'Not that again! Look, she said she had a vision of the house on fire, but she didn't say that until later, and even if she did, fat lot of good it did.' Shane's jaw was tight. A muscle fluttered in it. He punched a button to release the game from pause, and road noise poured out of the television speakers, closing out any chance of conversation on the subject.

Claire sighed. 'I'm going to bed.'

But she didn't. She was tired, and aching, and jittery...but her brain was way too busy picking over things. She finally nudged Shane over on the couch and sat next to him as he and Michael played, and played, and played...

'Claire. Wake up.' She blinked and realised that her head was on Shane's shoulder, and Michael was nowhere to be seen. Her first thought was, *Oh my God, am I drooling?* Her second was that she hadn't realised she was so close to him, snuggled in.

Her third was that although Michael's part of the couch was empty, Shane hadn't moved away. And he was watching her with warm, friendly eyes.

Oh. Oh, wow, that was nice.

Embarrassment flooded in a second later and made her pull away. Shane cleared his throat and scooted over. 'You should probably get some sleep,' he said. 'You're beat.'

'Yeah,' she said. 'What time is it?'

'Three a.m. Michael's making a snack. You want anything?'

'Um...no. Thanks.' She slid off the couch and then stood there like an idiot, unwilling to leave because he was still smiling and...she liked it. 'Who won?'

'Which game?'

'Oh. I guess I was asleep for a while.'

'Don't worry. We didn't let the zombies get you.'

This time, his smile was positively wicked. Claire felt it like a hot blanket all over her skin. 'If you want to stay up, you can help me kick his ass.'

There were not one but three empty beer bottles on the table in front of Shane. And three where Michael had been, too. No wonder Shane was still smiling at her, looking so friendly. 'That depends,' she said. 'Can I have a beer?'

'Hell no.'

'Because I'm sixteen? Come on, Shane.'

'Drinking kills brain cells, dumbass. And besides. If I give you one, that's one less for me.' Shane tapped his forehead. 'I can do the math.'

She needed a beer, to stay down here next to him, because she was afraid she was going to do or say something stupid, and at least if there was alcohol involved, it wouldn't be her fault, would it? But just as she opened her mouth to try to convince him, Michael came out of the kitchen with a bag of neon-coloured cheese puffs. Shane grabbed a handful and stuffed his mouth. 'Claire wants a beer,' he mumbled through orange goo.

'Claire needs to go to bed,' Michael said, and flopped down. 'Scoot over, man. I don't like you that much.'

'Dick. That's not what you said last night.'

'Bite me.'

'I want another beer.'

'You're cut off. It was my birthday present, not yours.'

'Oh, that's low. You really are a dick, and just for that, I'm totally thrashing you.'

'Promises, promises.' Michael glanced at Claire. 'You're still here. No beer. I'm not corrupting a minor.'

'But *you're* a minor,' she pointed out. 'At least for beer.'

'Yeah, and by the way, how much does it suck that I'm an adult if I kill somebody, and not if I want a beer?' Shane jumped in. 'They're all dicks.'

'Man, seriously, you are one cheap drunk. Three beers? My junior high girlfriend could hold her liquor better.'

'Your junior high girlfriend—' Shane brought himself up short without finishing that sentence, and flushed bright red. Must have been good, whatever it was. 'Claire, get the hell out of here. You're making me nervous.'

'Dick!' she flung at him, and went up the stairs before he could nail her with the pillow he grabbed. It plunked into the wall behind her and slithered down to the bottom of the stairs. She was laughing, but she stopped when a shadow suddenly blocked access to the hallway at the top.

Eve. And Miranda, looking weirder than ever.

'Miranda's leaving!' Claire called down. Which wasn't such a great idea, because Eve looked upset, and Shane was drunk, and letting some vampire-crazy maybe-psychic kid walk home by herself was…bad, at best.

'Miranda's not leaving,' Eve said, and clunked down the stairs, with Miranda drifting like a black-and-white ghost behind her. 'Miranda's going to do a séance.'

Below, in the living room, she heard Michael say, in outright horror, 'Oh, shit.'

CHAPTER TWELVE

Eve was so intense about it that not even Shane, three beers down, was able to exactly say no. Michael didn't say anything, just watched Miranda with eyes that were way too clear for somebody who'd had the same amount to drink as Shane. As Eve cleared stuff off the dining room table and set up a single black candle in the centre, Claire wrung her hands nervously, trying to get Michael's attention. When she did, she mouthed, *What do we do?*

He shrugged. Nothing, she guessed. Well, nobody but Eve believed in it, anyway. She supposed it couldn't really hurt.

'OK,' Eve said, and sat Miranda down in a chair at the end. 'Shane, Michael, Claire – sit down.'

'This is bullshit,' Shane said.

'Just – please. Just do it, OK?' Eve looked stressed. Scared. Whatever she and Miranda had been doing upstairs with those tarot cards had really made her nervous. 'Just do it for me.'

Michael slid into the chair at the other end, as far from Miranda as he could get. Claire sat next to him, and Shane grabbed a seat on the other side, leaving Eve and Claire the closest to Miranda, who was shaking like she was about to have a fit.

'Hold hands,' Eve said, and grabbed Miranda's left, then Shane's right. She glared at Claire until Claire followed suit, taking Miranda's other hand and Michael's. That left Shane and Michael, who looked at each other and shrugged.

'Whatever,' Michael said, and took Shane's hand.

'Oh, God, guys, homophobic much? This isn't about you being manly men, it's about—'

'He's dead! I see him!'

Claire flinched as Miranda practically screamed it out. All around the table, they froze. Even Shane. And then fought the insane urge to giggle – well, Claire did, and she could see Shane's shoulders shaking. Eve bit her lip, but there were tears in her eyes.

'Somebody died in this house! I see him. I see his body lying on the floor...' Miranda moaned, and thrashed around in her chair, twisting and turning. 'It's not over. It's never over. This house – this house won't let it be over.'

Claire, unable to stop herself, looked at Michael, who was staring at Miranda with cold, slitted eyes. His hand was gripping Claire's tightly. When she started to say something, he squeezed it even more. Right. Shutting up, she was.

Miranda wasn't. 'There's a ghost in this house! An unquiet spirit!'

'Unquiet spirit?' Shane said under his breath. 'Is that politically correct for *pissed off?* You know, like *Undead American* or something?'

Miranda opened her eyes and frowned at him. 'Somebody already died,' she proclaimed. 'Right here. Right in this room. His spirit haunts this place, and it's strong.'

They all just looked at one another. Michael and Claire avoided more eye contact, but Claire felt her breath get short and her heart race faster. She was talking about Michael! She *knew*! How was that even possible?

'Is it dangerous?' Eve asked breathlessly. Claire nearly choked.

'I – I can't tell. It's murky.'

Shane said, 'Right. Dead man walking, can't tell if he's dangerous because, wow, murky. Anything else?' And again, Claire had to choke back a hysterical giggle.

There was a bitter, unpleasant twist to Miranda's face now. 'Fire,' she said. 'I see fire. I see someone screaming in the fire.'

Shane yanked his hands away from Eve and Michael, slammed his chair back, and said, 'OK, that's it. I'm outta here. Feel free to get your psychic jollies somewhere else.'

'No, wait!' Eve said, and grabbed for him. 'Shane, wait, she saw it in the cards, too—'

He pulled free. 'She sees whatever you want! And she gets off on the attention, in case you didn't notice! *And* she's a fang banger!'

'Shane, please! At least listen!'

'I've heard enough. Let me know when you want to move on to table rapping or Ouija boards – those are a lot more fun. We could get some ten-year-olds to show us the ropes.'

'Shane, wait! Where are you going?'

'Bed,' he said, and went up the stairs. 'Night.'

Claire was still holding Michael's hand, and Miranda's. She let go of both, pushed her chair back, and went up after him. She heard his door slam before she made it to the top, and raced down the hall to bang her fist on the wood. There was no answer, no sound of movement inside.

Then she noticed that the picture on the wall hallway was crooked, and moved it to stare at the button underneath. Would he?

Of course he would.

She hesitated for a second, then pressed it. The panel across the hallway clicked open, letting out a breath of cold air, and she quickly slipped inside, latched it back, and went up the stairs.

Shane was lying on the couch, feet on the curved polished-wood armrest, one arm flung over his eyes.

'Go away,' he said. Claire eased herself down on

the couch next to him, because his voice didn't sound, well, right. It was quiet and a little bit choked. His hand was shaking. 'I mean it, Claire, go.'

'The first time you met me, I was crying,' she said. 'You don't have to be ashamed.'

'I'm not crying,' he said, and moved his arm. He wasn't. His eyes were hot and dry and furious. 'I can't stand that she pretends to *know*. She was Lyssa's friend. If she knew, if she really knew, she should have tried harder.'

Claire bit her lip. 'Do you mean she—?' She couldn't even say it. *Do you mean she tried to tell you?* And he couldn't admit it if she had. If he admitted that much…maybe his sister didn't have to be dead.

No, Claire couldn't say that. And he couldn't hear it.

Instead, she just reached out and took his hand. He looked down at their clasped fingers, sighed, and closed his eyes. 'I'm drunk and I'm pissed off,' he said. 'Not the best company right now. Man, your parents would kill us all if they knew about any of this.'

She didn't say anything, because that was absolutely true. And something she didn't want to think about. She just wanted to sit here, in this silent room where time had frozen still, and be with him.

'Claire?' His voice was quieter. A little smeared with sleep. 'Don't do that again.'

'Do what?'

'Go out like you did tonight. Not at night.'

'I won't if you won't.'

He smiled, but didn't open his eyes. 'No dates? What is this, the Big Brother house? Anyway, I didn't come back to Morganville to hide.'

She was instantly curious. 'Why *did* you come back?'

'Michael. I told you. He called, I came. It's what he'd do for me.' Shane's smile faded. He was probably remembering Michael not answering the phone, not coming to the hospital. Not having his back.

'It's more than that,' she said. 'Or else you'd have just taken off by now.'

'Maybe,' Shane sighed. 'Leave it, Claire. You don't have to dig into every secret around here, OK? It's not safe.'

She thought about Michael. About the way he'd looked at Miranda across the séance table. 'No,' she agreed. 'It's not.'

They talked for hours, about pretty much nothing – certainly not about vampires, or sisters dying in fires, or Miranda's visions, obviously. Shane delved into what Claire had always thought were the Boy Classics: debates about whether Superman could take Batman ('Classic Batman or Badass Batman?'), movies they liked, movies they hated. Claire tried him on books. He was light on the classics, but who wasn't? (She wasn't, but she was a freak of nature.) He liked scary stories. They had that in common, too.

Time just didn't seem to pass at all in that little room. The talk seemed to keep going, spinning out of them on its own, gradually getting slower as the minutes and hours slipped away. She got cold and sleepy, and dragged an afghan off the arm of a nearby chair, spread it around her shoulders, and promptly dropped off to sleep sitting on the floor with her back against the settee, where Shane was lying.

She woke up with a start when the settee creaked, and she realised that Shane was getting up. He blinked, yawned, rubbed at his hair (which did very funny things when he did) and checked his watch.

'Oh, God, it's early,' he groaned. 'Hell. Well, at least I can grab the bathroom first.'

Claire jumped to her feet. 'What time is it?'

'Nine,' he said, and yawned again. She reached over him, pushed the hidden button, dashed past him to the door, barely remembering to shed the afghan on the way. 'Hey! Dibs on the bathroom! I mean it!'

She wasn't worried about the bathroom so much as being caught. After all, she'd spent the entire night with a boy. A boy who'd been *drinking*. Most of that was against the house rules, she figured, and Michael would have freaked out if he'd known. Maybe...maybe Michael was too distracted from what Miranda had been spilling to worry about it, though, because she had to admit, Miranda had known exactly what she was talking about.

Just not by name, really.

Well, Michael was back to incorporeal in the light of day, so at least she didn't have to worry about running into him...but she did need to decide what to do about school. This was already the worst academic week of her life, and she had the feeling it wasn't going to get any better unless she acted quickly. Shane had made a deal with the devil; it only made sense to take advantage of it, until she could find a way to cancel it. Monica and her girls wouldn't be after her – not in a lethal way. So there was no reason not to get her butt in the library.

She grabbed her clothes and jumped in the bathroom just as Shane, still yawning, stumbled out of the hidden room.

'But I called dibs!' he said, and knocked on the door. 'Dibs! Damn girls don't understand the rules...'

'Sorry, but I need to get ready!' She cranked up the shower and skinned out of her old clothes in record time. The jeans *really* needed washing, and she was down to her last clean pair of underwear, too.

Claire was in and out of the shower fast, trusting that the waterproof bandage they'd put on her back would hold (it did). In under five minutes she was fluffing her wet hair and sliding past Shane in a breathless rush to grab her backpack and stuff it with books.

'Where the hell are you going?' he asked from the doorway. He didn't sound sleepy now. She zipped the bag shut, hefted it on the shoulder that wasn't aching and complaining, and turned toward him without answering. He was leaning on the doorframe, arms folded, head cocked. 'Oh, you've *got* to be kidding. What've you got, some kind of death wish? You really *want* to get knocked down another flight of stairs or something?'

'You made the deal. They won't come after me.'

'Don't be dense. Leave that to the experts. You really think they don't have ways around it?'

She walked up to him, staring up into his face. He looked enormously tall. And he was big, and in her way.

And she didn't care.

'You made a deal,' she said, 'and I'm going to the library. Please get out of the way.'

'Please? Damn, girl, you need to learn how to get mad or—'

She shoved him. It was dumb, and he had the muscle to stay right where he was, but surprise was on her side, and she got him to stumble a couple of steps back. She was already out the door and heading out, shoes in hand. She wasn't about to stop and give him another chance to keep her nice and safe.

'Hey!' He caught up, grabbed her arm, and spun

her around. 'I thought you said you wouldn't—'

'At night,' she said, and turned to go down the stairs. He let go...and she slipped. For a scary second she was off-balance, teetering on the edge of the stairs, and then Shane's warm hands closed around her shoulders and pulled her back to balance.

He held her there for a few seconds. She didn't turn around, because if she did, and he was right there, well, she didn't know...

She didn't know what would happen.

'See you,' she gulped, and went down the stairs as fast as she dared, on shaking legs.

The heat of the morning was like a toaster oven, only without any yummy food smells; there were a couple of people out on the street. One lady was pushing a baby stroller, and for a second, while Claire was sitting down to put on her battered running shoes, she considered that with a kind of wonder. Having babies in a town like this. What were people thinking? But she guessed they did it anywhere, no matter how horrible it was. And there was a bracelet around the woman's slender wrist.

The baby was safe, at least until it turned eighteen.

Claire glanced down at her own bare wrist, shivered, and put it out of her mind as she set off for campus.

Now that she was looking, just about every

person she passed had something around his or her wrist – bracelets for the women, watchbands for the men. She couldn't tell what the symbols were. She needed to find some kind of alphabet; maybe somebody had done research and put it somewhere safe...somewhere the vampires wouldn't look.

She'd always felt safest at the library, anyway. She went straight there, watching over her shoulder for Monica, Gina, Jennifer, or anybody who looked remotely interested in her. Nobody did.

TPU's library was huge. And dusty. Even the librarians at the front looked like they might have picked up a cobweb or two since her last visit. More proof – if she'd needed it – that TPU was first, and only, a party school.

She checked the map for the shelves, and saw that the Dewey decimal system reigned in Morganville – which was weird, because she'd thought all the universities were on the Library of Congress system. She traced through the listings, looking for references, and found them in the basement.

Great.

As she started to walk away, though, she cocked her head and looked at the list again. There was something strange about it. She couldn't quite put her finger on it...

There wasn't a fourth floor. Not on the list, anyway, and Mr Dewey's system jumped straight from the third floor to the fifth. Maybe it was offices, she thought. Or storage. Or shipping. Or…coffins.

It was definitely weird, though.

She started to take the stairs down to the basement, then stopped and tilted her head back. The stairs were old-school, with massive wooden railings, turning in precise L-shaped angles all the way up.

What the hell, she thought. It was only a couple of flights of stairs. She could always pretend she'd gotten lost.

She couldn't hear anything or anybody once she'd left the first floor. It was silent as – she hated to think it – the grave. She tried to go quietly on the stairs, and quit gripping the banister when she realised that she was leaving sweaty, betraying handprints behind. She passed the second-floor wooden door, and then the third. Nobody visible through the clear glass window.

The fourth floor didn't even *have* a door. Claire stopped, puzzled, and touched the wall. Nope, no door, no secrets she could see. Just a blank wall. Was it possible there was no fourth floor?

She went up to the fifth floor, made her way through the silent, dusty stacks to the other set of stairs, and went down. On this side, there was a door, but it was locked, and there weren't any windows.

Definitely not offices, she guessed.

But coffins weren't out of the question. Dammit,

she resented being scared in a library! Books weren't supposed to be scary. They were supposed to...help.

If she were some kick-ass superhero chick, she'd probably be able to pick the lock with a fingernail clipping or something. Unfortunately, she wasn't a superhero, and she bit her fingernails.

No, she wasn't a superhero, but she was something else. She was...resourceful.

Standing there, staring at the lock, she began to smile.

'Applied science,' she said, and ran down the stairs to the first floor.

She had a stop to make in chem lab.

Her TA was in his office. 'Well,' he said, 'if you really want to shatter a lock, you need something good, like liquid helium. But liquid helium isn't all that portable.'

'What about Freon?' Claire asked.

'No, you can't get your hands on the stuff without a licence. What you can buy is a different formulation, doesn't get as cold but it's more environmentally friendly. But it probably wouldn't do the job.'

'Liquid nitrogen?'

'Same problem as helium. Too bulky.'

Claire sighed. 'Too bad. It was a cool idea.'

The TA smiled. 'Yes, it was. You know, I have a portable liquid-nitrogen tank I keep for school demonstrations, but they're hard to get. Pretty expensive. Not the kind of thing you'd find lying around. Sorry.' He wandered off, intent on some postgrad experiment of his own, and he promptly forgot all about her. She bit her lip, stared at his back for a while, and then slowly...very slowly, moved back to the door that led to the supply room. It was unlocked so that the TA could easily move in and out if he needed to. Red and yellow signs on it warned that she was going to get cancer, suffocate, or die other horrible deaths if she opened the door...but she did it anyway.

It squeaked. The TA had to have heard it, and she froze like a mouse in front of an oncoming bird. Guilty.

He didn't turn around. In fact, he deliberately kept his back to her.

She let out a shaky breath, eased into the room, and looked around. The place was neatly kept, all its chemicals labelled and stored with the safety information for each hanging below it. He stored in alphabetical order. She found the LIQUID NITROGEN sign and saw a bulky, very obvious tank...and a small one next to it, like a giant thermos, with a shoulder strap. She grabbed it, then read the sign. USE PROTECTIVE GLOVES, the sign said. The gloves were right there, too. She shoved a pair in her backpack, slung the canister over her shoulder, and got the hell out of there.

The librarians didn't even give her a second look.

She waved and smiled and went into the stacks, all the way to the back stairs.

The door was just as she'd left it. She fumbled on the gloves, opened the top of the canister, and found that there was a kind of steel pipette that fit into a nozzle. She made sure it was in place, then opened the valve, held her breath, and began pouring supercooled liquid into the lock. She wasn't sure how much to use – too much was better than not enough, she guessed – and kept pouring until the outside of the lock was completely frosted. Then she cranked the valve shut, and – reminding herself to keep the gloves *on* – yanked on the doorknob.

Crack! It sounded like a gunshot. She jumped, looked around, and realised the knob had moved in her hand.

She'd opened the door.

Nothing to do now but go inside...but somehow, that didn't seem like such a great idea, now that she was actually able to do it.

Because...coffins. Or worse.

Claire sucked in a steadying breath, opened the door, and carefully looked around the edge.

It looked like a storeroom. Files. Stacks of cartons and wooden crates. No one in sight. *Great*, she thought. *Maybe I did just break into the file room*. That would be disappointing. Still, she stuffed the gloves in her backpack, just in case.

The cartons looked new, but the contents – when she unwrapped the string tying one closed –

appeared old. Crumbling books, badly preserved. Ancient letters and papers in languages she couldn't read, some of which looked like ancestors of English. She tried the next box. More of the same. The room was vast, and it was full of this kind of stuff.

The book, she thought. *They're looking for the book. Every old book they find comes here and gets examined.* Now that she looked, she saw that the crates had small red X marks on them meaning they'd been gone through? Initials, too. Somebody was being held accountable.

Which meant…somebody was working here.

She had just enough time to form the thought when two people walked out of the maze of boxes ahead of her. They weren't hurrying, and they weren't alarmed. *Vampires.* She didn't know how she knew – they weren't exactly dressed for the part – but the way they moved, loose and sure, screamed *predator* to her fragile-prey brain.

'Well,' said the short blond girl, 'we don't get many visitors here.' Except for the pallor of her face and the glitter in her eyes, she looked like a hundred other girls out on the Quad. She was wearing pink. It seemed wrong for a vampire to be wearing pink.

'Did you take a wrong turn, honey?' The man was taller, darker, and he looked really odd…really dead. It was because of his skin tone, she realised. He was black. Being a vampire bleached him, not to white, but to the colour of ashes. He had on a TPU purple T-shirt, grey sweatpants, and running shoes. If he'd been human, she'd have thought he was old – old enough to be a professor, at least.

They split up, coming at her from two different sides.

'Whose little one are you?' purred the pink girl, and before Claire could engage her brain to run, the girl had taken her left hand, examining her bare wrist. Then examining her right one. 'Oh, my, you really *are* lost, sweetie. John, what should we do?'

'Well,' John said, and put a friendly hand on Claire's shoulder. It felt colder than the liquid-nitrogen bottle hanging across her back. 'We could sit down and have a nice cup of coffee. Tell you all about what we do in here. That's what you want to know, right? Children like you are just so darn curious.' He was steering her forward, and Claire knew – just knew – that any attempt to pull free would result in pain. Probably broken bones.

Pink Girl still had hold of her other wrist, too. Her cool fingers were pressed against Claire's pulse point.

I need to get out of this. Fast.

'I know what you do here,' she said. 'You're looking for the book. But I thought vampires couldn't read it.'

John stopped and looked at his companion, who raised pale eyebrows back at him. 'Angela?' he asked.

'We can't,' she said. 'We're just here as...observers.

And you seem very knowledgeable, for a free-range child. Under eighteen, aren't you? Shouldn't you be under someone's Protection? Your family's?'

She seemed honestly concerned. That was weird. 'I'm a student,' Claire said. 'Advanced placement.'

'Ah,' Angela said, and looked kind of regretful. 'Well, then, I guess you're on your own. Too bad, really.'

'Because you're going to kill me?' Claire heard herself say it in a kind of dreamlike state, and remembered what Eve had told her. *Don't look in their eyes.* Too late. Angela's were a soft turquoise, very pretty. Claire felt a deliciously warm edge-of-sleep sensation wash over her.

'Probably,' Angela admitted. 'But first you should have some tea.'

'Coffee,' John said. 'I still like the caffeine.'

'It spoils the taste!'

'Gives it that zip.' John smacked his lips.

'Why don't you let me look through boxes?' Claire asked, desperately bringing herself back from the edge of whatever that was. The vampires were leading her through a maze of boxes and crates, all marked with red Xs and initials. 'You've got to let humans do it, right? If you can't read the book?'

'What makes you think *you* could read it, little one?' Angela asked. She had a buttery sort of accent, not quite California, not quite Midwest, not quite anything. Old. It sounded old. 'Are you a scholar of languages, as well?'

'N-no, but I know what the symbol is that you're looking for. I can recognise it.'

Angela reached down and drew her fingernails lightly over the skin of Claire's inner arm, looking thoughtful.

'No, I don't have the tattoo. But I've seen it.' She was absolutely shaking all over, terrified in a distant sort of way, but her brain was racing, looking for escape. 'I can recognise it. You can't, can you? You can't even draw it.'

Angela's fingernails dug in just a bit, in warning. 'Don't be smart, little girl. We're not the kind of people you should mock.'

'I'm not mocking. You can't see it. That's why you haven't found it. It's not just that you can't *read* it – right?'

Angela and John exchanged looks again, silent and meaningful. Claire swallowed hard, tried to think of anything that might be a good argument for keeping her unbitten (*Maybe if I don't drink any tea or coffee?*) and spared a thought for just how pissed off Shane was going to be if she went and got herself killed. On campus. In the middle of the day.

The vampires turned a corner of boxes, and there, in an open space, was a door that didn't lead out onto any stairwell she'd seen, an elevator with a DOWN button, a battered school-issue desk and chair, and...

'Professor Wilson?' she blurted. He looked up, blinking behind his glasses. He was her Classics of

English Literature professor (Tuesdays and Thursdays at two) and although he was boring, he seemed to know his stuff. He was a faded-looking man, all greys – thin grey hair, faded grey eyes – with a tendency to dress in colours that bleached him out even more. Today it was a white shirt and grey jacket.

'Ah. You're—' he snapped his fingers two or three times – 'in my Intro to Shakespeare—'

'Classics of English Lit.'

'Right, exactly. They change the title occasionally, just to fool the students into taking it again. Neuberg, isn't it?' Fright in his eyes. 'You weren't assigned here to help me, were you?'

'I—' Light dawned. Maybe letting mistaken impressions lie was a good idea right now. 'Yes. I was. By…Miss Samson.' Miss Samson was the dragon lady of the English department; everyone knew that. Nobody questioned her. As excuses went, this one was thinner than paper, but it was all she had. 'I was looking for you.'

'And the door was open?' John asked, looking down at her. She kept her eyes firmly fixed on Professor Wilson, who wasn't likely to hypnotise her into not lying.

'Yes,' she said firmly. 'It was open.' The only good thing about the canister on her back was that at least it *looked* like something a college student might carry around, with soup or coffee or something in it. And it didn't exactly look like something to break locks. By now, the liquid nitrogen in the lock would have sublimated into the air, and all evidence was gone.

She hoped.

'Well then,' Wilson said, and frowned at her, 'better sit down and get to work, Neuberg. We have a lot to do. You know what you're looking for?'

'Yes, sir.' John let go of her shoulder. After a reluctant second, Angela released her, too, and Claire went to the desk, dragged up a wooden chair, and carefully placed her backpack and canister on the floor.

'Coffee?' John asked hopefully.

'No, thank you,' she said politely, and pulled the first stacked volume toward her.

It was interesting work, which was weird, and the vampires became less and less frightening the more she was in their company. Angela was a fidgeter, always tapping her foot or restlessly braiding her hair or straightening stacks of books. The vampires seemed assigned only as observers; as Professor Wilson and Claire finished each mountain of books, they took them away, boxed them, and brought new volumes to check.

'Where do these come from?' Claire wondered out loud, and sneezed as she opened the cover of something called *Land Register of Atascosa County*, which was filled with antique, neat handwriting. Names, dates, measurements.

Nothing like what they were looking for.

'Everywhere,' Professor Wilson said, and closed the book he'd flipped through. 'Secondhand stores. Antique shops. Book dealers. They have a network around the world, and everything comes here for inspection. If it isn't what they're looking for, it goes out again. They even make a profit on it, I'm told.' He cleared his throat and held up the book he'd been looking at. 'John? This one is a first-edition Lewis Carroll. I believe you should put it aside.'

John obligingly took it and set it in a pile that Claire thought was probably 'rare and valuable'.

'How long have you been doing this, Professor?' she asked. He looked tired.

'Seven years,' he said. 'Four hours a day. Someone will come in to relieve us soon.'

Us, meaning that she'd get to walk out. Well, that was nice. She'd been hoping that she might at least slip a note out with the professor, something along the lines of IF YOU FIND MY BODY, I WAS KILLED BY MISS PINK IN THE LIBRARY, but that sounded too much like something out of that board game her parents liked so much.

'No talking in class,' John said, and laughed. When he did, his fangs came down. His were longer than Brandon's, and looked scarier, somehow. Claire gulped and focused on the book in front of her. The cover said *Native Grains of the New World*. A whole book about grain. Wow. She wondered how Professor Wilson had stayed sane all these years. *Corn is a member of the grass family and is native to the American continents...* She flipped pages. More about corn. She didn't know you could write so much about one plant.

Beside her, Professor Wilson swore softly under his breath, and she looked up, startled. His face had gone pale, except for two red spots high in his cheeks. He quickly faked a smile and held up a finger striped with red. 'Paper cut,' he said. His voice sounded high and tight, and Claire followed his stare to see Angela and John moving closer, watching the professor's finger with eerie concentration. 'It's nothing. Nothing at all.' He groped in his pocket, came out with a handkerchief, and wrapped it around his bloodied finger. In trying to attend to that, he knocked the book he'd been reviewing to the floor. Claire automatically bent to pick it up, but Wilson's foot hooked around it and scooted it out of her reach. He bent over and in the darkness under the desk...switched books.

Claire watched, open-mouthed. What the hell was he doing? Before she could do anything stupid that might give him away, there was a ding from the elevator across the room, then the rumble of opening doors.

'Ah,' Wilson said with evident relief. 'Time to go, then.' He reached down, picked up the hidden book, and slipped it into his leather satchel with such skill Claire wasn't absolutely sure she'd seen it. 'Come along, Neuberg.'

'Not her,' John said, smiling cheerfully. 'She gets to stay after class.'

'But—' Claire bit her lip and made desperate eye contact with the professor, who frowned and shifted his weight from one foot to the other. 'Sir, can't I go with you? Please?'

'Yes, of course,' he said. 'Come along, I said. Mr Hargrove, if you don't like it, please take it up with management. I have a class.'

He might have pulled it off, too, if Angela hadn't been so sharp-eyed, or suspicious; she stopped him half-way to the elevator, opened up his portfolio, and took out the book he'd stashed away. She leafed through it silently, then handed it to John, who did the same.

Both of them looked at the professor with calm, cool, oddly pleased eyes.

'Well,' Angela said, 'I don't know, but I think this may be a violation of the rules, Professor. Taking books from the library without checking them out first. Shame, shame.'

She deliberately opened the first page and read, 'It was the best of times, it was the worst of times...' and then flipped carefully through, stopping at random spots, to read lines of text. It all sounded right to Claire. She flinched when Angela pushed the book at her. 'Read,' the vampire said.

'Um...where?'

'Anywhere.'

Claire recited a few lines in a faltering voice from page 229.

'*A Tale of Two Cities,*' John said. 'Let me guess, Professor…a first edition?'

'Mint condition,' Angela said, and plucked it out of Claire's trembling hands. 'I think the professor has a nice retirement plan, composed of screwing us out of our rightful profits.'

'Huh,' John said. 'He didn't look quite so dumb as that. Got all those degrees and stuff.'

'That's just paper smarts. You never can tell about what's really in their heads until you open them up.' The two of them were talking like he wasn't even there.

Professor Wilson's pale skin had a sweaty gleam on it now. 'A moment of weakness,' he said. 'I really do apologise. It won't ever happen again, I swear that to you.'

'Apology accepted,' Angela said, and lunged forward, planted her hand on his chest, and knocked him flat to the floor. 'And by the way, I believe you.'

She grabbed his wrist, raised it to her mouth, and paused to strip off his gold wristwatch band and toss it on the floor. As it rolled, Claire's stricken eyes caught sight of the symbol on the watch face. A triangle. Delta?

Her shock broke at the sound of the professor's scream. Grown men shouldn't scream like that. It just wasn't right. Fright made her angry, and she dropped her book bag, took the canister off her shoulder, and yanked off the top.

Then she threw liquid nitrogen all over Angela's back. When John turned on her, snarling, she splashed what was left at his face, aiming for his eyes. Wilson rolled to his feet as Angela collapsed, shrieking and thrashing; John reached out for him, but she'd managed to hurt him, too – he missed. Wilson grabbed his satchel and she got her book bag; they ran for the elevator. A very surprised professor – someone she didn't recognise – was standing there, open-mouthed; Wilson yelled at him to stand aside, leapt into the cage, and pressed the DOWN button so frantically Claire was afraid it would snap or stick or something.

The doors rolled shut, and the elevator began to fall. Claire tried to get her breathing under control, but it was no good; she was about to hyperventilate. Still, she was doing better than the professor. He looked awful; his face was as grey as his hair, and he was breathing in shallow, hard gasps.

'Oh dear,' he said weakly. 'That wasn't good.' And then he slowly collapsed down the wall of the elevator until he was in a sitting position, legs splayed loosely.

'Professor?' Claire lunged forward and hovered over him.

'Heart,' he panted, and then made a choking sound. She loosened his tie. That didn't seem to help. 'Listen. My house. Bookshelf. Black cover. Go.'

'Professor, relax, it's OK—'

'No. Can't let them have it. Bookshelf. Black—'

His eyes got very wide, and his back arched, and she heard him make an awful noise, and then...

Then he just *died*. Nothing dramatic about it, no big speeches, no music swelling to tell her how to feel about it. He was just...gone, and even though she pressed her shaking fingers to his neck, she knew she wouldn't feel anything, because there was something different about him. He was like a rubber doll, not a person.

The elevator doors opened. Claire gasped, grabbed her books and the empty silver canister, and sprinted down the blank cinder-block hallway to the end, where a fire door opened into bright afternoon sunlight.

She stood there for a few long seconds, just shaking and gasping and crying, and then tried to think where to go. Angela and John thought her name was Neuberg, which was good – she supposed not so good for Neuberg, if one existed – but they'd find out who she was eventually. She needed to be home before that happened.

Bookshelf. Black cover.

Professor Wilson had been in that room for seven years, sorting through books. Probably slipping out those he thought might be worth something on the black market.

What if...?

No. It couldn't be.

Except...what if it was? What if a year ago, or five years ago, Professor Wilson had *found* that book the vampires were so intent on having, and decided to hang on to it for a rainy day? After all, she'd been basically planning to do the same thing, only for her it was already stormy weather.

She needed his address.

It wasn't far to the Communication Arts Building, and she ran as much of the way as she could before the pain in her still-bruised ankle and still-raw back made her slow down. Two flights of steps brought her to the offices, and she passed up Professor Wilson's closed and locked office to stop next to the cluttered desk out in the open between the corridors. The nameplate read VIVIAN SAMSON, but everyone just called her Dragon Lady, and the woman sitting behind it had earned the name. She was old, fat, and legendarily bad-tempered. There was no smoking in all university buildings, but the Dragon Lady had an overflowing ashtray on the corner of her desk and a glowing cigarette hanging out of the corner of her red-painted lips. Beehive hair, straight out of old movies. She had a computer, but it wasn't turned on, and as far as Claire could tell from the two-inch-long bright red nails, the Dragon Lady didn't type, either.

She ignored Claire and kept on reading the

magazine open in front of her.

'Um – excuse me?' Claire asked. She felt sticky with sweat from the run in the heat, and still kind of sick from what had happened at the library. The Dragon Lady turned a page in her magazine. 'I just need—'

'I'm on break.' The red-clawed hand took the cigarette out of the red-painted mouth for a trip to the ashtray to shed some excess. 'Not even supposed to be here today. Damn grad students. Come back in half an hour.'

'But—'

'No buts. I'm on break. Shoo.'

'But Professor Wilson sent me to get something from his house, but he didn't give me the address. *Please*—'

She slapped the magazine closed. 'Oh, for God's sake. I'm going to wring his neck when he gets back here. Here.' She grabbed a card from the holder on her desk and pitched it at Claire, glaring. 'If you're some nutcase, it's not my problem. You tell His Highness that if he wants to roll around with undergrads, he can damn well remember to tell them his own damn address from now on. Got it?'

'Got it,' Claire said in a very small voice. *Roll around with...* She wasn't going to think about that. Not at all. 'Thank you.'

The Dragon Lady puffed a cloud of smoke out of both nostrils and raised eyebrows plucked into more of a suggestion than an actual form. 'You're a polite one. Go on, get out of here before I remember I'm supposed to be off today.'

Claire escaped, clutching the card in her sweaty fingers.

CHAPTER THIRTEEN

'You know,' Shane said twenty minutes later, 'I'd feel a whole lot better about the two of us if you didn't think I was the go-to guy for breaking and entering.'

They were standing on the professor's back porch, and Claire was peering through a murky window into an equally murky living room. She felt a flash of guilt about the breaking-and-entering part – but she *had* called him – just before her heart did a funny little painful flip and she heard him say again in her head *the two of us*.

She didn't dare look at him. Surely he didn't mean that, exactly. That meant, you know, friendship or something. He treated her like a kid. Like his sister. He didn't – he couldn't—

But what if he could?

And she couldn't believe she was thinking this now, on the doorstep of a dead man. The memory of Professor Wilson's limp, rubbery body steadied her, and she was able to finally stand back from the window and meet Shane's eyes without fluttering like some scared sparrow. 'Well, I couldn't ask Eve,' she said reasonably. 'She's at work.'

'Makes sense. Hey, look, what's that?' Shane pointed. She whirled to stare. There was a sound of tinkling glass behind her, and when she turned back he was opening the back door. 'There. Now you can say you didn't know I was going to do it. Crime free.'

Well, not exactly. She was still carrying the metal cylinder over her shoulder. She wondered if the vampires had recovered yet, and if anybody had thought to question the TA at the chem lab. She hoped not. He was nice, and in his own way he was brave, but she had no illusions that he wouldn't sell her out in a hot second. There weren't a whole lot of heroes left in Morganville.

One of the last of them turned in the doorway and said, 'In or out, kid, daylight's burning.'

She followed Shane over the threshold into Professor Wilson's house.

It was kind of weird, really – she could see that he'd been here hours ago, living his life, and now the house seemed like it was waiting for him. Maybe not so much weird as sad. They came in through the kitchen, and there was a cereal bowl, a glass, and a coffee cup in the dish strainer. The professor had eaten breakfast, at least. When she touched the towel underneath the strainer, it was still damp.

'Hey,' Shane said. 'So what are we looking for in here?'

'Bookshelves,' she said.

'Yo. Found 'em.' He sounded odd. She followed him into the next room – the living room – and felt her stomach sink a little. Why hadn't she thought about this? He was a *professor*. Of course he'd have a jazillion books...and there were, floor to ceiling, all the way around the room. Crammed in together. Stacked on the floor in places. Stacked on tables. She'd thought the Glass House was a reader's paradise, but this...

'We have two hours,' Shane said. 'Then we're gone. I don't want to risk you out on the street after dark.'

She nodded numbly and went to the first set of shelves. 'He said it had a black cover. Maybe that will help.'

But it didn't. She began pulling out all the black-bound books and piling them on the table; Shane did the same. By the time they'd met in the middle of the shelves, an hour had passed, and the pile was huge.

'What the hell are we looking for?' he asked, staring at it. She didn't suppose *I don't know* would be an answer that would get any respect.

'You know the tattoo on Eve's arm?'

Shane acted like she'd stuck him in the butt with a fork. 'We're looking for *the* book? *Here?*'

'I—' She gave up. 'I don't know. Maybe. It's worth a try.'

He just shook his head, his expression something between *You're crazy* and *You're amazing*. But not in a good way. She pulled up a chair and began leafing through the books, one after another. Nothing...nothing...nothing...

'Claire.' Shane sounded odd. He handed her a black leather-bound book. 'Take a look.'

It was too new. They were looking for an old book, right? This was...this was a Holy Bible. With a cross on the front.

'Look *inside*,' he said. She opened it. The first few gold-leafed pages were standard, the same familiar words she'd grown up with, and still believed. Eve had said they had a few churches in Morganville, right? Maybe they had services. She'd have to check.

Midway through Exodus, the pages went hollow, and there was a tiny little volume hidden inside the Bible. Old. Very old. The cover was water-stained dirty leather, and scratched into it was a symbol.

The symbol.

Claire pulled it out of the Bible and opened it.

'Well?' Shane demanded after a few seconds. 'What about it?'

'It's—' She swallowed hard. 'It's in Latin.'

'So? What does it say?'

'I don't *read* Latin!'

'You're kidding. I thought all geniuses read Latin.

Isn't that the international language for smart people?'

She picked up a book without looking and threw it at him. He ducked. It flopped to the floor. Claire flipped pages in the small volume. It was handwritten in faded, coppery ink, the kind of beautiful perfect writing from hundreds of years ago.

She was actually holding it in her hands.

And here she'd been intending to just fake it.

'We'd better get going,' Shane said. 'Seriously. I don't want to be here when the cops come calling.'

'You think they will?'

'Well, if dear old Prof Wilson keeled over after stealing the vampires blind, yeah, I think they'll send a couple of cops over to inventory the goodies. So we'd better move it.'

She stuffed the journal back into the Bible and started to put it into her backpack, then paused in outright despair. Too much stuff. 'We need another bag,' she said. 'Something small.'

Shane came up with a plastic grocery sack from the kitchen, stuck the Bible inside, and hustled her out. She looked back at Professor Wilson's lonely living room one last time. A clock ticked on the mantel, and everything waited for a life that would never start up again.

She was right. It *was* sad.

'Run first,' Shane said. 'Mourn later.'

It was the perfect motto for Morganville.

⋈ ⋈ ⋈

They made it back home with half an hour or so to spare, but as they turned the corner on Lot Street, where the Gothic bulk of the Glass House pretty much dwarfed all of the other, newer houses around it, Claire's eyes went immediately to the blue SUV sitting at the curb. It looked familiar...

'Oh my God,' she said, and stopped dead in her tracks.

'OK, stopping? Not a great idea. Come on, Claire, let's—'

'That's my parents' car!' she said. 'My parents are here! Oh my *God*!' She practically squealed that last part, and would have turned around and run away, but Shane grabbed her by the neck of her shirt and hauled her around.

'Better get it over with,' he said. 'If they tracked you this far, they're not going to drive off without saying hello.'

'Oh, *man*! Let go!' He did. She twitched her shirt down over her shoulders and glared at him, and he did an extravagant bow.

'You first,' he said. 'I'm watching your back.'

She was, at least temporarily, more worried about her front.

When she cracked open the door to the house, she could hear Eve's anxious voice. 'I'm sure she'll be here any time – she's, you know, at class, and—'

'Young lady, my daughter is *not* in class. I've *been* to her classes. She hasn't been to class the entire afternoon. Now, are you going to tell me where she is, or do I have to call the police?'

Dad sounded *pissed*. Claire swallowed hard, resisted the urge to back up and close the door and run away – mainly because Shane was right behind her, and he was finding this way too funny to let her escape – and walked down the hall toward the voices. Just Eve and Dad, so far. Where was—

'Claire!' She'd know that shriek of relief anywhere. Before she could say *Hi, Mom*, she was buried in a hug and a wave of L'Oreal perfume. The perfume stayed longer than the hug, which morphed into Claire's being held at arm's length and shaken like a rag doll. 'Claire, *what have you been doing? What are you doing here?*'

'Mom—'

'We were so worried about you after that terrible accident, but Les couldn't get off work until today—'

'It wasn't that big a deal, Mom—'

'And we just had to come up and see you, but your room is *empty* in the dorm. You weren't in classes – Claire, what's happened to you? I can't believe you'd do something like this!'

'Like what?' she asked, sighing. 'Mom, would you quit shaking me? I'm getting dizzy.'

Mom let go and folded her arms. She wasn't very tall – just a couple of inches over Claire's height, even in mid-heeled shoes – and Dad, who was glowering at Shane in the background, was as tall and twice as broad. 'Is it him?' Dad asked. 'Did he get you into trouble?'

'Not me,' Shane said. 'I've just got that kind of face.'

'Shut *up*!' Claire hissed. She could hear that he thought all this was funny. She didn't. 'Shane's just a friend, Dad. Like Eve.'

'Eve?' Her parents looked at each other blankly. 'You mean—' As one, they cast horrified glances at Eve, who was standing with her hands folded, trying to look as demure as it was possible to look while wearing an outfit that looked like something a Goth ballerina might wear – all black netting in the skirt and red satin up top. She smiled sweetly, but it was kind of spoilt by the red lipstick (had she borrowed Miranda's?) and skull earrings.

Mom said faintly, 'Claire, you used to have such *nice* friends. What happened to Elizabeth?'

'She went to Texas A & M, Mom.'

'That's no reason not to still be friends.'

Mom logic. Claire decided that Shane had been right – there was no getting out of this one. She might as well jump into the pool; the sharks were circling no matter what she did. 'Mom, Eve and Shane are two of my roommates. Here. In this house.'

Silence. Mom and Dad looked frozen. 'Les?' Mom asked. 'Did she say she was *living here*?'

'Young lady, you are *not* living here,' Dad said. 'You live in the dorm.'

'I'm not. I'm living here, and that's my decision.'

'That's *illegal*! The rules said that you have to live *on campus*, Claire. You can't just—'

Outside the windows, night was slipping up on them, stealthy and quick as an assassin. 'I can,' Claire said. 'I did. I'm not going back there.'

'Well, I'm not paying good money just to have you squat in some old wreck with a bunch of—' Dad was at a loss for words to describe how little he thought of Eve and Shane. '*Friends*! And are they even in school?'

'I'm currently between majors,' Shane offered.

'Shut *up*!' Claire was nearly in tears now.

'All right, that's it. Get your things, Claire. You're coming with us.'

All the amusement faded out of Shane's face. 'No, she isn't,' he said. 'Not at night. Sorry.'

Dad got red-faced and even more furious, and levelled a finger at her. 'Is this why you're here? Older boys? Living under the same roof?'

'Oh, Claire,' Mom sighed. 'You're too young for this. You—'

'Shane,' Shane supplied.

'Shane, I'm sure you're a perfectly nice boy,' – she didn't sound especially convinced – 'but you have to understand that Claire is a very special girl, and she's very young.'

'She's a kid!' Dad interrupted. 'She's sixteen! And if you took advantage of her—'

'Dad!' Claire thought her face might be just as

red as his, for very different reasons. 'Enough already! Shane's my *friend*! Stop embarrassing me!'

'Embarrassing *you*? Claire, how do you think we feel?' Dad roared.

In the silence, Claire heard Michael say mildly, from the stairs, 'I think maybe we'd all better sit down.'

They didn't all sit down. Shane and Eve escaped to the kitchen, where Claire heard a clattering of pots and furious whispering; she was sitting uncomfortably on the couch between her parental bookends, looking mournfully at Michael, who was sitting in the armchair. He looked calm and collected, but then, he would. Mom, Dad, this is Michael, he's a dead guy... Yeah, that would really help.

'My name is Michael Glass,' he said, and extended his hand to Claire's dad like an equal. Dad, surprised, took it and shook. 'You've already met our other two roommates, Eve Rosser and Shane Collins. Sir, I know you're concerned about Claire. You should be. She's on her own for the first time, and she's younger than most kids coming to college. I don't blame you for being worried.'

Dad, defused, settled for looking stubborn. 'And who the heck are you, Michael Glass?'

'I own this house,' he said. 'I rent a room to your daughter.'

'How old are you?'

'A little over eighteen. So are Shane and Eve. We've known each other a long time, and to be honest, we didn't really want to let another person into the house, but...' Michael shrugged. 'We had an empty bedroom, and splitting costs four ways is better. I thought a long time about letting Claire stay here. We had house meetings about it.'

Claire blinked at him. He had? They did?

'My daughter's a minor,' Dad said. 'I'm not happy about this. Not at all.'

'Sir, I understand. I wasn't too happy about it, either. Even having her here is a risk for us, you understand.' Michael didn't have to go into it, Claire saw; her dad totally got it. 'But she needed us, and we couldn't turn her away.'

'You mean you couldn't turn her money away,' Dad said, frowning. For answer, Michael got up, went to a wooden box sitting on the shelf, and took out an envelope. He handed it to Dad.

'That's what she paid me,' he said. 'The whole amount. I kept it in case she wanted to leave. This wasn't about money, Mr Danvers. It was about Claire's safety.'

Michael glanced across at her, and she bit her lip. She'd been hoping to avoid this – desperately hoping – but she couldn't see any way out now. She nodded slightly and slumped back on the couch cushions, trying to make herself small. Smaller.

'Claire's dorm was girls-only,' Claire's mom put in. She reached over to stroke Claire's hair absently, the way she did when Claire was little. Claire endured it. Actually, she secretly liked it, a little, and had to fight not to relax against Mom's side and let herself be hugged. Protected. 'She was safe, wasn't she? That Monica girl said—'

'You talked to Monica?' Claire said sharply, and looked wide-eyed at her mother. Mom frowned a little, dark eyes concerned.

'Yes, of course I did. I was trying to find out where you'd gone, and Monica was very helpful.'

'I'll bet,' Claire muttered. The idea of Monica standing there smiling at her mom – looking innocent and nice, probably – was sickening.

'She said you were staying here,' Mom finished, still frowning. 'Claire, honey, why would you leave the dorm? I know you're not a silly girl. You wouldn't do it if you didn't have a reason.'

Michael said, 'She did. She was being hazed.'

'Hazed?' Mom repeated the word like she had no idea what it meant.

'From what Claire told me, it started small – all the freshmen girls get it from the older ones. Nasty stuff, but not dangerous. But she got on the wrong side of the wrong girl, and she was getting hurt.'

'Hurt?' That was Dad, who now had something to hold on to.

'When she came here, she had bruises like a road map,' Michael said. 'To be honest, I wanted to call the cops. She wouldn't let me. But I couldn't let her go back there. She wasn't just getting knocked around... I think her life was in danger.'

Mom's hand had frozen in Claire's hair, and she let out a little moan.

'It's not that bad,' Claire offered. 'I mean, look, nothing broken or anything. I had a sore ankle for a while, and a black eye, but—'

'A black eye?'

'It's gone. See?' She batted her eyelashes. Mom's gaze searched her face with agonising care. 'Honest, it's over. Done. Everything's fine now.'

'No,' Michael said. 'It's not. But Claire's handling it, and we're watching out for her. Shane especially. He – he had a little sister, and he's taken an interest in making sure Claire stays safe. But more than that, I think Claire's taking care of herself. And that's what she has to learn, don't you agree?' Michael leant forward, hands loosely clasped, elbows on his knees. In the glow of the lamps, his hair was rich gold, his eyes angel blue. If anybody *ever* looked trustworthy, it was Michael Glass.

Of course, he was dead and all, which Claire had to bite her tongue not to blurt out in sheer altered-state panic.

Mom and Dad were thinking. She knew she had to say something...something important. Something that would make them not drag her home by the ear. 'I can't leave,' she said. It came from her heart, and she meant every word. Her voice stayed absolutely steady, too – for once. 'Mom, Dad, I know that you're afraid for me, and I – I love you.

But I need to stay here. Michael isn't telling you this, but they put themselves on the line for me, and I owe it to them to stay until it's settled and I'm sure they won't get in trouble for me. It's what I have to do, you understand? And I can do it. I *have* to.'

'Claire,' Mom said in a small, choked voice. 'You're *sixteen*! You're a *child*!'

'I'm not,' she said simply. 'I'm sixteen and a half, and I'm not giving up. I never have. You know that.'

They did. Claire had fought all her life against the odds, and both her parents knew it. They knew how stubborn she was. More, they knew how important it was to her.

'I don't like this,' her dad said, but he sounded unhappy now, not angry. 'I don't like you living with older boys. Off campus. And I want these people who hurt you stopped.'

'Then *I* have to stop them,' Claire said. 'It's my problem. And there are other girls in that dorm getting hurt, too, so it isn't just about me. I need to do it for them, too.'

Michael raised his eyebrows slightly, but didn't answer. Mom wiped at her eyes with a handkerchief. Eve appeared in the doorway wearing a huge apron with a red-lips emblem that read KISS THE COOK, peered uncertainly at them, and gave Claire's parents a nervous smile.

'Dinner's ready!' she said.

'Oh, we couldn't,' Mom said.

'The heck we can't,' Dad said. 'I'm starved. Is that chilli?'

Dinner was uncomfortable. Dad made noncommittal grunts about the quality of the chilli. Shane looked like he was barely holding on to his laughter most of the time. Eve was so nervous that Claire thought she would jitter right out of the chair, and Michael... Michael was the calm one. The adult. Claire had never felt more like the kid at the big table in her life.

'So, Michael,' Claire's mother said, nibbling at a spoonful of chilli, 'what is it you do?'

Haunts the house where he died, Claire thought, and bit her lip. She took a fast sip of her cola.

'I'm a musician,' he said.

'Oh really?' She brightened up. 'What do you play? I love classical music!'

Now even *Michael* looked uncomfortable. Shane coughed into his napkin and drained Coke in huge gulps to drown out his hiccupping laughter.

'Piano and guitar,' he said. 'But mostly guitar. Acoustic and electric.'

'Humph,' Claire's dad said. 'Any good?'

Shane's shoulders were shaking.

'I don't know,' Michael said. 'I work hard at it.'

'He's *very* good!' Eve jumped in, eyes bright and flashing. 'Honestly, Michael, you should quit being so humble. You're really great. It's just a matter of time before you really do something big, and you know it!'

Michael looked…blank. Expressionless. That didn't quite hide the pain, Claire thought. 'Someday,' he said, and shrugged. 'Hey, Shane, thanks for dinner. Good stuff.'

'Yeah,' Eve said. 'Not bad.'

'Spicy,' Dad said, as if that was a flaw. Claire knew for a fact he ordinarily added Tabasco to half of what he ate. 'Mind if I get a refill?'

Eve jumped up like a jack-in-the-box. 'I'll get it!' But Dad was at the end of the table, closest to the kitchen, and he was already on his feet and heading that direction.

Michael and Shane exchanged looks. Claire frowned, trying to figure out what they were looking so alarmed about.

They sat in silence as the refrigerator opened, bottles rattled, and then it closed. Dad came back, one cold-frosted Coke in his hand.

In his other hand he held a beer. He sat it in the centre of the table and glared at Michael.

'You want to explain why there's beer in a refrigerator with a sixteen-year-old in the house?' he asked.

'Not to mention that none of you is old enough to be drinking it!'

Well, that was that. Some days, Claire thought, you just couldn't win.

✄ ✄ ✄

She had two days, and only because Dad agreed to allow her to go to the admissions office and file transfer paperwork. Michael tried his best, but even angelic good looks and complete sincerity weren't good enough this time. Shane had stopped finding it amusing at some point, and started yelling. Eve had gone to her room.

Claire had cried. A lot. Furiously.

She was so angry, in fact, that she barely cared that Mom and Dad were going to be driving out of Morganville in the dark, unprotected and unwarned. Michael took care of that, though, with a story about carjackers stealing SUVs in the area. That was the best anyone could do, and more than Claire wanted, anyway.

Dad had looked at her like she was a *disappointment*.

She'd never, ever been a disappointment before, and it totally pissed her off, because she didn't deserve it, not one bit.

Michael and Shane stood in the doorway, watching her parents hurry to their SUV in the dark. Shane, she saw, had a big hand-carved cross, and he was ready to charge to the rescue, even though he was mad as hell. He didn't need to, though. Mom and Dad got in their truck and drove away, into the hushed Morganville night, and Michael closed and locked the door and turned to look at Claire.

'Sorry,' he said. 'That could have been better.'

'You think?' she shot back. Her eyes were swollen and hot, and she felt like she might vibrate apart; she was so mad. 'I'm not leaving! No way!'

'Claire.' Michael reached out and put his hands on her shoulders. 'Until you're eighteen, you really don't have the right to say that, OK? I know, you're almost seventeen, you're smarter than ninety percent of the people in the world—'

'One hundred percent smarter than anybody else in this house,' Shane said.

'—but that doesn't matter. It will, but it doesn't right now. You need to do what they say. If you decide to fight them, it's going to get ugly, and Claire, we can't afford it. *I* can't afford it. You understand?' He searched her eyes, and she had to nod. 'Sorry. Believe me, it isn't the way I wanted it to happen, but at least you'll be out of Morganville. You'll be safe.'

He hugged her. She felt her breath leave for a second, and then he was gone, walking away.

She looked at Shane.

'Well, I'm not hugging you,' he said. He was standing close to her, so close she had to crane her neck way up to meet his eyes. And for a long few seconds, they didn't say anything; he just…watched her. In the living room, she heard Eve talking to Michael, but here in the hallway it was very quiet. She could hear the fast pounding of her heart, and wondered if he could hear it, too.

'Claire—' he finally said.

'I know,' she said. 'I'm sixteen. Heard it already.'

He put his arms around her. Not the way Michael had, exactly – she didn't know why it was different, but it was. This wasn't a hug; it was – it felt – *close*.

He wasn't holding himself back, that was it. And she relaxed against him with a breathless sigh, cheek against his chest, almost purring with relief. He rested his chin on the top of her head. She felt so *small* next to him, but that was all right. It didn't make her feel weak.

'I'm going to miss you,' he whispered, and she leant back to look up at him again.

'Really?'

'Yeah.' She thought – really thought – that he was going to kiss her, but just then, she heard Eve call, 'Shane!' and he flinched and pulled back, and the old Shane, the cocky Shane, was back. 'You made things exciting around here.'

He loped off down the hall, and she felt a pure burst of fury.

Boys. Why were they always such dumbasses?

The night did its usual tricks – creepy creaking sounds upstairs, wind hissing at the windows, branches tapping. Claire couldn't sleep. She couldn't get used to the idea that this room, this lovely room, was hers for only two more nights, and then she'd be carted off, humiliated and defeated, back home. No way would her parents let her go anywhere now. She'd have to wait out the next year and a half, which meant that her admission paperwork would have to be re-done, and she'd have to start all over…

At least it didn't matter now if she blew off classes, she thought, and punched her pillow into a more comfortable shape. Several times.

If she'd been asleep – even a *little* asleep – she'd have missed the knock on the door, as light as it was, but she was wired and full of restless energy, and she slipped out of bed and went to unlock it and swing it open.

It was Shane. He stood there, clearly wanting to come in, not daring to come in, as uncertain as she'd ever seen him. He was wearing a loose T-shirt and sweatpants, feet bare, and she felt a white-hot wave of – *something* – sweep over her. This had to be what he slept in. Or…maybe less than that.

OK, she *really* needed to stop thinking about that.

She became aware, a hot second later, that she was standing there in a thin oversized T-shirt – one of Michael's old ones – with bare legs from mid-thigh down. Half-naked wouldn't be overstating it.

'Hi,' she said.

'Hi,' Shane said. 'Did I wake you up?'

'No. I couldn't sleep.' She was acutely aware of the bed behind her, covers all twisted. 'Um, do you want to, um…come in?'

'Better not,' he said softly. 'Claire, I—' He shook his head, brown hair swinging loose around his face. 'I shouldn't even be here.'

But he wasn't leaving, either.

'Well,' she said, 'I'm sitting down. If you want to stand there, fine.'

She went to the bed and sat, careful how she did it. Legs together, prim and proper. Her toes barely brushed the carpet. She felt alive and tingling all over.

She looked down at her hands, at the ragged fingernails, and picked at them nervously.

Shane took two steps into the room. 'For the next two days, I don't want you leaving the house,' he said. Which was *not* what she was expecting him to say. Not at all. 'Your dad already thinks we're getting you drunk and staging orgies in the hallway. Last thing I want is to send you home with fang marks in your neck. Or in a coffin.' His voice dropped lower. 'I couldn't stand that. I really couldn't. You know that, right?'

She didn't look up. He came a step closer, and his bare feet and sweatpants came into her vision. 'Claire. You've got to promise me.'

'I can't,' she said. 'I'm not some little kid. And I'm not your sister.'

He laughed, low in his throat. 'Oh, yeah. That, I know. But I don't want to see you get hurt again.'

His hand cupped her chin in warmth, and tilted her face up.

The whole world hushed, one perfect second of stillness. Claire didn't even think her heart beat.

His lips were warm and soft and sweet, and the sensation just blinded her, made her feel awkward and scared. *I've never...nobody ever...I'm not doing it right...* She hated herself, hated that she didn't know how to kiss him back, knew he was measuring her against all those other girls, those *better* girls he'd kissed.

It stopped. Her heart was beating so fast it felt like a bird fluttering in her chest. She was flushed and hot and *warm*, so warm...

Shane pressed his forehead to hers and sighed. His breath warmed her face, and this time she kissed him, letting her instincts guide her, letting him pull her to her feet. Their hands were clasped, fingers laced, and parts of her – parts she'd only ever warmed up alone – were going full blast.

This time, when they came up for air, he pulled completely back. His face was flushed; his eyes were bright. Claire's lips felt swollen, warm, utterly deliciously damp. *Oh*, she thought. *I guess I should have done the tongue thing.* Putting theory into practice was hard when her brain kept wanting to short out entirely.

'OK,' Shane said. 'That – that shouldn't have happened.'

'Probably not,' she admitted. 'But I'm leaving in two days. It'd be stupid if I never even kissed you.'

She wasn't absolutely sure who kissed whom this time. Maybe it was gravity tilting, stars exploding. It felt like it. His hands were free this time, and they cupped her face, stroked her hair, her neck, down to her shoulders...

She gasped into his open mouth, and he moaned. *Moaned*. She had no idea a sensation could go through her like that, travelling through her skin and nerves like lightning.

His hands stopped right there, at her waist.

When their tongues touched, gentle and tentative and wet, it made her knees weak. Made her whole spine rattle like dry bones. Shane put his right arm around her waist, holding her close, and cupped the back of her head with his left.

OK, this was *kissing*. Serious kissing. Not just a kiss before moving out, not a goodbye, this was *Hello, sexy*, and wow, she'd never even *suspected* that it could feel this way.

When he let go, she fell back to sit on the bed, utterly weak, and she thought that if he followed her, she'd fall back and...

Shane took two giant-sized steps backward, then turned and walked out into the hall. Facing away from her. In a kind of dreamlike trance she watched the strong, broad muscles of his back moving under his shirt as he took deep breaths.

'OK,' he said finally, and turned around. But staying well out in the hall. 'OK, that really shouldn't have happened. And we're not going to talk about that, right? Ever?'

'Right,' she said. She felt like there was light dripping from her fingertips. Spilling out of her toes. She felt full of light, in fact, warm buttery sunlight. 'Never happened.'

He opened his mouth, then closed it, and closed his eyes. 'Claire—'

'I know.'

'Lock the door,' he said.

She got up and swung it mostly closed. One last look at him through the gap, and then she clicked it shut and flipped the dead bolt.

She heard a thump against it. Shane was slumped on the other side; she just knew it.

'I am *so* dead,' he muttered.

She went back to bed and lay there, full of light, until morning.

CHAPTER FOURTEEN

No sign of Shane on Monday morning, but she got up way early – just after Michael would have evaporated into mist, in fact. She showered and grabbed a Pop-Tart from the cabinet for breakfast, washed the dishes that had been dumped in the sink from last night's disaster of Parental Dinner – hadn't that been Michael's job? – and emptied out her backpack to stuff in the metal canister (to return to the chem lab, which made it borrowing, not stealing) and the Bible with its concealed secret.

And then she thought, *It won't do any good if they just steal it from me*, and took it out again and put it on the shelves, wedged in between an old volume 10 of the *World Encyclopaedia* and some novel she'd never heard of. Then she stepped out, locked the door, and began walking toward the school.

The chem lab was busy when she arrived between classes, and she had no trouble slipping into the supply room to put the canister back in place, after carefully wiping her fingerprints from everything she could think of. That moral duty done, she hustled to the admissions office to put in her paperwork to withdraw from school. Nobody seemed surprised. She supposed that there were a lot of withdrawals. Or disappearances.

It was noon when she walked down to Common Grounds. Eve was just arriving, yawning and bleary-eyed; she looked surprised to see Claire as she handed over the cup of tea. 'I thought you weren't supposed to leave the house,' she said. 'Michael and Shane said—'

'I need to talk to Oliver,' Claire said.

'He's in the back.' Eve pointed. 'In the office. Claire? Is there anything wrong?'

'No,' she said. 'I think something's about to be right for a change.'

The door marked OFFICE was closed. She knocked, heard Oliver's warm voice telling her to enter, and came in. He was sitting behind a small desk in a very small room, windowless, with a computer running in front of him. He smiled at her and stood up to shake her hand. 'Claire,' he said. 'Good to see you're safe. I heard there had been some…unpleasantness.'

Oliver was wearing a tie-dyed Grateful Dead T-shirt and blue jeans with faded patches on the knees – not so much style as wear, she figured. He looked tired and concerned, and she thought suddenly that there was something about him a lot like Michael. Except that he was here in the daytime, of course, and at night, so he couldn't be a ghost. Could he?

'Brandon is very unhappy,' he said. 'I'm afraid that there's going to be retaliation. Brandon likes striking from an angle, not straight on, so you'd better watch out for your friends, as well. That would include Eve, of course. I've asked her to be extra careful.'

She nodded, heart in her throat. 'Um…what if I have something to trade?'

Oliver sat down and leant back in his chair. 'Trade for what? And to whom?'

'I – something important. I don't want to be more specific than that.'

'I'm afraid you're going to have to be, if you want me to act as any kind of go-between for you. I can't trade if I don't know what I'm offering.'

She realised she was still holding her teacup, and put it down on the corner of the desk. 'Um…I'd rather do it myself. But I don't know who to go to. Whoever can order Brandon around, I guess. Or even higher than that.'

'There is a social order to the vampire community,' Oliver agreed. 'Brandon's hardly at the top. There are two factions, you know. Brandon is part of one – the darker side, I suppose you could say. It depends on your viewpoint. Certainly, from a human standpoint, neither faction is exactly lily-white.' He shrugged. 'I can help you, if you'll let me. Believe me, you don't want to try to contact these people on your own. And I'm not sure they'd even allow you to do so.'

She bit her lip, thinking about what Michael had said about the deals in Morganville. She wasn't good at it; she knew that. And she didn't know the rules.

Oliver did, or he'd have been dead a long time ago. Besides, he was Eve's boss, and *she* liked him. Plus, he'd been able to keep Brandon from biting her at least twice. That had to count for something.

'OK,' she said. 'I have the book.'

Oliver's grey eyebrows came down into a straight line. 'The book?'

'You know. The *book*.'

'Claire,' he said slowly, 'I hope you understand what you're saying. Because you can't be wrong about this, and you absolutely can't lie. Bluffing will get you, and all your friends, killed. No mercy. Others have tried, passing off fakes or pretending to have it, then running. They all died. *All of them*. Do you understand?'

She swallowed again, convulsively. Her mouth felt very dry. She tried to remember how it had felt last night, being warm and full of light, but the day was cold and hard and scary. And Shane wasn't here. 'Yes,' she whispered. 'I understand. But I have it, and I don't think it's a fake. And I'm willing to trade for it.'

Oliver didn't blink. She tried to look away, but

there was something about him, something hard and demanding, and she felt a real surge of fear. 'All right,' he said. 'But you can't do this by yourself. You're too young, and you're too fragile. I'll undertake this for you, but I'll need proof.'

'What kind of proof?'

'I need to see the book. Take photographs of at least the cover and one inside page, to prove that it's legitimate.'

'I thought vampires couldn't read it.'

'They can't, at least according to legend. It's the symbol. Like the Protection symbols, it has properties that humans can't really understand. In this case, it confuses the senses of vampires. Only humans can read the words inside – but a photograph removes the confusion, and vampires will be able to see the symbol for what it is. Wonderful thing, technology.' He glanced at the clock. 'I have a meeting this afternoon that I can't postpone. I'll come to your house this evening, if that's all right. I'd like a chance to speak with Shane and Eve, as well. And your other friend, the one I've never seen come in – Michael, correct? Michael Glass?'

She found herself nodding, a little alarmed and not even sure why she should be. It was OK, wasn't it? Oliver was one of the good guys.

And she had no idea whom else she could turn to, not in Morganville. Brandon? Right. There was a good option.

'Tonight,' she echoed. 'OK.'

She stood up and walked out, feeling strangely cold. Eve looked up at her, frowned, and tried to come after her, but there were people crowding at the coffee bar, and Claire hurried to the door and escaped before Eve could corner her. She didn't want to talk about it. She was sickly certain she'd just made a terrible mistake, but she didn't know what, or why, or how. She was so caught up in it, lost in her own head and lulled by the hot safety of the sun, not to mention people on the streets, that she forgot not all the dangers came at night in Morganville. The first warning she had, in fact, was the low rumble of an engine, and then she was being knocked off-balance and stumbling against the sun-heated finish of a van door, which slid aside.

She was being pushed from one side, pulled from the other, and before she could do more than yelp, she was in the van, bodies were piling on top of her, and the van door slammed shut on the sun. She slid on the carpeted floor as the van accelerated off, and heard whoops and laughter.

Girls' laughter.

Somebody was kneeling on her chest, making it hard to breathe; she tried to twist and throw her off, but it didn't work. When she blinked away stars she saw that the person on top of her was Gina, looking freshly made-up and fashion perfect, except for the sick gleam in her eyes. Monica was kneeling next to her, smiling a tight, cruel little smile.

Jennifer was driving. There were a couple of other girls in the van, too, ones she remembered from the basement confrontation at the dorm. Apparently, Monica was still recruiting, and these two had made the cut to Advanced Psycho School.

'Get off me!' Claire yelled, and tried to bat at Gina; Monica grabbed her hands and yanked them over her head, painfully hard. 'Bitch, get *off*!'

Monica punched her in the stomach, driving out what little air she had, and Claire whooped for breath. Gina's weight made it incredibly hard to breathe. Could you kill somebody like this? Smother a person like this? Maybe if the victim was small...like her...

The van was still going, taking her farther and farther away from safety.

'You,' Monica said, leaning over her, 'really pissed me off, fish. I don't forget things like that. Neither does my boyfriend.'

'Brandon?' Claire wheezed. 'Jeez, at least get one with a pulse!'

For that, she got punched again, and this time it hurt bad enough she started to cry, furious and helpless. Gina put a hand around her neck and began to squeeze. Not enough to kill her, just enough to hurt and make it even harder to gasp for precious little air.

They could keep this up for hours if they wanted. But Claire thought they probably had a lot more in store.

Sure enough, Monica reached in her pocket and brought out a lighter, one of those butane ones with a long, bright flame. She brought it close to Claire's face. 'We're going to have a barbecue,' she said. 'Roast freak. If you live, you're going to be hideous. But you shouldn't worry about that, because you probably won't live, anyway.'

Claire screamed with whatever she had, which wasn't much; it startled Monica, and it positively scared Jennifer, who was driving; she twisted to look back, turning the wheel while she did.

Mistake.

The van careened to the right, and smashed into something solid. Claire flew through the air, with Gina riding her like a magic carpet, crashed into the padded back of the seats, and Monica and Gina rolled in confusion as the van skidded to a stop.

Claire shook off her panic and lunged for the van door. She bailed out. The van had ploughed into the rear of another car, parked along the side, and car alarms were going off. She felt dizzy and almost fell, then heard Monica yelling furiously behind her. That pulled her together, fast. She began running.

This part of downtown was mostly deserted – shops closed, only a few pedestrians on the street.

None of them would look at her at all.

'Help!' she yelled, and waved her arms. 'Help me! Please—'

They all just kept walking, as if she were invisible. She sobbed for a second in horror, and then pelted around the corner and skidded to a stop.

A *church*! She hadn't seen a single one the entire time she'd been in Morganville, and there one was. It wasn't a big one – a modest white building, with a small-sized steeple. No cross on it, but it was unmistakably a church.

She darted across the street, up the steps, and hit the doors at a run.

And bounced off.

They were locked.

'No!' she yelled, and rattled the doors. 'No, come on, please!'

The sign on the door said that the church was open from sundown to midnight. What the hell…?

She didn't dare think too much. She jumped off the steps and ran around the side, then the back. Next to the dumpster there was a back door with a glass window in it. It was locked, too. She searched around and found a broken piece of wood, and swung it like a baseball bat.

Crash!

She scraped her arm reaching through the broken window for the lock, but she made it, and slammed the door behind her. She locked it, frantically looked around, and found a piece of black poster board to prop against the blank space where the window had been. Hopefully, it would pass a quick glance.

She backed away, sweating, aching now from the

crash and the run, and turned to go into the chapel. It was unmistakably a chapel, with abstract stained-glass windows and long rows of gleaming wood pews, but there was no cross, no crucifix, no symbol of any kind. The ultimate Unitarian church, she guessed.

At least it was empty.

Claire sank down on a pew midway back through the sanctuary and then stretched full length on the red velvet padding. Her heart was beating fast, so fast, and she was still so very scared.

Nobody knew where she was. And if she tried to leave, Monica might...

They were going to burn me alive.

She shivered and wiped tears from her cheeks and tried to think, think of *something* she could do to get out of this. Maybe there was a phone. She could call Eve or Shane? Both of them, she decided. Eve for the car, Shane for the bodyguard duty. Poor Shane. He was right – she really ought to stop calling him every time she needed brute strength. Didn't seem fair, somehow.

Claire froze, unable to breathe, as she heard a soft noise in the chapel. Like fabric moving. A bare whisper, maybe just a curtain moving in the air-conditioning breeze, right? Or...

'Hello,' said the very pale woman leaning over the pew and looking down on her. 'You would be Claire, I believe.'

✄ ✄ ✄

Once the paralysing terror receded just a little, Claire finally placed her. She knew she'd seen her; it had been just a split-second glance, but this was the woman – the vampire – who'd been brought to Common Grounds in a limousine after closing time.

What was she doing in a *church*?

Claire slowly sat up, unable to take her eyes off of the woman, who was smiling slightly. Light filtered in softly from the stained-glass windows and gave her a golden glow.

'I followed you,' the woman said. 'Although in truth, I do like this church quite a bit. Very peaceful, don't you think? A sacred place. And one that grants those within it a certain...immunity from danger.'

Claire licked her lips and tasted salt from sweat and tears. 'You mean you won't kill me here.'

The smile stayed intact. If anything, it widened a little. 'I mean exactly that, my dear. The same goes for my guards, of course. I assure you, they're present. I am never left alone. It is part of the curse of the position I hold.' She smiled and tilted her head an elegant fraction. Everything about her was elegant, from the shining golden crown of her hair to the clothes she was wearing. Claire wasn't much for noticing fashion, unless it was worn by girls kicking the crap out of her, but this outfit looked like something out of old formal photographs from her mother's time. Or grandmother's.

'My name is Amelie,' the woman continued. 'You

are, in a sense, already acquainted with me, although you might not be aware of it. Please, child, don't look so frightened. I absolutely assure you that no harm will come to you with me. I always give very clear warning before I do anything violent.'

Claire had no idea how to look any less frightened, but she clasped her hands in her lap to stop them from shaking. Amelie sighed.

'You are very new to our town,' she said, 'but I have rarely seen anyone disturb quite so many hornets in such a short time. First Monica, then Brandon, and then I hear you turn to my dear Oliver for advice...and now I see you running for your life through my streets... Well, I find you interesting. I find myself wondering about you, Claire. About who you are. *Why* you are.'

'I'm – nobody,' Claire said. 'And I'm leaving town. My parents are taking me out of school.' It suddenly seemed like a really good idea. Not so much running away as retreating.

'Are they? Well, we'll see.' Amelie made a shrug seem like a foreign gesture. 'Do you know who I am?'

'Somebody important.'

'Yes. Someone very important.' Amelie's eyes were steady in the dim light, of no real colour – grey, maybe? Or blue? It wasn't colour that made them powerful. 'I am the oldest vampire in the world, my dear. In a certain sense, I am the only vampire who matters.' She said it without any particular sense of pride. 'Although others may have differing opinions, of course. But they would be sadly, and fatally, wrong.'

'I – I don't understand.'

'No, I do not expect you to.' Amelie leant forward and put lean, elegant, white hands on the wooden pew in front of her, then rested her pointed chin on top of them. 'Somehow you have become mixed up in our search for the book. I believe you know the one I mean.'

'I – uh – yes.' No way was she going to confess what she had sitting at home. She'd made that mistake once already. 'I mean, I know about all the—'

'Vampires,' Amelie supplied helpfully. 'It is not a secret, my dear.'

'Vampires looking for it.'

'And you just happened to stumble into the operation at the library, in which we were combing through volumes to find it?'

Claire blinked. 'Does it belong to you?'

'In a way. Let's say that it belongs to me as much as it belongs to anyone alive today. If I am, strictly speaking, living. The old word was *undead*, you know, but aren't all living things undead? I dislike imprecision. I think we may have that in common, young lady.' Amelie tilted her head a little to the side. Claire was reminded, with a chill, of a nature film. A praying mantis studying its food-to-be.

'*Vampire* is such an old word. I believe I shall commission the university to find another term, a more – what is the new saying? – *user-friendly* term for what we are.'

'I – what do you want?' Claire blurted. And then, ridiculously, '...sorry.' Because she knew it sounded rude, and however scary this vampire, or whatever, might be, she hadn't been *rude*.

'That's quite all right. You're under a great deal of stress. I shall forgive your breach of manners. What I want is just the truth, child. I want to know what you have found out about the book.'

'I – um, nothing.'

There was a long silence. In it, Claire heard distant noises – somebody tugging on the front door of the church.

'That's unfortunate,' Amelie said quietly. 'I had hoped I would be able to help you. It appears that I cannot.'

'Um – that's it? That's all?'

'Yes, I'm afraid it is.' Amelie sat back again, hands folded in her lap. 'You may go the way you came. I wish you luck, my dear. You are going to need it. Unfortunately, mortal life is very fragile, and very short. Yours could be shorter than usual.'

'But—'

'I can't help you if you have nothing to offer me. There are rules to life in Morganville. I can't simply adopt strays because they seem winsome. Farewell, little Claire. Godspeed.'

Claire had no idea what *winsome* meant, but she got the message. Whatever door had been opened – whether it led to good things or bad – had slammed shut on her now. She stood up, wondering what to say, and decided that saying nothing might be the very best thing...

...and she heard the back door crash open.

'Oh, crap,' she whispered. Amelie looked at her in reproach. 'Sorry.'

'We are in a house of worship,' she said severely. 'Really, did no one teach your generation any sort of manners?'

Claire ducked behind a pew. She heard fast footsteps, and then Monica's voice. 'Ma'am! I'm sorry, I didn't know you were—'

'But I am,' Amelie said coolly. 'Morrell, aren't you? I can never keep any of you straight.'

'Monica.'

'How charming.' Amelie's voice changed from cool to ice-cold. 'I'll have to ask you to leave, Miss Morrell. You do not belong here. My seal is on this place. You know the rules.'

'I'm sorry, ma'am. I didn't think—'

'Often the case, I suspect. Go.'

'But – there's this girl – did she—?'

Amelie's voice turned to a hiss like sleet on a frozen window. *'Are you questioning me?'*

'No! No, so sorry, ma'am, it won't happen again, I'm sorry...' Monica's voice was fading. She was backing away, down the hall. Claire stayed where she was, trembling.

She almost screamed when Amelie's pale form rose up over the edge of the pew again and gazed down at her. She hadn't heard her move. Not at all.

'I suggest you go straight home, little Claire,' Amelie said. 'I would take you there, but that would imply more than I think I can afford just now. Run, run home. Hurry, now. And – if you have lied to me about the book, remember that many people might want such a valuable thing, and for many reasons. Be sure of why they want it before you give it over.'

Claire slowly took her hands away from her head and slid onto the seat of the pew, facing the vampire. She was still scared, but Amelie didn't seem…well…evil exactly. Just cold. Ice-cold.

And old.

'What is it?' Claire asked. 'The book?'

Amelie's smile was as faded as old silk. 'Life,' she said. 'And death. I can tell you no more. It wouldn't be prudent.' The smile vanished, leaving behind only the chill. 'I believe you really should go now.'

Claire bolted up and hurried away, checking over her shoulder every other step. She saw other vampires coming out – she hadn't spotted them, not one of them. One of them was John, from the library. He grinned at her, not in a friendly way. One of his eyes was milky white.

She ran.

✄ ✄ ✄

Wherever Monica and her friends had gone, it wasn't the way Claire ran – and run she did, the whole way to Lot Street. Her lungs were burning by the time she turned the corner, and she was nearly in tears with gratitude at the sight of the big old house.

And Shane, sitting on the front steps.

He stood up, not saying a word, and she threw herself at him; he caught her and held her close for a few seconds, then pushed her back for a survey of damage.

'I know,' she said. 'You told me not to go. I'm sorry.'

He nodded, looking grim. 'Inside.'

Once she was in, with the door safely locked, she babbled out the whole story. Monica, the van, the lighter, the church, the vampire. He didn't ask any questions. In fact, he didn't even blink. She ran out of words, and he just looked at her, expressionless.

'You,' he finally said, 'had better like the inside of your room, because I'm locking you in there, and I'm not letting you out until your parents come to load you in the car.'

'Shane—'

'I mean it. No more bullshit, Claire. You're staying alive no matter what I have to do.' He sounded flatly furious. 'Now. You need to tell me about Michael.'

'What?'

'I mean it, Claire. Tell me, right now. Because I

can't find him anywhere, and you know what? I can never find him during the day – damn! Did you feel that?' She did. A cold spot, sweeping across her skin. Michael, trying to tell her something. Probably *Hell no, don't tell him.* 'We can't get through this if we're not straight with each other.' Shane's Adam's apple bobbed as he swallowed. 'Is he – you know – one of them? 'Cause I need to know that.'

'No,' she said. 'No, he's not.'

Shane closed his eyes and slumped against the wall, hands to both sides of his head. 'God, thank you. I was going nuts. I thought – I mean, it's one thing to be a night person, but Michael – I was – I thought—'

'Wait,' Claire said, and took a deep breath. Cold settled over her again – Michael, trying to stop her. She ignored it. 'Quit it, Michael. He needs to know.'

Shane took his hands away from his head and looked around, then frowned at her. 'Michael's not here. I checked. I searched the damn place from top to bottom.'

'Yes, he is. Cold spot.' She held out her hand and waved it through the refrigerated air. 'I figure he's standing…right here.' She looked at her watch. 'He'll be back in about two hours, when the sun goes down. You can see him then.'

'What in the *hell* are you talking about?'

'Michael. He's a ghost.'

'Oh, come on! Bullshit! The dude sits here and eats dinner with us!'

She shrugged, threw up her hands, and walked

away. 'You wanted to know. Fine. Now you know. And by the way? I'm fine.'

'What do you mean, he's a ghost?' Shane caught up with her, came around her, and blocked her path. 'Oh, come on. Ghost? He's as real as I am!'

'Sometimes,' she agreed. 'Ask him. Better yet, watch him at dawn. And then tell me what he is, because ghost is about all I know to call him. The thing is, he can't leave the house, Shane. He can't help us. He's stuck here, and during the day, he can't even talk to us. He just – drifts.' She batted away the cold air again. 'Stop it, Michael. I know you're pissed. But he needs to know.'

'Claire!' Shane grabbed her and shook her out of sheer frustration. 'You're talking to thin air!'

'Whatever. Let go, I've got things to do.'

'What things?'

'Packing!' She pulled free and went upstairs, two steps at a time. Shane always slammed his door when he was mad; she tried it out. It helped.

The cold spot followed her. 'Dammit, Michael, get out of my room, you pervert!' Could you even be a pervert if you were dead? She supposed you could, if you had a working body half the time. 'I swear, I'm going to start taking my clothes off!'

The cold spot stayed resolutely put until she got the hem of her T-shirt all the way up to her bra line, and then faded away. 'Chicken,' she said, and paced the room, back and forth. Worried and more than a little scared.

Shane pounded on the door, but she stretched out on her bed, put a pillow over her face, and pretended not to hear him.

Dusk came, pulling a blue gauze over the sky; she watched the sun sink halfway down the horizon, then unlocked her door and stormed out. Shane was just coming out of Michael's bedroom. Still looking for someone he wasn't going to find. Not the way he thought, anyway.

'Michael!' Claire yelled from her end, and felt the cold settle around her like an icy blanket. Shane spun around, and she felt the mist gather, thick and heavy, and then she actually saw it, a faint grey shape in the air...

Eve's door flew open. 'What in the *hell* is going on around here?' she yelled. 'Could you guys keep it down to aircraft-carrier noise?'

...And then Michael just...appeared. Midway between all three of them, forming right out of a thick grey heavy mist, taking on colour and weight.

Eve screamed.

Michael collapsed to his hands and knees, retching. He fell on his side, then rolled over to stare up at the ceiling. 'Shit!' he gasped, and just stayed there, fighting for breath. His eyes looked wet and terrified, and Claire realised that it was like this for him every day. Every night. Frightening beyond anything she could even imagine.

Claire looked down the hall at Shane. He was frozen in place, mouth open, looking like a cartoon of himself. Eve, too, from her angle.

Claire walked over, held out a hand to Michael, and said, 'Well, I guess that settles things.'

He gave her a filthy, wordless look, and took her hand to pull himself up. He staggered and leant against the wall for support, shaking his head when she tried to help. 'In a minute,' he said. 'Takes a lot out of you.'

Eve said, in a high, squeaky, airless voice, 'The ghost! You're the ghost Miranda was talking about! Oh my God, Michael, you're the *ghost*! You *bastard*!'

He nodded, still concentrating on breathing.

Eve got control of her voice and squealed, 'That is without a doubt *the coolest damn thing I have ever seen in my entire life*!'

Shane looked...pale. Pale and shaken and – how predictable was this? – pissed. Michael met his eyes, and the two of them looked at each other for a long, silent second before Shane said, 'This is why you asked me to come back.'

'I—' Michael coughed. When he sagged this time, Eve threw his arm around her shoulders. He looked surprised, then pleased. 'Not just because—'

'I get it,' Shane said. 'I get it, man. I do. What the hell happened while I was gone?'

Michael just shook his head. 'Later.'

No, it wasn't that Shane was pissed after all, Claire realised. He turned away and pounded down the stairs before she could say anything, but she'd seen his eyes.

She knew.

He lost Alyssa. Now he thinks he's lost Michael, too. She didn't know how that felt, not really; she could imagine, but she was – she knew it – sheltered. She'd never really lost anybody, not even a grandparent. Grief was something in TV shows, in movies, in books.

She had no idea what to say to him. She'd thought that he'd just take it in stride, the way Shane seemed to take things, but...

'Claire,' Michael said. 'Don't let him leave.'

She nodded and left Eve supporting Michael in the hallway, the two of them looking surprisingly comfortable with the whole living-dead-not-dead thing. She supposed that if a ghost had to have a girlfriend, well, Eve was just about the best choice there was.

Shane was standing downstairs, just...standing. Not paying much attention to her or anything else. She reached out, ready to tap him on the shoulder, let him know she was here even if she was no help at all, but just then, there was a knock on the front door.

'I swear to God, if that's Miranda—' he grated. His fists were clenched at his sides.

'No, I think it's for me,' Claire said, and darted around him to run down the hallway. She checked the peephole first, and sure enough, there was Oliver, standing on the doorstep and looking uncomfortable. She supposed he had good reason... Jeez, hanging around *anywhere* after dark in

Morganville had to be like hanging an EAT ME sign on your back.

She unlocked the door and swung it open.

'I don't have a lot of time,' he said. 'Where are they? Shane and Eve?'

'Inside,' she said, and pulled it open wider, the universal signal for *Come in*. He didn't. He held up a hand instead, waved it in the air in front of him with a puzzled frown. 'Oliver?'

'I'm afraid you'll have to ask me in,' he said. 'It seems this house has some very detailed Protections in place. I can't come in unless you ask.'

'Oh. Sorry about that.' She was about to ask him inside when it occurred to her that maybe it wasn't the best idea, just asking people in without okaying it with the rest of the Glass House first. Especially since she was living here only another day. 'Um, can you wait just a second?'

'No, Claire, I really can't,' Oliver said impatiently. He was still wearing the hippie gear from Common Grounds, but somehow he looked…different. Odd. 'Please invite me in. I don't have time to wait.'

'But I—'

'Claire, *I can't help you if you won't trust me*! Now quickly, before it's too late, let me in!'

'But I—' She pulled in a deep breath. 'All right. I invite you—'

'No!' It was a roar from behind her, absolutely terrifying, and she threw herself to one side and covered her mouth with both hands to hold in her scream. It wasn't Shane bearing down on her; it was Michael. Shane was behind him, and Eve. 'Claire, get back!'

Michael looked like an avenging angel, and nobody argued with angels. Claire scurried backward, still holding her hands over her mouth, as Michael strode past her, right up to the doorway. The edge of his territory.

Oliver looked disappointed but, she saw, not particularly surprised. 'Ah, Michael. Good to see you again. I see you're surviving nicely.'

Michael didn't say anything, but from Claire's vantage point to the side, she saw the look he was giving Oliver, and it frightened her. She hadn't thought Michael could get that angry.

'What do you want here?' he asked tightly. Oliver sighed.

'I know you won't believe me,' he said, 'but in truth, I had the best interests of your young friend at heart.'

Michael laughed bitterly. 'Yeah. I'll bet.'

'Also your friend Shane—' Oliver's eyes darted past Michael to lock on Shane, then Eve. 'And of course my dear sweet Eve. Such a fine employee.'

Michael turned slowly to look at Eve, whose eyes were wide with what Claire hoped was horror. Or at least confusion. 'You know each other?' Eve blurted. 'But – Michael, you said you didn't know Oliver, and—'

'I didn't,' Michael said, and turned back, 'until he killed me. We were never formally introduced.'

'Yes,' Oliver said, and shrugged. 'Sorry about that. Nothing personal about it; it was an experiment of sorts that didn't quite work out. But I'm pleased to see you survived, even if not quite in the form that I'd hoped.'

Michael made a sound Claire hoped never to hear again from any person, living or dead. It was Eve's turn to clap her hands over her mouth, then quickly take them away to yell, 'Oh my *God*! Oliver!'

'We can discuss my moral shortcomings later,' he said. 'For now, you need to let me inside this house, and as quickly as possible.'

'You have *got* to be kidding,' Michael said. 'I think one of us dead in here is good enough. I'm not letting you in to kill the rest.'

Oliver studied him silently for a long moment. 'I'd hoped to be able to avoid this,' he finally said. 'Your little Claire is quite the prodigy, you know. She says she's found the book. I think she has quite a promising future in Morganville...provided she survives the night.'

Michael looked like he wanted to vomit. His eyes darted to Claire, then away. 'Doesn't matter. Go away. Nobody's asking you in.'

'No?' Oliver smiled widely, and his fangs came down with lazy slowness. That was absolutely the scariest thing Claire had ever seen, that and the sincerity in his eyes. 'I think someone will. Sooner or later.'

'I'd say over my dead body, but I think you already made that point,' Michael snapped. 'Thanks for the visit. Now fuck off, man.'

He started to close the door. Oliver held up a hand – not like he was trying to stop him physically, just a warning – and his fangs folded up to leave his face kind and trustworthy again. Like...the face of a really cool teacher, the kind who made school worth living through. That, Claire thought, was a bigger betrayal than anything else.

'Wait. Do they understand why they're here, Michael? Why you risked exposing your secrets to them?' Michael didn't stop. The door was swinging closed on Oliver. 'Shane, listen to me! *Michael needed someone living to activate the house Protection!* You think he cares about you, he doesn't! You're just arms and legs for him! Beating hearts! He's no different from me!'

'Except for the not-bloodsucking part, you freak!' Shane yelled, and then the door slammed shut on Oliver's face. Michael threw the bolt with shaking fingers. 'Christ, man. Why didn't you tell us?'

'I – about what?' Michael asked, not turning to face him. He looked pale, Claire saw. Scared.

'*Any damn thing!* How did this happen, Michael? How did you get to be—?' Shane made a gesture that was vague enough to mean anything.

'Was he trying to, you know, vamp you out?'

'I think so. It didn't work. This is as far as I got.' Michael swallowed hard and turned to face him. 'He's right about the Protections. The house won't enforce any Protection unless there's someone living in it. I don't exactly count. I'm – part of it now. I did need you.'

'Whatever, man. I don't care about that. I care that you went and got yourself drained by some damn leech while my back was turned—'

'He can't be a vampire,' Eve said suddenly. 'He can't. He's my *boss*! And...and he works days! How is that even possible?'

'Ask him,' Michael said. 'Next time you go to work.'

'Oh, right, as if I didn't just quit that job!' Eve moved up beside Michael and put her arms around him. He hugged her back, like it was the most natural thing in the world. Like they'd been doing that all along which, Claire admitted, maybe they had and she just hadn't known. Michael stroked Eve's hair. 'God, I am *so* sorry!'

'Not your fault,' he said. 'Not anybody's fault except his.'

'How'd you—?'

'I played a set at Common Grounds. I didn't know he owned the place. I was dealing with a guy named Chad—'

'Oh. Right. Chad died,' Eve said.

'Wonder how *that* happened?' Shane put in acidly.

'This guy – Oliver, but I never knew his name – said he was a musician and he was looking for a room to rent. I thought it was a good idea. He came over to see the house.' Michael closed his eyes tight, like he couldn't bear to see the pictures in his head again. Not that it would help, Claire knew. 'As soon as I asked him in. I felt it. But it was too late, and – he had friends.'

Shane cursed, one harsh word that boomed off the wood floor like a gunshot, and leant back against the wall, head down. Slumped. 'I should have been here,' he said.

'Then we'd both be dead.'

'And you still will be,' said Oliver's voice through the door. 'Eve, my dear. Listen to me. Listen to my voice. Let me in.'

'Leave her alone!' Michael roared, and turned to face the door.

Claire saw something happen in Eve's face – the will go out of it, the light go out of her eyes. *Oh no*, she thought, frozen, and tried to open her mouth to warn Michael.

Before she could do it, Eve said, 'Yes, Oliver. Come inside.'

And the lock snapped on the door with a crisp, bright ringing sound, and the door drifted open on the night, and Oliver stepped over the threshold.

CHAPTER FIFTEEN

Claire didn't even see Michael move; he was that quick. Until that moment she'd thought he was just a normal guy, really... OK, one who disappeared into mist during the day. But nobody moved that fast. Nobody human.

And *nobody* was that strong, either. Michael grabbed Oliver by the shoulders, lifted him into the air, and launched him headfirst down the hall to crash into the far wall. Claire dived out of the way. So did Shane, and Eve, although Eve was diving *toward* Oliver, not away. Shane got hold of her ankle and dragged her backward, kicking and screaming.

Michael went after Oliver. As the vampire was rolling to his feet, Michael smashed into him. Oliver was strong, and fast, but in this house Michael was unstoppable, and he was really, really angry.

'You fool!' Oliver screamed at him. 'Do you

understand what I said? *Claire has the book!*'

'I don't care!'

'You have to care! If you don't give it over, they'll rip all of you apart to get it! I'm trying to save you!'

Michael slammed his fist into his face two or three times, quicker than Claire could blink. Oliver went down again, scrabbling at the floor, then rolled over and stared furiously through tangled greying hair up at them. Vampires bled, after all, but it didn't quite look right – not red enough, and too thick. It trickled from the corners of Oliver's mouth as he snarled, fangs down, and tried to drag Michael close enough to bite. Michael hit him so hard that one of the fangs broke off and skittered away across the floor like an ivory dagger. Oliver shouted in surprise and pain and rolled, trying to protect himself.

'Eve!' Michael yelled, and dragged him by one foot down the hallway toward the door. 'Revoke the invitation! Do it!' Oliver was fighting him wildly now, ripping long raw scratches in the wooden floor with his fingernails, snarling and twisting to get free. '*Eve!*'

Shane lunged for Eve, pulled her to her feet, and shook her hard. That didn't work. She just stared right past him, her face still and dead.

Claire moved him out of the way and slapped Eve hard.

Eve yelped, clapped a hand to her wounded

cheek, and blinked. 'Hey! What the hell...?' And then she looked past Claire to the furious battle going on in the hallway, lips parted in amazement.

'Eve!' Michael yelled again. 'The invitation! You have to withdraw it *now*!'

'But I didn't—' Eve didn't waste time arguing. 'Hey! Oliver! Get the hell out of our house!'

Oliver went still. Completely still, like a dead man. Michael picked him up by an arm and a leg, and threw him out into the dark. Claire heard the vampire hit the pavement outside and curse as he rolled back to his feet and came back at the door.

He bounced off a solid cushion of air in the doorway.

'You're not welcome,' Michael grated. He had a cut on his face, bleeding a thick thread down the side of his neck, and he was breathing hard. 'And by the way? Eve quits.'

He slammed the door in Oliver's snarling face, and collapsed against it, shaking. He didn't look all-powerful anymore. He looked terrified. 'Michael?' Eve asked, breathless. 'You OK?'

'Peachy,' he said, and got it together. 'Eve, stay away from the door. He got to you once; maybe he can do it again. Claire! You, too. Stay away from the door.' He grabbed her by the arm and pulled her down the hall – which was a mess, wow, the floor all ripped up, the walls scraped and scratched – and shoved her down to a sitting position on the couch. 'Claire.'

'Um…yes?' Things were moving too fast. She didn't know what he was waiting to hear.

'The book?'

'Oh. Yeah. Well – see, there was this floor in the library where they were going through books, and Professor Wilson was stealing things, and—'

He held up a hand to stop her. 'Do you have the book?'

'Yes.'

'Please tell me you didn't bring it here.'

She blinked. 'Well – yes.'

Michael fell into the armchair, leant forward, and buried his face in his hands. 'Sweet baby Jesus, do you not pay *any attention* to what goes on in this town? You really have the book?'

'I…guess so.' She got up and started to retrieve it, but he raised his head and grabbed her wrist as she moved by him.

'No,' he said. 'Leave it, wherever it is. The less we know, the better. We need to figure out what we're going to do, because Oliver wasn't kidding around. He wouldn't have come here if he hadn't intended to kill us all for that book. As it was, he took a big chance. He knows how powerful the Protection is on this house.'

'That how come you could beat him?' Shane asked. 'Because you know, I'm your best friend, but you're just not that badass, man.'

'Thanks, asshole. Yeah. I'm part of the house, and that means I can use what the house has. It's strong. Really strong.'

'Good to know. So what's the plan?'

Michael took in a deep breath, then let it out. 'Wait for daylight,' he said. 'Eve. You ever see Oliver outside in the sun?'

'Um…' She thought hard. 'No. Mostly he stays in his office, or in the bar area, away from the windows. But I didn't think vampires could be awake during the day!'

Claire thought about the church Monica had chased her into, and the elegant, ancient woman sitting in the pews. 'I think they can,' she said. 'If they're old. He must be really old.'

'I don't care how old he is – he's not tanning,' Shane said. 'We wait for dawn, and then we get Claire and the book out of here.'

'She can't go home. They'll go there first,' Eve said. Claire went cold.

'But – my parents! What about my parents?'

Nobody answered her for a second or two, and then Shane came and sat down next to her. 'You think they'll listen? If we tell them the truth?'

'What, about Morganville? About vampires?' She laughed, and it sounded hysterical. 'Are you kidding? They'd never believe it!'

'Besides,' Eve said, and sat down on her other side to take her hand, 'even if you convinced them, they'd forget all about it once they were out of town. It's hard to be paranoid when you don't remember they're out to get you.'

'Ouch,' Shane agreed. 'OK, then. Running's out – for one thing, we can't throw Claire's parents to the vampire wolves...right?'

Michael and Eve nodded.

'And besides, same problem for Claire. Even if we got her out of town, she'd forget why she was running. They'd catch her.'

More nods.

'So what do we do?'

'Trade the book,' Claire said. They all looked at her. 'What? I was going to, anyway. In exchange for some things.'

'Like what?' Michael asked, amazed.

'Like – Brandon not holding Shane to his deal. And Monica and her freaks backing off of me. And... Protection for all the dorms on campus, so that the students are safe.' She blushed, because they were all staring at her like they'd never seen her before. 'That's how Oliver knew I had the book. I messed up. I was trying to make a deal, but I thought he was just, you know, a good guy who could help. I didn't know he was one of the vampires.'

'Oh, he's not one of them,' Michael said. 'He *is* them.'

Shane frowned. 'How do you know that, man?'

'Because in a way I'm one of them,' Michael replied. 'And something in me wants to do what he says.'

'But – not a big part, right?' Eve ventured.

'No. But he's definitely in charge.'

Shane got up and walked to the windows, twitched back the curtain, and looked out. 'No kidding,' he said.

'What've you got?'

'Vamp city, man. Check it out.'

Michael joined him at the window, then Eve. When Claire squeezed in, she gasped, because there were *dozens* of people in view, all standing or sitting facing the house. Unnaturally still. Eve dashed to another set of windows. 'Same here!' she called. 'Hang on!'

'Shane,' Michael said, and jerked his head after her. Shane loped off in pursuit. 'Well, so much for sneaking out. I think we're here for the night, at least. Most of them have to go underground during the day. Those that don't won't be able to stay out in direct sunlight – I hope – so maybe we'll have more options then.'

'Michael—' Claire felt like crying. 'I didn't know. I thought I was doing something good. I really did.'

He put his arm around her. 'I know. It's not your fault. It might have been a dumb idea, but at least it was a sweet one.' He kissed her cheek. 'Better get some rest. And if you hear voices, try not to listen. They're going to be testing us.'

She nodded. 'What are we going to do?'

'I don't know,' he said quietly. 'But we'll think of something.'

❧ ❧ ❧

Claire curled up on the corner of the couch, piled under an afghan; Eve took the other end. Nobody felt much like going upstairs to bed. Shane paced a lot, talking in low whispers with Michael, who hadn't once gotten out his guitar. The two of them looked wired. Ready for anything.

Claire didn't mean to fall asleep – she thought she was too scared – but she did, eventually, as night spun on toward morning. Voices whispered to her – Michael's, she thought, and then Shane's. *Get up*, the voices said. *Get up and open the door. Open the window. Let us in. We can help you if you'll just let us in.*

She whimpered in her sleep, sweaty and sick, and felt Shane's hand on her forehead. 'Claire.' She opened her eyes and saw him sitting there next to her. He looked tired. 'You're having a nightmare.'

'Don't I wish,' she muttered, tried to swallow, and discovered she was burning-up thirsty. She felt feverish and weak, too. Well, *this* was a perfect time to be catching the flu...

'Michael!' Oliver's voice came faint through the front door. 'Something you should see, my boy! Look out your windows!'

'Trap,' Shane said instantly, and reached out to grab Michael's arm as he walked by. 'Don't, man.'

'What's he going to do? Make faces at me?'

'If you start doing what he wants, it's hard to stop. Just don't.'

Michael considered that for a few seconds, then

pulled away and went on to the windows.

Where he stared out, frowning. There were red and blue flashing lights shining on the glass and reflecting on his skin.

'What is it?' Claire asked, and got up.

'Hey! Seriously, guys. Quit playing their game—'

'Cops,' Michael said. He sounded blank and shocked. 'They've got the whole street blocked off. They're moving people out.'

'What people? The vampires?' Eve wanted to know. She piled on at the window, too.

'Sheesh,' Shane said grumpily. 'Fine. Don't listen to me. If a vampire tells you to jump off a cliff...'

'They're evacuating the neighbourhood,' Michael said. 'Getting rid of witnesses.'

'Oh, shit,' Shane said, and jumped up and craned to look over Claire's shoulder. 'So just how screwed are we?'

'Well, the cops aren't vampires. And the Protections won't keep them out.'

As Claire watched, the six police cars, all with their lights running in blood-red and vein blue flashes, were joined by two long, skeletal fire trucks. One at each end of the block.

Michael said nothing, but his eyes narrowed.

'Oh, *shit*!' Shane whispered. 'They wouldn't.'

'Yeah,' Michael said. 'I think they would. If this book is that important, I think they'd do just about anything to get it.'

Oliver's face suddenly popped up in front of the

window. They all screamed – even Michael – and jumped back. Shane tried to push Claire behind him. She smacked at him until he left her alone.

She wanted to hear what Oliver had to say.

'It's nearly five o'clock,' Oliver said, his voice muffled by the window glass. 'We're running out of time, Michael. Either invite me in and give me the book, or I'm afraid this is going to get unpleasant.'

'Wait!' Claire balled her hands into fists. 'I want to trade for it!'

His eyes weighed her, and dismissed her. 'I'm very sorry, my dear, but that opportunity has come and gone. We're in much rougher waters now. Either hand over the book, or we'll come in and get it. I promise you, this is the best deal you're likely to get this side of hell.'

Michael yanked down the shade. 'Shane. You, Eve, and Claire get into the pantry room. Move it.'

'No way!' Eve declared. 'I'm not leaving you!'

He took her hand and locked eyes with her, in a way that made Claire's knees go weak even at several feet away. 'They can't hurt me, except by hurting the house itself. They can't kill me, except by destroying the house. Understand? You guys are the vulnerable ones. And I want you safe.'

He kissed her hand, darted a self-conscious look at Claire and Shane, and then kissed her lips, too.

'Huh,' Shane said. 'Thought so.' He took Claire's hand. 'Michael's right. Better get you girls someplace safe.'

'You, too, Shane,' said Michael.

'No way!'

'Not the time to be proving anything, dude. Just take care of them. I can take care of myself.'

Maybe, Claire thought. And maybe he just wanted them out of the way in case he couldn't.

Either way, she didn't have a chance to protest. Shane steered her and Eve into the kitchen, loaded them down with water and pre-packaged food like Pop-Tarts and energy bars, and helped them stack things in the dark, gloomy hiding place where Claire had spent her first morning in the Glass House.

She didn't know if Shane really might have followed Michael's orders – it was possible, she guessed – but just as they were pushing the last of the supplies into the narrow little doorway, there was a loud crashing of glass from the living room.

'What the hell?' Shane blurted, and ducked out to see what was going on. Claire went after him, and when she looked back, Eve was following, too.

But they didn't get very far, because the kitchen window smashed into splinters, and Claire and Eve stopped and turned to look.

Oliver was standing just outside the window. They heard more glass breaking, all over the house.

'Girls,' he said. 'I'm sorry to do this. Truly I am. But you're not giving me much choice. Last chance. Invite me in, and this can end peacefully.'

'Bite me!' Eve taunted. 'Oh, wait...you can't, can

you? Not from way out there!'

His eyes flared, and his fangs snapped down. *Threat display*. That was what it was called when a rattlesnake shook its tail, or a cobra spread its hood. He was giving them a clear sign that he didn't find them very funny.

'The book,' he said. 'Or your lives. That's the only deal you're going to get, Claire. I suggest you make the right choice quickly.'

'It's OK,' Eve said. 'They can't come inside.' Oliver nodded, his faded, curling hair blowing in the hot night wind. 'That's true,' he said. 'But then, I'm hardly all alone.'

And he stepped aside as a policeman, in uniform, broke out the remaining glass with a nightstick and hopped up on the windowsill to climb through.

Eve and Claire screamed and ran.

The living room was a mess of broken furniture, scattered papers, struggling bodies – Shane punched out some guy in a black jacket, who flew back out of the window and into the arms of some waiting, snarling vampires. Michael was fighting a couple more, whom he just bodily picked up and threw out. As Eve and Claire skidded into the room and broke right and left, the cop in pursuit ran headlong into Michael and got tossed out, as well.

'They're coming in!' Eve screamed, and slammed the kitchen door and jammed a chair under the handle. Michael grabbed the nearest bookcase – not the one with the Bible on it, Claire saw – and pulled it over to block the window, then leant the sofa against it.

'Upstairs!' he yelled. 'Move it!'

Shane grabbed Claire by the hand and pounded up the steps, half dragging her; she missed a step and stumbled, and pulled him off-balance just at the right moment, because the bat that was swung at his head missed and thumped into the wall with a crack of wood. Another person hiding at the top of the stairs, this one female and tall. Shane grabbed the bat away from her and menaced her with it, driving her back down the hallway. Claire recognised her – one of the dorm girls, Lillian.

'Don't!' Lillian yelled, and put up her arms when Shane pulled back the bat.

'Hell,' Shane spit in disgust. 'I can't hit a girl. Here, Claire. *You* hit her.' He tossed her the bat. Claire grabbed it and came to a clumsy batting stance, wishing she'd paid more attention in phys ed. Lillian screamed again and ran into the open doorway of Eve's room. Eve, coming up the stairs, screamed, too, for different reasons.

'Hey! That's *my* room, bitch!' And she flew in to grab Lillian by the hair, swing her around, and throw her out into the hall, then shoved her toward the stairs. 'Michael! This one needs to go out!'

She shoved her again. Lillian tottered down the steps, and shrieked once more before leaving the building at speed, propelled by Michael-power.

'Check the rooms,' Shane panted. 'If one got in, there are probably more. Don't take chances. Yell for help.'

Claire nodded and hurried to her room. It looked quiet, thank God – the windows were unbroken, and there was no sign of anybody hiding in the closets or under the bed. Same for the bathroom, although she had a bad shower-curtain moment. She heard crashing from down the hall. Shane had found somebody. She ran out into the hall and started to come to his defence, then hesitated when she saw that Eve's door was now open a crack.

She'd left it closed.

She opened it slowly, as silently as she could, and peeked around the edge...

...and saw Eve up against the wall, and Miranda holding a knife at Eve's throat. She recognised the bruises and bite marks on her neck first, then the faded blue eyes as the girl's head turned toward her.

'Don't,' Miranda said. 'I have to do this. Charles says I need to. To make the visions stop. I want it to *stop*, Claire. You understand, right?'

'Let her go, Miranda, OK? Please?' Claire swallowed hard and stepped into the room. She could hear fighting from down the hall. Shane and Michael were busy. 'You don't want to hurt Eve. She's your friend!'

'It's too much,' Miranda said. 'So many people dying, and I can't do anything. Charles said he'd make it go away. All I have to do is—'

'What? Kill Eve? Really, don't – you don't want to – to do anything—' Panicked, she looked to Eve for help. One thing was for sure: the pallor in Eve's face wasn't make-up.

'Yeah,' Eve said faintly. 'I'm your friend, Mir. You know that.'

Miranda shook her head so hard her dark hair flew. The knife trembled against Eve's throat, and she squeezed her eyes shut, whispering something that sounded like, '*Charles*,' and when she opened her eyes again she looked different. Not scared. Focused.

She's going to do something. I need to— Claire didn't have time to figure it out; she just moved, because Eve was moving, her arm flashing up and smacking Miranda's elbow. In the second that the knife was away from Eve's throat, Claire grabbed a thick handful of Miranda's hair and yanked, hard, dragging her backward. Miranda shrieked and slashed wildly at them. Eve's upraised arm got a bloody cut, and Claire moved backward, gasping, holding on to Miranda's hair and trying to stay out of cutting range.

Miranda swept the knife around and cut off the clump of hair a couple of inches away from Claire's knuckles. *Oh no...*

Miranda lunged at her, knife held out, and Claire ran into the black bedside table, toppled over onto the black satin comforter, and saw the knife coming for her.

'Hey!' Eve screamed, and spun Miranda around and slapped her, hard, across the face. Twice. When Miranda tried to stab her, Eve smacked the girl's hand into the wall and twisted her wrist until Miranda's fist opened and the knife dropped to the wood floor.

Miranda started crying. It was a hopeless, helpless sound, and if Claire hadn't been angry-scared, she might have actually felt sorry for her. 'No, no, I don't want to see it anymore, I don't want to – he said he'd make it stop—'

Eve grabbed her by the arm, opened up the closet door, and stuffed Miranda inside, then jammed a wooden chair under the door handle to hold it shut. She looked furious and really, really hurt. Her arm was bleeding all over the place – not spurting, but flowing pretty freely. Claire grabbed up a black towel lying on the bureau and pressed the makeshift bandage to the wound; Eve blinked, like she'd forgotten all about it, and held it in place.

'Maybe she was just under his spell. Like you were, when you—' OK, maybe it hadn't been smart to bring that up, Claire thought.

'That's why I slapped her,' Eve said. 'But I don't think that's it. Miranda's always been crazy. I just thought – well, I thought she wasn't *that* crazy.'

Eve looked better. More colour in her face, anyway...and then Claire thought, no, she looked *too* good.

Claire's eyes turned to the broken window.

Outside, there was a slight edge of sunlight climbing above the horizon, and the sky had turned a deep blue-grey.

'Michael!' she blurted. 'Oh my God!'

She left Eve and ran into the hall. Shane was just coming out of his room, shaking out his right hand. His knuckles were bloody. 'Where's Michael?' she yelled.

'Downstairs,' he said. 'What the hell is that?'

Claire realised with a shock that somehow she was still holding the handful of Miranda's severed hair. She made a face and let go, then fluttered her hand to shake off the clingy strands. 'You don't *even* want to know. Oh, Miranda's locked in Eve's closet, by the way.'

'Well, that's a bonus. Sorry, but I really don't like that kid.'

'She's not growing on me, either,' Claire admitted. 'Come on, we need to get to Michael.'

'Trust me, he's doing OK without us.'

'No, he's not,' she said grimly. 'The sun's coming up.'

He didn't get it for a second, and then he *did*, and oh, boy. He was gone before she could yell at him to wait for her.

She reached the bottom of the staircase a few seconds behind, and saw him race across to where Michael was grabbing another – presumably, human – intruder on his way in through the broken-down front door.

'I don't need you!' he yelled at them both, and tossed the guy halfway to Kansas. 'Get upstairs! Shane, show her where!'

Shane ignored him, plunged past him and into the hallway. Guarding the front door. Michael started to follow him, and stepped into the growing light from the back window.

He spun to look at it, then wordlessly at Claire. She saw the outright fear in his eyes. 'No,' he said. 'Not *now*!'

She couldn't say or do anything to help, and she knew it. 'How long...?'

The terrible look on his face pretty much answered the question, but he said it anyway. 'Five minutes. Maybe less. *Dammit!*'

As if the vampires knew, there was a rattle at the window behind the bookcase blocking it. It heaved uneasily, then started to topple forward. Michael got in between it and the floor, caught it, and flung it back upright, then braced it again with the sofa.

'Back up!' Michael ordered her, and she retreated to the stairs. She could hear Shane fighting in the hall again. 'Claire, you and Eve need to find a way to block everything. Seal it up. Don't let Shane—'

She wasn't sure what he was going to say, but just then he gasped and doubled over, and she knew that it was lost. He looked pale. Paler.

Mist.

Gone, along with a fading ghost of a scream.

Eve skidded to a stop beside her, eyes wide. 'He's gone,' she whispered, as if she really couldn't believe it. 'He left us.'

'He couldn't help it.' Claire took her hand. 'Come on, Eve, let's get the bookcase down the hall. We need to wedge it in the doorway.'

Eve nodded numbly. It was like all the fight had gone out of her, and Claire understood why... What hope was there now? Michael had been handling things, but without him...?

'Help me,' she said to Eve, and she meant it in every way she could.

Eve gave her a tiny little smile and squeezed her fingers. 'You know I will.'

Between the three of them, they managed to block the front door pretty thoroughly, wedging the bookcase in place and bracing it with two more at an angle. Sweaty, panting, scared, they looked at each other.

It got quiet. Weirdly quiet.

'Well?' Eve looked around the corner. 'I don't see anything...'

'Can we get to the pantry?' Claire asked. 'I mean, I don't hear anybody...'

'Too risky,' Shane said. He grabbed the phone from a pile of debris and started dialling on the fly, then dropped it. 'They cut the line.'

Eve pulled her cell phone out of a holster on her belt. Shane grabbed for it, checked the signal, and held up his hand for a high five. He was already dialling when they smacked it. 'Come on,' he muttered, pacing, listening. 'Pick up, pick up, pick up...'

He stopped in mid-step. 'Dad? Oh, damn, it's the machine – Dad, listen, if you get this, it's Shane, I'm at Michael Glass's house in Morganville, and I need shock and awe, man – come running. You know why.'

He flipped the phone shut and threw it to Eve. 'Upstairs, both of you. Get in the secret room. Michael? Are you with us?'

Claire shivered in a sudden cold draft. 'He's here.'

'Watch out for them,' Shane said. 'I – I kind of have a plan.' He said it as if he was half surprised.

'Girls. Upstairs. Now.'

'But—'

'Go!' He'd learnt how to yell orders from Michael, and it seemed to work, because Claire was moving for the stairs without any conscious decision to do it. The cold chill stayed around her, and she saw Eve shivering, too.

The upstairs was quiet, as well, except for the distant knocking sound of Miranda hammering on her door. 'I don't like this,' Claire said. 'Oliver knows Michael can't do anything after dawn, right?'

'I don't know,' Eve said, and chewed at her

bottom lip. Most of her make-up had sweated off or gotten wiped away; even her lips were normal lip colour now, for nearly the first time Claire could remember. 'You're right. It's weird. Why would they just give up now?'

'They haven't,' said a voice that Claire's tingling spine recognised before her brain. Michael's bedroom door opened, and standing there, smiling, was Monica Morrell. Gina and Jennifer were behind her.

They were all holding knives, and that was a hell of a lot scarier than Miranda, no matter how crazy she might be.

Eve got in between Claire and Monica and began backing her away, down the hallway. 'Get in your room,' Eve said. 'Lock the door.'

'Won't do you any good,' Monica said, leaning around Eve. 'Ask me why. Go on, ask me.'

She didn't have to. She heard the door open behind her, and whipped around to see a man in a police uniform stepping out into the hallway with his gun drawn.

'Meet my brother, Richard,' she giggled. 'Isn't he cute?' He might have been, but Claire couldn't look anywhere but at the gun, which was big and shiny and black. She'd never had a gun pointed at her before, and it scared her in ways that even knives didn't.

'Shut up, Monica,' he said, and nodded toward the far end of the hall. 'Ladies. Downstairs, please.

We don't have to make this bloody.' He sounded harassed more than anything else, like mass home invasion was just something standing between him and morning coffee.

Claire backed up, touched Eve, and whispered, 'What do we do?' She was asking Michael, too, for all the good it would do.

'I guess we go downstairs,' Eve said. She sounded defeated.

The chill swept across them stronger than ever.

'Um, I think that's a no?' Warm air flooded in. 'That's a yes?' More warm air. 'You're kidding me, Michael. *Stay here?*' Fine, if you were already a ghost, but how the hell were the two of them supposed to fight off three girls with knives and a cop with a gun?

Eve fainted. She did it convincingly, too, so well that Claire wasn't totally for sure that she wasn't really out. Monica, Gina, and Jennifer looked down at her, frowning, and Claire bent over her, fanning at her face. 'She got cut,' she said. 'She's lost a lot of blood.' She hoped that was an exaggeration, but she wasn't too sure, because the black towel had fallen away from Eve's arm and it looked soaked.

'Leave her,' said Monica's brother. 'We only need you, anyway.'

'But – she's bleeding! She needs—'

'Move.' He shoved her, and she nearly ran into the knife Gina was holding out. 'Monica, for God's sake, back the hell off, will you? I think I can handle some little girl!'

Monica frowned at him. 'Oliver said we could have her when it's over.'

'Yeah, when it's over. Which isn't now, so *back the hell off*!'

She shot him the finger, then stepped back to let Claire move past her. Claire did it as slowly as she could, manufacturing a crying jag and some shaking that, once started, felt too real to stop.

'See?' Monica said over her shoulder to Jennifer. 'Told you she was a punk.'

Claire doubled over, moaning, and very deliberately puked all over Monica's shoes. That was all it took. Monica screamed in horror and slapped her, Gina grabbed her, Jennifer stepped away, and Richard, confused by all the sudden girl fighting, took a couple of steps back so he wouldn't put a bullet in the wrong one.

'Hey!' Shane's voice, loud and angry. He was on the stairs, looking through the railing at them. 'Enough already. I'll give you the damn book. Just leave them alone.'

'Not fair,' Monica muttered, glaring at him. He glared right back, looking like he'd take back that hitting-a-girl rule, just once. Gladly. 'Richard, shoot him.'

'No,' Richard said wearily. 'I'm a *cop*. I only shoot who I'm told to shoot, and you aren't the chief.'

'Well, I will be. One day.'

'Then I'll shoot him when you are,' he said. 'Shane, right? Get up here.'

'Let them walk out of here first.'

'Not going to happen, so just get your ass up here before I decide I don't need either one of them.' Richard cocked the gun for emphasis. Shane slowly came up to the top of the steps and stopped. 'Where is it?'

'The book? It's safe. And it's someplace you'll never get it if you piss me off, Dick.'

Richard fired the gun. Everybody – even Monica – screamed, and Claire looked down at herself in shock.

He'd missed. There was a smoking round hole in Michael's door.

Oh. He *hadn't* missed.

'Kid,' Richard said wearily, 'I am *not* in the mood. I haven't slept in thirty-six hours, my sister's crazy—'

'Hey!' Monica protested.

'—and you're not *my* high school crush—'

'He is *not* my high school crush, Richard!'

'The point is, I couldn't give a crap about you, your friends, or your problems, because for me this isn't personal. Monica will kill you because she's nuts. I'll kill you because you make me kill you. Are we straight?'

'Well,' Shane said, 'that's kind of a personal question.'

Richard aimed directly at Claire. It wasn't much

of a change, but she definitely felt it, like being in the centre of the spotlight instead of just on the edges, and she heard Shane say, 'Dude, I'm kidding, all right? Kidding!'

She didn't dare blink, or move her eyes away from the gun. If she could just keep staring at it, somehow, that would keep him from shooting her. She knew that didn't make sense, but...

In her side vision she saw Shane reach behind his back and pull out a book. Black leather cover. *Oh no. He's really going to...he can't. Not after all this.* Although she didn't have any answers for how he was supposed to avoid it, either.

Shane held up his left hand, showing it empty, and held out the black Bible with his right.

'That's it?' Richard asked.

'Swear to God.'

'Monica. Take it.'

She did, scowling at Shane. 'You are *not* my high school crush, idiot.'

'Great. I can die happy, then.'

'I'm shooting the next person who talks who isn't my sister,' Richard said. 'Monica?'

She opened the Bible. 'There's a hole in it. And another book.' She stopped, staring at the inside. 'Oh my God. It really is. I thought for sure she was bull-shitting us.'

'She knows better. Let me see.'

Monica tilted the open Bible toward him, and Claire's last faint hope went away, because yes, that was the cover, with its scratchy home-engraved symbol.

Shane had done it. He'd given it up.

Somehow she'd expected better.

'So. We're square, right?' Shane asked tensely. 'No shooting or anything.'

Richard reached out, took the Bible from Monica, and flipped it close to tuck it under one arm. 'No shooting,' he agreed. 'I meant what I said. I'll only kill you if you make me. So thanks, I really didn't need the paperwork.'

He walked past Shane to the stairs, and started down.

'Hey, wait!' Shane said. 'Want to take your psycho sister with you?'

Richard stopped and sighed. 'Right. Monica? Let's go.'

'I don't want to,' she said. 'Oliver told me I could have them.'

'Oliver's not here, and I am, and I'm telling you that we have to go. Right now.' When she didn't move, he looked back. 'Now. Move, unless you want to fry.'

She blew Claire and Shane a mocking kiss. 'Yeah. Enjoy the barbecue!'

She followed her brother down. Gina went after, and that just left Jennifer standing there, looking oddly helpless even with a knife in her hands.

She bent over and put it on the floor, held up her hands, and said, 'Monica set a fire. You should get out while you can, and run like hell. It probably won't help, but – I'm sorry.'

And then she was gone. Shane stared after them for a frozen second, then moved over to kneel next to Eve. 'Hey. You OK?'

'Taking a nap,' Eve said. 'I thought maybe if I stayed down, you'd have it easier.' She sounded shaky, though. 'Help me up.'

Shane and Claire each took a hand and pulled her up; she swayed woozily. 'Did I get that right? You actually handed it over?'

'You know what? I did. And it kept you guys alive, so there you go. Hate me.' He was going to say something else, but then stopped and frowned and nodded down the hallway.

There was a thin thread of smoke curling out from underneath the door of Claire's bedroom.

'Oh my God!' she gasped, and ran for it; the knob was hot. She instantly let go and backed away. 'We have to get out of here!'

'Like they're going to let us go?' Shane asked. 'And no way am I letting this house burn. What about Michael? He can't leave!'

She hadn't even thought of that, and it hit her hard. Michael was trapped. Would he die if the house burnt? *Could* he? 'Fire trucks!' she yelled. 'There are fire trucks outside—'

'Yeah, to keep everything *else* from going up,' Eve said. 'Trust me. This is their easy answer. The Glass House goes up in flames, along with all their problem kids. Nobody's going to help us!'

'Then we have to do it,' Shane said. 'Yo, Michael! You there?'

'Here's there,' Eve said. 'I'm cold.'

'Anything you can do?'

Eve looked puzzled. 'Yes? No? Oh. Maybe. He says maybe.'

'Maybe's not good enough.' Shane opened the door to Eve's room and grabbed the black comforter off the bed. 'Blankets, towels, whatever, get it in the bathroom and soak it down. Oh, and let Miranda out, will you? We can hate her later.'

Claire kicked the chair out of the way from under the doorknob. The closet door flew open, and Miranda spilt out, coughing. She took one look at them and ran for the stairs.

'My clothes!' Eve yelped, and grabbed a double armful of hangers, then ran to Michael's room to dump them in a pile.

'Yeah, way to stay focused, Eve!' Shane yelled. He had the tap going in the bath, and seconds later he was back, dragging the soaking wet bundle. 'Stay back.'

He kicked open the door, and behind it Claire saw fire licking from the curtains up toward the ceiling. Her bed was on fire, too. It looked like that was where Monica had started it, since it was mostly in flames.

'Be careful!' she yelled, and hesitated to watch as Shane yanked the curtains down, threw the wet comforter over the bed, and began stomping down flames.

'Don't just stand there!' he said. 'Blankets! Towels! Water! *Move!*'

She dashed off.

CHAPTER SIXTEEN

The whole house smelt like smoke and burnt mattress, but on the whole, it could have been a lot worse. Claire's room was a mess, and her bed and curtains were a dead loss. Scorches on the floor and smoke damage on the ceiling.

Still.

Shane dumped more water on the mattress, which was already a sodden mess, and collapsed against the wall next to Claire and Eve.

'They've got to be wondering why we're not all screaming and burning by now,' Eve said. 'I mean, logically.'

'Go look.'

'You go look. I've had a tough night.'

Claire sighed, got up, and went to the unbroken window at the far end of the room. She couldn't see anything. No vampires, obviously, since the sun was blazing in the sky by now, but no human flunkies, either. 'Maybe they're all out front,' she said.

In the silence, she distinctly heard...the doorbell. 'You're kidding me,' Shane said. 'Hey, did you order pizza? Good thinking. I'm starved.'

'I think you have brain damage,' Eve shot back.

'Yeah, because I'm starved.'

There was a crash from downstairs, and Shane stopped smiling. His eyes went dark and focused. 'I guess this is it,' he said. 'Sorry. Last stand at the Alamo.'

Eve hugged him and didn't say a word. Claire walked over and hugged each of them in turn, Shane last so she could spend more time doing it. There really wasn't enough time, though, because she heard footsteps coming up the stairs, and she felt a strong chill sweep over her. Michael was with them. Maybe that was his version of a hug.

'Stay strong,' she heard Eve whisper in her ear. She nodded and took Eve's hand. Shane stepped out in front, which was – she knew by now – just what Shane did. He picked up the baseball bat he'd retrieved from down the hall and got ready.

'There's no need for that,' said a light, cool voice from the hallway. 'You must be Shane. Hello. My name is Amelie.'

Claire gasped and peeked around his broad back. It was the blond vampire from the church, looking perfectly cool and at ease as she stood there, hands folded.

'You can put that away,' Amelie said. 'You won't need it, I assure you.'

She turned and left the doorway. The three of them looked at one another.

Is she gone? Eve mouthed. Shane edged up to the doorway and looked out, then shook his head. *What's she doing?*

That was obvious one second later, as there was a faint click and the panelling on the other side popped free.

Amelie opened the hidden door and went up the steps.

'I think you have some questions,' she called down. 'I have some, as well, as it happens, and it would be prudent if we indulged each other. If not, then of course you are free to go but I must warn you that Oliver is not happy. And when Oliver is unhappy, he tends to be rather childish about lashing out. You are not, as they say, out of the woods quite yet, *mes petits*.'

'Vote,' Shane said. 'I'm for leaving.'

'Stay,' Eve said. 'Running won't do us any good, and you know it. We need to at least hear what she has to say.'

They both looked at Claire. 'I get a vote?' she asked, surprised.

'Why wouldn't you? You pay rent.'

'Oh.' She didn't even have to think about it. 'She

saved my life today. I don't think she's – well, maybe she's bad, but she's not, you know, *bad*. I say we listen.'

Shane shrugged. 'Whatever. You go first.'

Amelie had settled herself on the antique Victorian settee. There were two other vampires in the room, standing very quietly in the corner, both wearing dark suits. Claire swallowed hard and fought an urge to back up and change her vote. Amelie smiled at her, lips closed, and gestured elegantly at the chair next to the sofa. 'Claire. Ah, and Eve, how lovely.'

'You know me?' Eve asked, surprised. She took a look around at the other two vampires.

'Of course. I always pay attention to the dispossessed. And your parents are particular favourites of mine.'

'Yeah, great. So who the hell are you?' Shane asked, blunt as ever. Amelie regarded him for an instant in surprise.

'Amelie,' she said, as if that explained everything. 'I thought you knew whose symbol you wore from birth, my dear.'

Shane looked pissed off. Of course. 'I don't wear any symbols.'

'That's true. You don't now.' She shrugged. 'But everyone in this town did once, including those from whom you sprang. One way or another, you are owned, body and soul.'

Shane, for once, didn't try a comeback. He just stared at her with dark, angry eyes. She didn't seem bothered.

'You have a question,' Amelie stated. Shane blinked.

'Yeah. How did you get in here? Oliver couldn't.'

'An excellent question, well phrased. And were I any other vampire, I would not be able to do so. However, this house is *my* house, first and foremost. I built it, as I built several such in Morganville. I live in each of them in turn, and while I am in residence the Protections will defend me from any enemy, either human or vampire. While I am absent, they will exclude vampires, if the residents are human, and of course humans if the residents are vampires. Unless the proper permissions are given.' She inclined her head. 'Does that answer your question?'

'Maybe.' Shane chewed on it a little, then said, 'Why didn't it protect Michael?'

'He gave Oliver permission to enter, and, in doing so, forfeited the house's Protection. However, the house did what it could to preserve him.' Amelie spread her hands. 'Perhaps it helped that Oliver was, in fact, not trying to destroy him but to change him.'

'Into a vampire,' Eve said.

'Yes.'

'Yes! I always wanted to ask why that doesn't work. I mean, the vampires keep on biting, but...?'

Amelie said nothing. She seemed to be thinking, or remembering; either way, it was a long and uncomfortable silence before she said, 'Have you children any concept of geometric progression?'

Claire raised her hand.

'And how many vampires would it take to turn the entire world into vampires, if it was so simple as that?' Amelie smiled as Claire opened her mouth. 'My dear, I do not expect you to answer, though if you would like to work out the math of it and tell me someday, I should be most interested to see it. The truth is that we came very near to it, in my younger years, when humans were much fewer. And it was agreed – as it has lately been agreed among you humans – that perhaps conservation of game is a wise idea. So we – removed the knowledge of how to create more vampires, simply by refusing to teach it. Over time, the knowledge was lost except to the Elders, and now it is lost altogether, except in two places.'

'Here?' Claire asked.

'Here,' Amelie said, and touched her temple. 'And there.'

She pointed at Shane.

'What?' Claire and Eve both blurted, and Claire thought, *Oh my God I kissed him and he was a vampire*, but Shane was looking odd, too. Not lost, exactly.

Guilty.

'Yeah,' he said, and put his hand in the pocket of

his blue jeans. He pulled out a small book. The cover – Claire could read it from where she sat – read *Shakespeare Sonnets*. 'It was all I could think of.'

He tipped it sideways, and the pages slid out, away from the cover. Sliced neatly at both edges of the binding.

'Very clever,' Amelie said. 'You gave them the cover, filled with words they did not want, and kept for yourself what was important. But what if I told you that it was the cover they were after, and not the contents?'

He looked shaken. 'I had to play the odds.'

'Wise gamesmanship,' she said. 'In fact, I told you that Oliver is unhappy, and so he is, because he has allowed *that*' – she nodded toward the pages – 'to slip through his fingers. And so I find that I come to you for a favour.'

His eyes lit up, and he said, 'A favour? Like a deal?'

'Yes, Shane. I shall make a deal for what you hold in your hand, and I promise you that it is the only deal that matters, as I am the only vampire that matters. I will take the book, and destroy the last written record of how vampires may be created, which will ensure my continued survival against my enemies, who will not dare to move against me for fear of losing what only I know.' She sat back against the puffed cushions, studying him very calmly. 'And for this, you and all in this house will receive my Protection for as long as you should choose to have it. This will cancel any other, lesser contracts you might have made, such as the agreement you made with Oliver, through Brandon.'

'Oliver – is Brandon's boss?' Claire asked.

'Boss?' Amelie considered that, and nodded. 'Yes. Exactly. While I do not command Oliver, neither can he command me. Until he discovers the secrets I hold, he cannot unseat me in Morganville, and he cannot create his own followers to overwhelm mine. We are...evenly matched.'

Shane looked down at the book in his hand. 'And this would have changed that.'

'Yes,' she said softly. 'That book would have destroyed us all in the end. Vampires as well as humans. I owe you a debt for this, and I will pay it as well as circumstances will allow.'

Shane thought about it for an agonising second, then looked at Eve. She nodded. Claire nodded when he checked for her approval, and then he held the book up. 'Michael?' he asked. 'Yes or no?' After another long second, he sighed. 'Guess that's a yes. Well, anything that pisses off Oliver is a good deed, so...' He held it out to Amelie.

She made no move to take it. 'Understand,' she said, and her eyes were bitter cold, 'that once this is done, it is done. Your Glass House will remain, but you are bound together. None may leave Morganville, after. I cannot risk your knowledge escaping my control.'

'Yeah, well, if we go now, we're toast anyway, right?' Shane kept holding it out. 'Take it. Oliver was right about one thing: it's nothing to us but death.'

'*Au contraire*,' she said, and her pale white fingers took it from his. 'It is, in fact, your salvation.'

She stood, looked around the room, and sighed a little. 'I have missed this place,' she said. 'And I believe it has also missed me. Someday I will come back.' She pressed the hidden catch on the arm of the settee, and without another word to them turned to leave.

'Hey, what about the cops?' Shane asked. 'Not to mention all those people who tried to kill us today?'

'They answer to Oliver. I will make it known that you are not to be troubled. However, you must not further disturb the peace. If you do, and it is your fault, I will be forced to reconsider my decision. And that would be…unfortunate.' She gave him a full smile. With fangs. '*Au revoir*, children. Do take care of the house more carefully in the future.'

Her two vamp guards went with her. Smoke and silence. There was no sound on the stairs after. Claire swallowed. 'Um…what did we just do?' she asked.

'Pretty much all we could,' Shane said. 'I'm checking the street.'

They ended up going down together, in a group – Shane with the bat, Eve with the knife Jennifer had abandoned, and Claire armed with a broken chair leg sharp on one end.

The house was deserted. The front door was standing open, and out on the street, cop cars were pulling away from the curb around the big black Cadillac. A limousine was leaving, too. Its tinted windows cast back blinding reflections of the sun.

It was all over in seconds. No cars, no vampires, nobody hanging around. No Monica. No Richard. No Oliver.

'Crap,' Shane said. He was standing on the porch, looking at what was hanging next to the doorbell. It was a black lacquered plaque with a symbol on it. The same symbol that had been on the book cover he'd sent to Oliver. 'Does that mean she wrote the damn book, too?'

'I'll bet she did, for back-up,' Eve said. 'You know, the symbol's also on the well in the centre of town. It's the Founder symbol.'

'She's the Founder,' Shane said.

'Well, somebody had to be.'

'Yeah, but I figured it was a *dead* somebody.'

'Funny,' Claire said, 'but I think it *is* a dead somebody.'

Which made Shane laugh, and Eve snort, and Shane slung his arm over her shoulders. 'You still quitting school?' he asked.

'Not if I can't leave town.' Claire smacked herself in the head. 'Oh my *God*! I can't leave town! I can't *ever leave town?* What about school? Caltech? *My parents?'*

Shane kissed her on the forehead. 'Tomorrow's problems,' he said. 'I'm going with let's just be glad there's a tomorrow, at this point.'

Eve closed the front door. It swung open again in the breeze. 'I think we're going to need a new door.'

'I think we're going to need Home Depot.'

'Do they sell stakes at Home Depot here?' Claire asked. Shane and Eve looked blank. 'Dumb question. Never mind.'

CHAPTER SEVENTEEN

Clean-up took pretty much all day, what with the broken furniture, the shattered windows, the front and back doors, and hauling Claire's damaged mattress out to the curb. They were just sitting down to dinner when the sun went behind the horizon, and Claire heard the sound of a body hitting the floor, followed by dry retching.

'Michael's home,' Eve said, as if he'd just come back from school. 'You guys dig in.'

It took a while before she came back with Michael. Holding hands. Shane got up, smiling, and held up his hand. Michael high-fived it.

'Not bad, brother,' Michael said. 'The girls gave you enough time for the switch.'

'Even though they didn't know. Yeah. Worked out,' Shane said, pleased. 'See? My plans don't all suck. Just most of them.'

'So long as we keep on being able to tell the difference.' Michael pulled up a chair. 'What's for –

oh, you're kidding me. Chilli?'

'Nobody wanted to go to the store.'

'Yeah, I guess.' Michael closed his eyes. 'I'm saying a prayer. Maybe you ought to, too. It's going to take us a miracle to get through this.'

Whether he was serious or not, Claire sent the prayer up toward heaven, and she thought the others did, too. So it seemed kind of miraculous when the doorbell rang.

'At least they're getting more polite when they try to kill us,' Shane said. Michael got up and went to the door. After a second's hesitation, they all got up and followed.

Michael swung the new door open. Outside, in the glow of the porch light, stood a middle-aged man with a scraggy beard and a huge scar down one side of his face, dressed in black motorcycle leather. Behind him were two more guys, not quite as old and a whole lot bigger and meaner-looking.

Bikers. Claire nearly choked on her bite of chilli. The man nodded.

'Son,' he said, looking past Michael right at Shane. 'Got your message. Cavalry's here.' He walked right in, past the threshold, and ignored Michael like he wasn't even there. 'About time you got your ass in gear. Been waiting for you to call for six damn months. What kept you? Took you this long to find the head bloodsucker?'

They followed him into the living room. Michael turned to look at Shane, who was turning red. Not meeting anybody's eyes, really. 'Things have changed, Dad,' he mumbled.

'Nothing's changed,' Shane's dad said, and turned to face them, hands on hips. 'We came to kick us some ass and kill us some vampires, just like we planned all along. Time to get some payback for Alyssa and your mother. Nothing's going to change that.'

'Dad, things are *different* now, we can't—'

Shane's father grabbed him by the hair, quick as a snake. There were tattoos on his hand, ugly dark blue smudges, and he forced Shane's head back. 'Can't? *Can't?* We're going to burn this town down, boy, just like we agreed. And you're not changing your mind.'

'Hey!' Michael said sharply, and reached out for Shane's dad. When he touched him, something happened, something like an electric shock that flared blue white in the room and raised the hair on Claire's arms. Michael flew back and hit the wall, too stunned to do anything.

'No!' Shane yelled, and tried to pull free. He couldn't. 'Dad, no!'

Shane's dad nodded to one of his biker buddies. 'Yep. He's one of them,' he said. 'Take care of it.'

The biker guy nodded back, pulled a knife from his belt, and advanced on Michael.

'*No!*' Shane screamed it this time. Claire took a hesitant step forward, and stopped when Michael's wide blue eyes locked on hers. Eve was screaming, and so was Shane.

Miranda saw this, she thought. Michael was even standing on the rug Miranda had pointed to when she'd said, *And he died...right...there.* It hadn't been his first death.

It was his second.

'Guys, stay out of it!' Michael said sharply when Eve tried to lunge toward him and get between him and the biker. He was still backing away, and this time, he looked afraid. He hadn't been afraid of the vampires and all their minions, but this time...

The biker moved faster than anybody Claire had ever seen, except vampires; she didn't even see what happened, just heard the heavy thud as Michael hit the floor. The biker went down with him, holding him flat with one huge hand while the other one raised the knife.

'No, Dad, God, I'll do whatever you want!'

'Shut up,' Shane's dad said, and threw Shane toward the sofa. He sprawled there, and Claire ran over to him and put her arms around him. 'You bet you will. You three are going to tell me which vamps to strike first. Because it's us against them now, and don't you forget it.'

'Three?' Eve said faintly. Her huge eyes were locked on Michael, and the biker, and the knife.

'Three,' said Shane's dad, and nodded to the biker.

They all screamed as the knife came down.

From the diary of Eve Rosser
Autumn 2006

A word about birthdays. I was kinda disappointed when Michael didn't even hint around that his was coming up and he was all grown-up and everything, turning nineteen – not that we didn't know! Shane gave him some magazine neither one of them wanted me to see – like, thanks, guys, I can't figure out porn. Also, a twelve-pack of beer that neither one of them was old enough to buy. Trust Shane to come up with an all-illegal celebration.

Good thing I was on the case, because I bought Michael a cake. OMG, it was totally adorable, too: it was all layers with black and purple icing and the cutest little vampire couple on top. OK, so I think it was a wedding cake, maybe, but when I saw it in the store I had to have it. Anyway, it was cream frosting and really great cake. I got ice cream, too, and we totally skipped dinner and pigged out and the boys drank beer, but I don't even like the stuff, so I had coffee.

I love living here. I just hope we can hold it together for another month, because the money? Not really coming in that fast. My paycheque stretches to rent and my share of the groceries and utilities, and Shane ponies up his fair share – don't even ask me how because all I ever see the boy do is slack.

But Michael's pretty much flat broke now, and taxes are coming due. He could lose the house!!!! We have to think of something fast. He said he'll call his 'rents, but he's not sure if they'll have the money, either. I don't know why he doesn't just give up the music thing and go get a day job for a while! I mean, wouldn't you?

I don't want to move.

Weird thing today: couldn't find Michael. Shane was out doing whatever Shane does, who the hell knows, and the utility company called and left a message that the light bill was overdue, and sheesh, I may be Goth but I don't want to sit around in the dark by candlelight. So when I came home for lunch I tried to get him up, and yeah, I know he sleeps like the dead but as far as I can tell he's not *actually* dead, and banging on the door ought to give him a clue. So I got worried. One thing about having Jason the Psycho for a brother, you learn a thing or two about locks...how to pick them, and how to jam them so he doesn't pick them. So I picked the lock on Michael's door.

He wasn't there. The bed hadn't even been slept in, or he was way neater than any boy I'd ever seen. So granted, maybe he went out shopping or driving or something, but the point is, *why did he lock his door?* I mean, it locks from the inside.

Weird.

False alarm. Michael's back tonight, says he went out today to try to land some gigs at clubs (no luck, the bastards) and forgot to unlock his door when he slammed it shut. Guess he's as good at picking it as I am; he didn't seem too upset.

Have I mentioned how hot Michael is? Hot, hot, hot. I mean, all guitar players are crushworthy – it's like it's issued with the talent – but I've been noticing lately that he is totally Hottie McHott of Hotland.

Not that I could tell him that. Luckily, he's a boy. Hence, too dense to figure out why I'm staring at his ass.

We have a new roomie! Well, I hope, anyway. She's kind of small and scrawny and I totally felt bad for her standing outside crying on the sidewalk. She had the kind of bruises you don't get from just being clumsy – I should know, I ran into Dad's fist a lot, and then Jason's when he tried to be the man. I didn't really pick up on Claire's whole underage vibe, which must have been dumb because it took Michael exactly one second or something when he saw her.

Shane - who knows about Shane? Planet Shane is a lovely place a long way from here.

Michael says she can stay, but only until she finds something else. I think he's got a soft spot for her, though, 'cause he didn't toss her out on the street, and he didn't even know she'd gotten her ass beat by *Monica Morrell*.

I repeat: *Monica Morrell OMG!!!!!*

Shane didn't take that well, which I can understand. He thought Monica the Monster was out of reach, and now he has to get up tomorrow and think about her being here, maybe right down the street, someplace close enough to hurt. I know Shane *wants* to hurt her, and hey, I wouldn't put it all the way past him, either. After listening to his baby sister scream for help when he couldn't get to her, because of the fire? Hey. If he wants to get a little vengeance, I don't blame him. I'd hold her down.

Poor Claire, caught in the middle. She doesn't even know what she's stepped into. She doesn't even know about the vamps.

Sure hope she makes it. I like her, and we can kind of use the rent money.

OMG OMG OMG, Shane is totally crushing on the new roomie! I can't believe it. Somehow I always pictured Shane going after the blond beach hotties. Who knew he liked big brains in teeny little bodies? Although, to be fair, she *is* cute as a button. (Why do we say that? What's so cute about a button, anyway?) She's like a little wee pocket fairy, only fierce and stubborn. I've never really been hanging with the smart geeks before. Goths tend to be more artsy-fartsy, less brainy-wainy. It's sorta fun trying to freak Claire out, 'cause she totally doesn't believe in the supernatural.

Or she didn't, anyway. Kinda hard to stick to that once you get to Morganville.

Man, when Claire flips, she just *flips*. Yesterday she was all, *Oh, poo, supernatural!* And today she's all *Let's talk about how to kill vamps.* Which I love, don't get me wrong, but she scares me a little. I wasn't really ready to join the Morganville Vampire Hunter's Club. Not sure Michael's signing up for it, either, and by the way, did I mention again how *hot* that boy is? I stare at him all the time now; I'm sure he's going to notice, but Michael seems to be happily living in the zip code of Oblivious.

Which, hey - more free staring for me, right?

Anyway, back to Claire: she thinks she's going to find the Book!!!!! I didn't have the heart to tell her that she might as well ask Santa Claus for it. My family used to devote like six weeks a year, twenty-four/seven, to looking for the Book, because there's this enormous reward for any Protected family that finds it. It's what we did instead of vacations. Poor Claire. Well, at least it'll keep her busy and away from Monica Morrell, hopefully.

Saw a vamp today...average height, dark hair, dark eyes. He was buying sheets at McMann's. I wanted to ask him, 'Don't you have people to do that for you?' but he seemed embarrassed enough to be there without me piling it on. I mean, sure, there are a few vamps who slum it with the breathing population, but not a lot, and I didn't recognise this one. If he comes into Common Grounds, he does it during VIP hours, when it's vamps only (and Oliver, of course).

The vamp in McMann's stared at me. I guess he didn't like the Goth look. Most of them don't; somehow they think I'm making fun of them.

Which I totally am.

Otherwise, I bought a new toothbrush and did my blood donation. Nothing to report.

Claire totally almost got us killed today. She got into something with Brandon, and next thing you know, he's all stalky and he *follows us home!* I can't believe that I'm back in this nightmare again – I really thought that I'd gotten out of it. Brandon was my family's Protector (ha!) and I had this horrible crush on him until I was nearly sixteen, and then he did things...things he shouldn't have done. That's when I dyed my hair and turned Goth, since he liked that innocent-little-schoolgirl thing, and I figured it might turn him off. Seemed to work, mostly. At least it got me thrown out of the house early, which was a bonus, because at least then I could fight back!

But now all of a sudden Brandon's back, and he's got a hard-on for Claire. I think he was really just messing with us. If he'd wanted, he could have picked us off outside the house – me, Claire, and Shane. Michael didn't come out, which was smart. Did I mention that Shane totally got all hero-type, charging out to the rescue? I take it all back, what I said about him being slacker-boy.

Michael held me when I got inside, because I was shaking all over. That felt so good. Warm all the way down. Did I mention Michael's feet? They're all the way sexy, and he's always barefoot – he hates shoes. I wish he hated pants and shirts, too.

See, that totally made me feel better about almost getting killed.

If I didn't hate Monica before, now I absolutely for certain hate her. I mean, it was possible she'd reformed a little, right? Evolved from flesh-eating amoeba to some kind of higher form, like penicillin, right? But, no, she has her pet crazy person Gina what's-her-face throw acid on my *friend!* I can't believe it. Shane sounded awful when he called; he was totally freaked out. He says it was just a little bit that got on Claire, but he's pissed and he's scared. Can't find Michael anywhere, *again*, and this time I think Shane's not going to forgive him, because right now Shane needs his buds.

Going to go pick Shane and Claire up at the hospital. No way is it safe for anybody to be walking home. It's getting dark.

I can't believe Shane did that. He made a deal with Brandon. With *Brandon*. Claire says we have to stop him, and I agree, we do. I'm not letting Brandon get his fangs in my friends. No way. I'll kill him first.

To make things even more festive, Michael and Shane got in a fight, and Miranda showed up, OMG, all wigged out about some visions she'd had. I know the kid's got real ability, but she is so annoying. And Shane really, really doesn't like her, which doesn't surprise me a bit.

She's just a kid, and the vamps are starting to chow down on her. She's never going to last.

Poor Mir.

I want to stab this town *right through the heart.*

Don't even know where to start, but I'll try.

Michael's a ghost, which...OK, I still think is pretty amazingly cool, but – he's a *ghost.* Can't leave the house, misty half the day. Which completely explains all those times I looked for him, now that I think about it. Out looking for gigs, right. I asked him, straight up, if he ever floated around invisible and watched us, watched – *me* – when we thought he wasn't around. He got this funny look on his face that I could have sworn was guilty, guilty, guilty, but then he changed the subject and we had plenty of other subjects to talk about.

Like, for one, my boss. Oliver. Kind, friendly, funny Oliver, who gives me days off and takes my side when the preppies get in my face and—

He's a vamp. I never knew, or if I did, he made me forget. He could have made me do a lot of things, it looks like, and I haven't felt this sick and empty since Brandon...since Brandon. Oliver wants the Book. He thinks Claire has it, which doesn't seem real likely, but so long as he thinks it, we're in big, big trouble because if Oliver is who he says he is, he can just tear this house apart. And us with it. We've got nobody on our side.

Nobody but each other.

I cried a lot while Claire was asleep, and Michael held me. I tried to tell him how bad I felt, but there just aren't any words for this stuff, and in the end I just curled up in his arms and it felt good, so good, and when I looked up, he kissed me. Fast and wild, like he couldn't believe he was doing it and he wasn't sure I wouldn't freak out about it but he couldn't stop himself. OMG, our world was coming apart and it was the best kiss I've ever had. Sweet and hot and it made me tremble all the way to my toes. I think Michael would have dragged me back to his room right then and there, but we were kind of in a crisis, and it would have been kind of rude to Shane and Claire. Still, there was kissing. Lots of kissing and holding and touching, and wow. I was right. Boy is *hottttt*.

Of course, we could all die soon. I'm writing this because Michael's patrolling the house and Shane and Claire are asleep. It may be the last chance I have to write anything down.

So in case that's true, I want to say that I love Shane and Claire, and I *love* Michael, and staying here in the Glass House has been the best time of my entire life. I'd like to say I'll miss my folks, but I won't. And they won't miss me, either. But if it all ends here, at least it's ending with the people I really love.

I don't think I can write this down, but I'm going to try, because maybe the sorta nice vamp Amelie will read it later, when this is all over. It wasn't Shane's fault, OK? He never meant for any of this to happen, and if he could have stopped it, he would have. I know that. I have to believe that.

I think something happened to Michael, but I can't remember what it was, and I can't stop crying when I try to think about it. Claire tells me it's OK, but it's not, I know it's not. Shane isn't saying anything, just staring at the floor. His dad – the dad from hell! – hit him a couple of times for trying to stand up to him.

They're here to kill vamps, I guess, which makes sense – Morganville screwed their family royally, didn't it? First Lyssa dying in the fire, and then Shane's mom just drifting off like she couldn't deal with anything. And then taking a razor to the bath to drift off forever. I can't understand how Shane's dad remembered Morganville, though, or what he'd be dealing with. Guess they figured out some way to make it work. No wonder Shane came back to town – he was doing advance work for his dad, the Great White Vamp Hunter.

Shane looks like he's lost the taste for it. Too late now.

We're in trouble. Bad trouble. All those vamps out there, they've got no idea what's coming for them, and we're going to be caught in the middle.

I wish Michael would come back soon.

But I'm afraid – really afraid – that he won't.

Welcome to Morganville.
Just don't stay out after dark.

Morganville is a small college town filled with unusual characters. But when the sun goes down, the bad come out. Because in Morganville, there is an evil that lurks in the darkest shadows ...

The Dead Girls' Dance

Claire Danvers has her share of challenges. Like being a genius in a school that favours beauty over brains; homicidal girls in her dorm, and finding out that her college town is overrun with the living dead. On the up side, she has a new boyfriend with a vampire-hunting dad. But when a local fraternity throws the Dead Girls' Dance, hell is really going to break loose.

Midnight Alley

Claire Danvers' college town may be run by vampires but a truce between the living and the dead made things relatively safe. For a while. Now people are turning up dead, a psycho is stalking her, and an ancient bloodsucker has proposed private mentoring. It's giving night school a whole new meaning . . .

Feast of Fools

In the town of Morganville, vampires and humans live in relative peace. But Claire Danvers has never felt too relaxed about it — especially with the arrival of Mr Bishop, an ancient, old-school vampire who cares nothing about harmony. What he wants from the town's living and its dead is unthinkably sinister. It's only at a formal ball, attended by vampires and their human dates, that Claire realises the elaborately evil trap he's set for Morganville.

Lord of Misrule

Bishop, the master vampire, once again threatens to abolish all order in Morganville, revive the forces of the evil dead, and let chaos rule. But Bishop isn't the only threat; violent black cyclone clouds hover over the town, promising a storm of devastating proportions as student Claire Danvers and her friends prepare to defend Morganville against elements both natural and unnatural.

Carpe Corpus

Bishop has kept a death grip on Morganville ever since he arrived. Now an underground resistance is brewing, and in order to contain it, Bishop must go to even greater lengths. He vows to obliterate the town and all its inhabitants – the living and the undead. Claire Danvers and her friends are the only ones who stand in his way . . .

Fade Out

Life has changed dramatically in Morganville. The vampires have made major concessions to the human population, and with their newfound freedom, Claire and her friends start to feel comfortable again – almost. Yet when one of Eve's castmates in the local theatre company goes missing, Eve suspects the worst . . .

Kiss of Death

Trouble seems to follow Claire and her friends like a shadow and tonight is no exception to the rule. They must find the most difficult documents for a vampire to acquire; people passes that will allow 'bad ass' Morley and his two friends to leave Morganville. But it's proving incredibly problematic, and with the odds seemingly stacked against them, the biggest question of all is . . . will they survive?

Ghost Town

With Shane's vampire father back in town and her crazy boss Myrnin acting even crazier than usual, living in Morganville isn't easy. And when Claire gets on the wrong side of a vamp while protecting her friend Eve, her punishment is severe and her future is in her own hands.

Bite Club

Claire Danvers has come to realise that for the most part, the undead just want to live their lives. But someone else wants them to get ready to rumble. There's a new extreme sport being broadcast over the Internet: bare-knuckle fights pitting captured vampires against one another – or against humans. But what started as an online brawl soon threatens everyone in Morganville. And if Claire and her friends want to survive, they'll have to do a lot more than fight . . .

Last Breath

There is a question Claire has long been asking: why do vampires live so far out in a sunny desert when they're sensitive to sunlight? The reason doesn't have to do with sunlight but water - and an ancient enemy who has finally found a way to invade the vampires' landlocked community. Vampires aren't the top predator on earth. There's something worse that preys on them . . . something much worse. Which means if Claire, and Morganville, want to live, they will have to fight on to the last breath.

Black Dawn

When a tide of ferocious draug, the vampire's deadliest enemy, floods Morganville, its eclectic mix of residents must fight to save their town from devastation. Things take a turn for the worse when vampire Amelie, the town's founder, is infected by the master draug's bite. Unless Claire and her friends can find an antidote to save Amelie and overcome the draug, Morganville's future looks bleak . . .

The Morganville Vampires series

Check out our website for free tasters and exclusive discounts, competitions and giveaways, and sign up to our monthly newsletter to keep up to date on our latest releases, news and upcoming events.

www.allisonandbusby.com